STRIPPED
BARE

EMMA HART
new york times bestselling author

STRIPPED BARE

STRIPPED
BARE

*What happens when you mix a bachelorette party,
the queen of dating disasters, and a stripper so hot
he was forged from the fires of hell? Screwed. You
get screwed.*

Cocky. Commanding. Powerful. Relentless.
Those four words all summed up West Rykman
perfectly.
So did filthy, dirty, sexy, and addictive.
He was supposed to be my one night stand...not my
new marketing client.
He was definitely not supposed to be back inside my
pants, not that anybody told him that.
I knew one thing: What West Rykman wanted, West
Rykman got.
And he wanted me.

What happens in Vegas... might just make you stay.

STRIPPED BARE is a standalone, erotic novel with romcom elements. Although the book completes Mia & West's story, please be aware **that the epilogue leads into the companion novel,** STRIPPED DOWN, out August 30th.

More information about STRIPPED DOWN, including the blurb, is at the end of the book.

STRIPPED BARE

"**I** don't want to see a bunch of naked penises writhing at me!"

My best friend's words slid right over my head, but their meaning didn't: Taking my virgin best friend to Las Vegas for her bachelorette party might not have been the greatest idea.

All right. "Might not have been the greatest idea" was a total understatement. Las Vegas was the worst idea I'd ever had, mostly because the entire plan was a night at a strip club. On the Strip. Strippers on the Strip. Pole-dancing, hip-grinding, booty-shaking male strippers.

It was proving to be pretty damn hard convincing her to go.

"Since when were penises not naked?" Jaz snorted, putting her mascara wand down and flipping her jet-black hair over her shoulder. "They're not usually suited and booted with a bow tie, Al."

My blond best friend and bride-to-be pouted glossy, pink lips and crossed her arms in annoyance. "I know that. I'm not a total virgin. I just... I don't know. I didn't know a cock fest was on the agenda." She punctuated that with a dark look at me, but her heart wasn't in it.

Allie's trying to be angry at me was like trying to be angry at a puppy. It was literally impossible. That's what twenty-four years of being attached at the hip will do to you.

"It's your bachelorette party! What did you expect me to do? Buy you pajamas and fluffy socks for a slumber party?" I raised my eyebrows and handed her a

1

glass of the Long Island Iced Tea I'd just finished shaking.

Yeah—we'd brought our own alcohol. We were...resourceful that way.

Plus, all of my cash may or may not have been in one-dollar bills, and I didn't want to check out the next day and find I had eight hundred dollars of alcohol on my bill.

Not that I'd found myself there before. Just, you know. Hypothetically.

"Allie, it's just a strip club," Lucie reasoned, taking her glass from me. She tucked her dark-brown hair behind her ear, and not for the first time, I found myself mildly amused that, with my fiery, auburn hair, we were like a walking Pantene advertisement or something. "Besides," she added, sipping on the cocktail. "It's not gonna hurt you to see some real-time peen."

Twenty-seven years old or not, Allie had decided at fifteen—after a disastrous blow job incident when her mom had walked in on her—that she wasn't going to have sex until marriage. Her fiancé, Joe, was a reformed Christian and a supposedly born again virgin and I respected that, but lord... The girl needed a bit of peen in her life.

It was a wonder we were best friends at all.

"You guys act like I've never seen a cock before. I've seen a lot of cocks. I've touched a lot of cocks. I just don't want to see or touch...stripper cocks." She shuddered as she spoke and then took a long drink through her straw. "Who knows where they've been?"

"Inside their tighty-whiteys, ready to play peekaboo for a good portion of my life savings?" I offered, fighting the smile my lips were threatening to form.

"I have no idea how I've tolerated you for this long." Allie sighed and put her glass down.

"Because she's the crazy to your straitjacket?" Jaz suggested, pulling three pairs of heels out of her suitcase.

"The one-click to your Amazon?" Lucie added cheerfully.

"The smut book to your Kindle?"

"The bra to your boobs?"

"All right, all right," Allie grumbled and picked her glass right back up. "These are strong. If I didn't know better, I'd say you're trying to get me drunk, Mia."

I whistled low and turned around to check out Jaz's shoes. She had the best shoes known to man, and god only knows where she freakin' found them. She's the ultimate shoe hunter. She could make a career out of that shit.

Meanwhile, I wasn't even going to dignify Allie's comment with a response—honestly, she should have known I was damn well trying to get her drunk.

All right, so maybe the cocktails were a little stronger than I'd intended, but since we hadn't even left the room yet and we were already fighting about the club, it's not a bad thing. She was gonna need to be a little giggly—as in sober enough to walk but drunk enough to forget the plan.

"You know Joe's gonna be going to one, right?" Lucie slid her gaze over to Allie. "It's pretty much a given for most guys. Or one will be brought to him."

I put one of Jaz's red shoes down and moved to my own. The red-soled, pointed Louboutins were born of the devil, but good lord, they looked like heaven when they were on. They'd also gotten me my current job and let me keep it, so I was pretty sure my baby toes had finally come to an agreement with them.

My friends all thought I was crazy for wearing those things for a minimum of five days a week, but I called it love. And made the shoes promise to never, ever break on me, because it had taken me forever and a day to break them in.

"If Darren is in charge, they'll strip-club hop until five in the morning," I reminded her.

"You said his name without spitting. I'm impressed." Allie skipped right over the club thing. Maybe that drink was hitting her already...

"I'm a mature adult." I slammed both of my shoes down on the table. "I can speak about my ex-boyfriend without wanting to scoop his balls out with a potato masher." *Just.*

"You sure about that? 'Cause, now, I'm more worried about taking *you* to a strip club than getting *her* out the door," Jaz said, one scarlet-red heel hanging off her finger while she pointed between me and Allie.

"Look." I gripped my glass a little too tightly, feeling the familiar buzz of frustration that zinged to life whenever my cheating son-of-a-bitch ex was mentioned. "This is one wedding where the maid of honor isn't gonna get it on with the best man, because she's already been there, done it, and got the 'fuck you, heart' T-shirt. So let me have tonight, will ya? I'm not getting it on the wedding night because I'm gonna be sitting by my phone, waiting for somebody to call me."

Allie's cheeks flushed bright red. "I'm not going to call you right after I lose my virginity to my husband!"

3

"Uh... Yeah... You will. You're gonna call me and ask me why the hell you waited so long. You know...once you've forgotten that it kinda hurts."

"Mia!" Jaz gasped. "You can't tell her that!"

"Sure I can! It's practically in the Best Friend Code of Ethics. It's my responsibility to make sure she's prepared for that night, and if that means telling her that her taco might get a crack, that's what I'm gonna do."

"My taco might get a crack?" Allie half screeched. "The hell kinda explanation is that?"

"Oh, Allie." I turned to her and sighed heavily, gently waving my glass. "It's a polite way to tell you that's it gonna hurt like a motherfucking bitch."

"There we go. Break it to her gently, why don't you?" Lucie rolled her eyes and took a new, full glass of Long Island Iced Tea to Allie. "Drink this. With any luck, you'll forget her crap by tomorrow morning."

"My crap? I take offense at that. You can't tell me it didn't hurt when you lost your V-card."

"No idea," she replied as she perched on the edge of the bed, her light-brown eyes lifting to meet mine. "I was crammed into the back seat of a Corolla and uncomfortable enough without thinking about the pain my vagina might have been experiencing."

"A Corolla? Really?" Allie asked, her nose wrinkled.

Lucie shrugged a shoulder. "Junior prom. Where else was I gonna lose it?"

"In a bed. Like normal people," Jaz fired at her, buckling one of her heels at her ankle before sitting up straight.

"You lost it on your dad's sofa." Allie frowned delicately. "And I know for a fact Mia lost it in a tent when we went camping the summer before senior year."

I groaned and covered my face with my hand. Why'd she have to go and bring that up? She knew how I felt about that awful night.

"How did we go from convincing Allie to go to strip club to the worst two and a half minutes of my entire life?"

"Two and a half minutes?" Jaz snorted. "You lucky duck."

"Lucky? How is it lucky? He screwed me like he was a drill and I was a solid-brick wall. Then I hit my head on a rock I didn't know was in the tent. I still have freaking nightmares about it."

4

"I had ten minutes of relentless pounding that felt like he was trying to break into Fort Knox via my cervix," she said dryly, grabbing her glass. "I was thirty seconds away from calling the FBI to report an attempted break-in when I clenched, yelled, and he finally came."

"You're all insane." Allie sighed and ran her hand through her sleek, blond hair, messing it up.

Yep. She was getting drunk.

"If she's messing up her hair already, does that mean she's tipsy enough that we can go?" Lucie asked hopefully. "Because I've got a clutch full of ones ready and waiting."

"No!" Jaz exclaimed. "Wait!" She grabbed her case and pulled out a hot-pink sash from the top. Then she shoved it in Allie's direction, a big grin on her face. "You've gotta look the part."

Allie's eyes widened as she took in the bright pink satin sash. "No. I'm not wearing that."

"Why not?"

"It's pink."

"And? Your cheeks are gonna be too the second one of these hunks grinds his butt in front of you."

"She has a point." I tipped my empty glass toward her. "You're gonna blush like...well, a virgin when you go in there and see their erections."

Allie froze. "They're gonna have erections?"

"Obviously. No one wants to see a guy with a softie strip, do they?"

Several thoughts visibly flitted across her face. And, yep--she was definitely tipsy, because she actually looked like she was considering it.

Jesus. She was considering it. She was more than tipsy.

Allie pushed herself to standing, still clutching her empty glass in her hand. "Fuck it," she announced, surprising me by not slurring her words in the slightest. "Let's go!"

Well. I was ready.

She looked a little like...a virgin in a strip club.

I couldn't stop laughing.

I had no idea what she'd expected to find, but I didn't know if this was it. In fact, I was pretty sure it wasn't it.

Rock Solid, the strip club of my choice, was nestled at the far end of the Strip. When I had been researching, I'd assumed that meant it'd be quieter than the ones in the middle, but I had been wrong.

So. Wrong.

The place was stupid busy, and it wasn't hard to see why. We'd been there for a little over an hour. The drinks were great, the atmosphere was great, and the lighting was great. Our booth, with smooth, dark-brown leather seats, allowed us a ton of room, and the reserved sign that glared out at everyone walking past meant none of the ladies forced into standing up could take our space.

But really—who was paying attention to that?

Not me.

The stage, which generously allowed us a flawless view of some of the most perfect men I'd ever seen in my goddamn life, stretched almost entirely through the center of the club. At least fifteen feet wide and god knows how long, it was the only part of the club aside from the bathrooms that was completely lit. The strobe lights that flashed across it occasionally, in time with the pounding, wall-vibrating music, only lent a hand to its vibrancy.

And the ripped, defined men dancing on the stage in various stages of undress, both against and between the poles, were the sole cause of the vibrant, electric atmosphere.

Jaz tapped the bottom of her cigarette packet on the table before opening it and drawing one out. "Hot. Damn." She whistled appreciatively as a tall man wearing nothing but black dress pants approached our table with a bottle of champagne and four flutes balanced on a round, black tray.

"Your second bottle, ladies. Would you like me to pour it for you?" His smile was dazzling as he set everything out on the table and swept the table for our empty glasses and bottle.

"No, we're good, thank you," Lucie answered, passing Jaz a lighter.

"Perfect. Can I get you anything else?"

"Yes!" Allie clapped her hands. "One round of tequila shots, please."

Oh, Jesus...

The server nodded, that same, hot smile plastered on his face. Then he disappeared.

Jaz blew smoke to the side and raised an eyebrow at Allie. "Al, the last time you had tequila shots, you threw up inside my shoes."

"So keep your shoes away from me." She grinned, not caring at all. "It's my party, and if I wanna drink until I vomit, I'm gonna."

"That's the spirit," I muttered, unable to fight my smirk as I reached for the champagne bottle. My fingers closed around the ice-cold neck of the bottle, and the ice in the bucket crunched as I lifted it out.

What? She was in the strip club. I was calling the night a win, so if she vomited, then, well, I knew I'd have to hold her hair.

Hashtag best friend *ever*.

"Note to self: Keep Allie away from shoes later," Lucie muttered, shoving her glass in front of my face.

Dutifully, I poured. "Preach it, sister. Preach it."

Allie rolled her eyes as Hot Server brought the shots out and set them in front of us. Jaz grinned again as he lifted his tray and winked at her. I'd have sworn his smile grew a little.

"Twenty bucks says you're taking him back to your room tonight," Lucie piped up.

"Nooo..." Jaz said slowly, putting her cig out in the ashtray. Her gaze followed Hot Server as he walked away. "It's my best friend's bachelorette party. I can't do that."

"Yeah, you can, and you will." Allie laughed loudly and lifted her shot.

We downed them in sync, and I shuddered as the strong, cold liquid burned a harsh path down my throat. Should have gotten a Blow Job instead... I'd never mixed well with tequila, but I knew, if I'd refused, there were three of them and one of me.

I'd refused once before.

I'd ended up very, very drunk.

7

"Are we going down to the stage?" Lucie asked as I finished my previously interrupted champagne-pouring and put the bottle back. "These one-dollar bills aren't going to tuck themselves into boxers, you know."

"In a minute." I couldn't help the grin that formed on my face. I was going to be killed a hundred times over for the shenanigans I was about to pull, but what kind of best friend would I be if I didn't organize a lap dance for Allie?

That's right. I'd be a shit one. Besides, I'd booked it when I'd called and paid over the phone, so it wasn't like I could cancel. She was gonna be all kinds of pissed off, but one day, she'd thank me for it. Hopefully, that day was tomorrow.

A guy wearing nothing but tight, black briefs approached the table, and from beneath dark, floppy hair, brown eyes scanned the four of us. Allie paused when his gaze zeroed in on her and her bright-pink sash, and he grinned slowly, totally sexily, and closed the distance between them.

Her eyes shot to me, and it was a mix between horror and excitement. My own smile was literally glued to my face as he leaned down and whispered something in her ear and she nodded. Jaz's following laugh was loud as she realized along with Lucie what was about to happen.

Allie was about to get some real-time peen.

The girl in question was blushing furiously as the stripper pulled her to the edge of the seat and all but straddled her. She was torn between obviously wanting to kill me and wanting to see what was going to happen next, and given the fact that she was under probably one hundred and eighty pounds of ripped muscle, she was waiting to see what would happen next... Whether she liked it or not.

The stripper flexed his hips, light glinting off his flawless skin. His muscles rippled with each move he made as he treated Allie to some fine-ass moves. Seriously—no man should have been able to move as easily as he did. The last time I saw hips snaking like that was while watching a Shakira music video on MTV—a long-ass time ago.

He encouraged Allie to touch him, which only made her cheeks blaze brighter. Still, she looked more delighted than I'd thought she would after running her hands over some guy's abs.

"Fifty bucks says Joe doesn't have abs like that," Lucie yelled into my ear as Allie once again touched the stripper's stomach as he sat on her and ground his hips against her.

"Joe doesn't have abs at all," Jaz threw in. "He has one ab, and it's his entire stomach. She's probably rethinking her choice of man. Look at her, all happy and shit."

I felt a little smug. She'd been so apprehensive about this plan, but she was happy now.

I guessed having a hot, naked guy grinding his junk in her face would do that to a girl.

Hell, I wasn't even grumpy and I could guarantee it'd cheer me the fuck up.

When he finally finished his dance, Allie continued to blush so many shades of red that a paint color chart would have been jealous. Then she turned her flustered face toward me.

"I can't believe you did that to me!"

"Moi?" I gasped and pressed my hand to my chest. "Why do you think it was me?"

"Because!" She threw a perfectly pressed napkin at me. "You're the only whore who'd dare book me a freakin' lap dance!"

I considered this for the briefest moment. "Yeah, you're right." I was grinning again, but I couldn't help it. It was almost an illness, how amused I was.

"Ugh!" She grabbed her glass and downed the champagne before looking at us. "I'm going to get something stronger than mosquito piss. Anyone else?"

"Yep!" Jaz stood, grabbing another cigarette and lighting it. "Mia, wine?" she directed to me on an exhale of smoke.

Drunk Jaz resembled a choo-choo train where nicotine was involved.

"Yep." I picked my champagne up as they disappeared, Lucie yelling her order of a cocktail after them. I sure as hell needed something stronger than just champagne. A bottle seemed a lot when it was for one person—split between four people? Not so much.

It was like splitting a bottle of water between the sand grains of the Sahara or something. Almost certainly an exaggeration, but whatever.

"I can't believe she went through with it," Lucie said quietly, snorting as she held her champagne flute against her lips. "I thought for sure she'd push him away and then bottle you."

"Ha!" I clapped my hand over my mouth as the laugh barked out of me. "Me too."

Seriously though. That had honestly been my first thought when she'd realized she was about to get a lap dance. I'd thought she'd kill me.

She probably had inside her head.

Allie came back to the table, a cigarette-free Jaz on her heels, both of them clutching drinks. The smile that stretched across my blond best friend's face instantly made me pause, but it was the glint in her eye that got me.

Bitch was up to something.

"Here you go." She set my drink in front of me and took her seat.

"What did you do?" I asked immediately.

"Who said I did anything?"

Lucie choked on her drink. "The guy approaching our table and staring at Mia."

I snapped my head up and looked out at the crowd. Shit, she was right.

The guy though.

Six foot three, at least. Dark hair. Strong jaw lined with a sexy five-o'clock shadow. Blue eyes the color of the Caribbean. And a body that fit the white shirt he was wearing to perfection.

And Lucie was right.

He was headed right for me.

"Allie!" I snapped, looking back at her. "What the hell did you do?"

"Think of it as...a thank-you for such a great party."

I wanted to slap that grin right off her face and spit on it. Oh. My. God. "You booked me a lap dance?" I was a little horrified.

Sure, I'd booked one for her, but she was the bride-to-be. It was supposed to be the bride-to-be with the lap dance, not the maid of honor. Right?

"No." Jaz leaned forward. "She booked you a *private* lap dance."

"You did what?" I could barely breathe, but it didn't matter, because the guy who was obviously about to give me said lap dance approached the table before I could say another word.

"Mia?" he asked, hitting me with a hot gaze.

I nodded. Speaking seemed like a stupid idea because I'd only end up sounding like a mouse. If I was lucky.

He held one hand out for me, looking at me expectantly. *Fuck all my friends*, I thought as I reluctantly placed my hand in his. His rough fingers wrapped around mine, and he tugged me up, his plump lips twitching into a smile.

"Don't worry about your drink," he said into my ear. "You won't have time to drink it."

My stomach flipped. Holy. Shit. That was the sexiest thing I'd ever heard.

As he led me away, I glanced over my shoulder to look at my friends. They were all laughing, and my teeth sank into my lower lip.

I was equal parts nervous and excited. I'd never had a lap dance before, but I guessed it was fair. Even if I did know how Allie felt now.

But this guy was...hotter. The guy who'd shown up for hers was handsome, sure, but he had a different...feel than the man who was currently leading me down a small, dimly lit hallway. The guy whose fingers were gently wrapped around mine oozed power and sexuality, and with every step I took, a little more of my nervousness disappeared.

The control he exercised as he led me into a room and shut the door made a shiver run down my spine. I didn't know why—maybe it was how smoothly he moved. Or maybe it was the way he looked down into my eyes, a dirty, suggestive smirk on his lips.

Yep. It was the smirk. Without a doubt.

"Take a seat, Mia." He let my hand go.

I stood awkwardly for half a second before doing what he'd said.

"Let me guess. You've never been to a strip club before."

"No..." I said slowly, pushing some hair from my face. "And I wasn't really planning on this happening."

"Nervous?"

"If I say yes, will you still do it?"

"Yes." His smirk grew, and he undid the top two buttons of his shirt, keeping his eyes on me. "I don't bite, darlin'. Unless you ask me to."

That sounded a little too tempting. He did have perfect teeth.

I watched as he unbuttoned every last button on his crisp, white shirt, exposing the hottest body I'd ever seen. Swear to god, it had to have been surgery, because no man on this planet could have gotten abs so perfect otherwise.

Stripper or not.

"Maybe I'll ask." The words slipped right off my tongue.

He walked toward me and put his hands on the back of the sofa. His strong body leaned right over me, and involuntarily, I leaned back against the plush cushions behind me and looked up at him. It only served to make him dip his head so his lips were close to mine, and he whispered, "Maybe, for you, I'll do it anyway."

I drew in a deep breath. My heart pounded in my chest when he didn't move away for several seconds.

Were lap dances supposed to be this quiet?

He answered my question by getting up and moving toward a side table. There, he picked up a remote control, and instantly, the room magically filled with loud music. After another push of a button, the lights dimmed just enough that I was pretty confident he wouldn't see me when I inevitably blushed.

I was going to blush. I knew it.

I think he did too, this nameless man who was currently walking toward me. The predatory glint in his eye was thrilling and scary, and honestly, I was no weak woman, but I knew one thing.

If I'd met this man anywhere else, he'd have probably eaten me for breakfast.

I'd also have probably opened my legs and let him. Lunch, dinner, and snacks too.

He moved.

Not...to me. Against me. He flexed his hips, making a grinding motion. It should have been cheesy or wrong or stupid, but it wasn't. His muscles rippled and danced along with him, tensing and becoming more obvious with each move, and I couldn't look away. It was mesmerizing.

My teeth sank into my bottom lip as he moved closer to me and opened my legs with one nudge of his knee. I obliged, my eyes focused on his body and the way his hips moved perfectly in time with the music.

My fingers twitched with the urge to touch him, but he beat me to it. He ran one of his hands through my hair and fisted it at the nape. The tug was gentle, but it felt good as he pulled my head back and forced me to look into his eyes. The bright sea of blue cut through the dim light, and he reached up, slowly sliding his shirt over his shoulders and down his arms. It fell to the floor in a flash of white, and he bent to open my legs further.

I swallowed hard as he popped the button on his pants and gripped the back of the sofa again.

"You can touch me," he murmured into my ear. His breath was hot against my skin.

Touch him? Whoa. I didn't plan on that. What if my fingers burned with his hotness?

EMMA HART

His strong hand brushed my knee and up my thigh. He pushed my dress up, and his touch seared against me as he edged my legs farther apart and got even closer.

Oh my god. I'm so turned on.

I hadn't thought it was possible, but there I was, desire bolting through my veins as he slid his hand up my side and brushed the underside of my breast. I fought the urge to physically respond to him, but he held his hand behind his head, and as the music slowed to something more intimate, his movements slowed until every one flawlessly matched the beat.

"Mia," he murmured, this time *against* my ear. "Touch me, angel. I can see you want to."

I did. Shit, I did, but it was awkward.

His chuckle was low as he grabbed my hand and flattened it against his own stomach. My eyes widened at how solid the muscle was—fuck me, he was made of stone—but he didn't notice as he guided my hand up his body. He all but showed me how to touch him, how he wanted to be touched.

I ran my second hand up his body, my eyes flitting up toward his like I was asking for permission. Fucking hell, was I twenty-five or eighteen?

I knew my way around a man's body. Just not one this hot. That was all.

"Down." The word sounded so hot. "You want my pants off?"

I nodded. Freakin' right I did.

"Sorry. I don't speak silence." He was teasing me now, still dancing against me.

"Yes. Take your pants off." It came out a little more demanding than I had been going for, but honestly, I was happy I'd found my voice again.

I bit down hard on the inside of my cheek as he moved back. His eyes were hot on me. They had been the whole time, but my gaze dropped to the sway of his lower body as he eased his pants down over his thighs.

Holy shit.

He was hard.

And he was big. The outline of his erection was obvious as it pushed against his white boxer briefs. His cock was long and thick, and I could see a teasing hint of the head of it through the material.

My clit ached. I didn't realize how turned on I was until just now. Was he turned on too? By me? He had to be. I knew getting hard was part of a stripper's

4

job, but he didn't strike me as the everyday stripper.

The music changed in the background from the unknown tune to the erotic, slow beat of The Weeknd's "High For This." It only served to turn me on a little more. I was aching everywhere, my pussy almost painfully so.

I resolved there and then that the next guy I dated would be a stripper.

The man in front of me drew me back to him by running his hand down his stomach and along the side of his cock. My lips felt dry, and when my tongue flicked out to wet them, he grasped my chin. Slowly, he shook his head and ran his other hand up my thigh.

Then he climbed on top of me. Kind of. He wasn't actually sitting on me, but his knees were on the sofa cushions either side of my hips, and his erection came dangerously close to brushing my stomach as he thrust his hips forward.

Bravely, I touched his body, running my hands across the deep valleys indented between his muscles, exploring every solid inch as he continued dancing against me. My clit literally throbbed as my skin tingled with warmth, even when his breath cascaded across my skin.

He dipped his mouth toward my ear. "Tell your friend I'm not charging her for this." He wound his hand in my hair, and I involuntarily tilted my head back. "It's on me."

"No, you can't."

"I can." He flicked his tongue against my earlobe, making me shiver.

He couldn't do it for free.

"I insist."

"I insist it's free."

"Why?"

He moved back the smallest amount and looked into my eyes. "I'm a man of great restraint, Mia, but dancing for you is pushing the boundaries of my self-control. You're beautiful, and very, very tempting." He ran his thumb across the curve of my jaw and cupped my chin. "Now, let me finish before it breaks."

"Wait," I heard myself say. No... I wasn't going to proposition him, was I?

Fuck it.

I was.

I trailed my fingers across his stomach, and my baby finger caught in the sharp

Sex-God-V-Line muscle that disappeared beneath his boxers, my touch missing his erection by half an inch. His hips half jerked away from me. He wasn't dancing anymore.

"I have a room at Planet Hollywood," I murmured, staring at his cock. "Eight oh two."

"Are you inviting me to fuck you, angel?"

I raised my eyes to his. The slight hint of amusement reflected back at me, but his gaze was primarily heated lust.

"Yes," I answered boldly. Fuck it. I was there now. "I've never been this turned on in my entire life, and I've been known to suck until I swallow. Your choice."

He froze for a split second before lowering his face back to mine. His lips were inches from mine, his breath dancing across them. "I've never done this," he said in a low voice. He stood and, grasping my thigh, knelt forward. Then he hooked my leg over his hip. Wrapping one hand around the back of my neck, he grazed his mouth along to my jaw to my ear, and I fought back a harsh shiver. "But I'll leave there ten minutes after you and meet you there."

My face turned toward his, my teeth sinking into my lower lip for the hundredth time that night, and I grazed my nails across his lower stomach. "How will you know when I go?"

"I have my ways." That dirty smirk formed on his lips again, and after squeezing my leg, he got up. He grabbed his pants and, as he pulled them up, said, "Now, go back out there and enjoy yourself. I'll make sure another bottle of champagne finds its way to your table. For the bride-to-be, of course."

I grasped the bottom of my dress and met his eyes, my mouth tugging up into a coy smile on one side. "Of course."

I stared at my hotel room door, wringing my hands in my lap.

I was insane. I mean, I'd known it for a long time, but my actions earlier had cemented it. Proposing sex to a stripper?

In my defense, and it was all I had left, if the man moved his hips like that in the club, I was kinda interested in how he moved them in a bed. If it was anything like he moved them there...

I slapped my hand against my forehead. God, I really was insane. The second we landed back in San Diego, I needed to call a therapist and get my head checked. Random one-night stand with a guy whose name I didn't know? Mind you, though, the dating-guys-whose-names-I-did-know thing wasn't exactly working out for me. I had a long list of break-ups and equally shitty reasons to go with them.

"You make more money than I do." Sorry you felt like I emasculated you with my career I'd worked hard for while you flipped burgers part time.

"I kinda sorta slept with someone else." Kinda sorta? What'd you do? Put it in her belly button? Her ear?

"I accidentally kissed my ex-girlfriend, and now, we're getting back together." 'Cause you slipped and fell on her mouth, right?

And my personal favorite: *"I'd rather see other people. Men. I'm gay."* Nothing like being the girl to make a guy realize he no longer had to be confused about his sexuality.

Yes. Maybe random one-night stands were definitely the way to go

Was I slut if my whorishness was justifiable? Did one one-night stand make me a slut? I had no idea. I was a serial dater, not a serial screwer.

I turned my attention to the clock on the nightstand and tapped my nails against my knee. I'd been back for eight minutes. Yes, eight. I was precise.

He said that he'd leave the club ten minutes after I did, and the club was around ten minutes away if you walked.Basically, this has been the longest eight minutes of my life. Except the two that were about to happen. No doubt those one hundred and twenty seconds would be like a hundred and twenty *thousand.*

What was I doing?

Oh my god.

I'd invited a stripper back to my hotel to fuck me.

That was not normal behavior.

That was fucked up.

What was wrong with me?

The last time I'd had no-strings sex was with my best friend's fiancé's best friend, and look where that had gotten me. I had to pair my ass up with him at said best friend's wedding because of being best man and maid of honor.

I had time to get outta here, right? I knew that Lucie was alone, and Allie definitely was. Jaz... Well, she'd left with Hot Server, as we'd all assumed she would.

It was one a.m. and I was—

Knock. Knock.

—no longer waiting for the stripper to show up.

I blew out a long breath as I got up and headed for the door. I peeked through the little peephole and cussed myself out when my heart thumped a little too hard at the sight of the hot guy standing on the other side of the door.

"Nine minutes," I said approvingly, opening the door. "I'm impressed."

His instantly eyes caught mine, a slow, sexy smile curving his lips. "I don't like to keep a lady waiting."

"Come in." I stepped away from the door. "Would you like a drink?"

"No, thank you." He shut the door behind him. The white shirt he was wearing had the sleeves rolled up to his elbows, and its tailored fit perfectly hugged his muscular body.

I swigged from the glass of wine I'd poured myself from the fully stocked mini fridge and then gulped it down. The glass clinked as I put it down on the counter, but before I could turn, I felt the warmth of his hard body behind me.

He rested his hands on the edge of the counter and leaned into me. His breath was hot as it skittered across my neck, and his lips brushed my earlobe as he spoke. "Nervous again, Mia?"

I paused, sucking my lower lip between my teeth. There was no use in denying it. I was. "A little. There was a good chance I was under the influence of, well, you when I proposed this earlier tonight."

"Would you like me to leave?"

"Whoa now. That's a little rash." I turned around so I was perching on the counter instead.

My gaze traveled across his upper body, from his slender waist to his broad shoulders and his toned arms, to his sharp, stubble-dusted jaw and the perfect, soft-looking, pink lips that were quirked up in amusement.

"I'm gonna go with no. Don't leave."

"Are you sure?"

I was still watching his lips. If they were that hot when he spoke, how hot would they be elsewhere? Namely, between my legs?

"Positive."

"Good." That was all he said before he slid his hand around the back of my neck and pulled my face toward his.

Our lips met, and my first thought was that they were as soft as I'd imagined, and the second was, *Oh, fuck me.*

My hands found their way up his body and around his neck. He kissed me so firmly that my head swam as his tongue flicked against the seam of my mouth. The simple touch sent a bolt of fiery lust hurtling through me, and I wound my fingers in his hair and pressed my body against his.

The kiss deepened, so our tongues met, and he wrapped his arm around my waist, holding me in place. It took only seconds for the kiss to grow to something more, and my body reacted in a startlingly strong way.

He swung me around and pushed me back toward the bed, releasing the back of my neck. Then he fell with me, and as my leg bent, my dress rode up my thigh. He took it as an invitation, and his rough palm trailed up it, taking the dress up even farther until it was bunched around my waist.

"You didn't mention your name," I gasped when he kissed his way down my neck. My hands moved to undo the buttons of his shirt, my back arching.

"West," he replied, the word a murmur against my skin. "Now you know what to scream when I fuck you."

Yes. Yes, I did.

His teeth grazed across my pulse point, and I pushed my body against him. I undid the final button of his shirt, and my hands explored his body as his mouth moved across my chest. My heart thundered in my chest when he pulled the straps of my dress down over my shoulders. The tingles left in the wake of his fingertips scorched, and before I knew it, my dress was bunched around my hips, my bra was unclasped, and his mouth was around my nipple.

His tongue roughly teased it, and he rolled the tip over the sensitive, hardened bud. I arched beneath him, but my hips bucked at the same time, so my pussy pushed right up against his hard cock.

Fuck. It felt bigger than it'd looked earlier.

I felt his smile rather than saw it as he moved down my body. He was swift and exercised control in every movement he made, whether it was a kiss or a grab of my thigh. It was erotic—a total turn-on. My breathing sped up as he dropped to his knees, grabbed my ankles, and yanked my ass to the edge of the bed.

I could read him, or maybe he was reading aloud to me.

He loved control.

I loved it everywhere but...there.

West trailed a fingertip up the inside of my thigh, his mouth deftly following behind it. He didn't kiss me—rather, he dragged his lips across the ticklish skin until his face was close to the apex of my thighs and I felt his breath over my panties as he exhaled.

He hooked one finger beneath the lacy fabric and moved it to the side. My chest heaved as his gaze settled on my aching, wet pussy, and he touched one finger to it.

"Mia," he murmured, moving his mouth to the top of my thigh and kissing, pushing the finger inside me. "Look how fucking wet you are."

I couldn't answer. Only throw my arm over my eyes.

"Jesus..." He pushed a second finger inside me, and the easy stretch as my pussy took the pressure felt so damn good. "You feel that, angel? Your tight little pussy is so fucking wet for me."

The low huskiness of his voice only served to turn me on more. I writhed beneath him as he withdrew his fingers only to push them back inside me. The rhythmic movement combined with his slow, hot exhales teased me to the brink of pleasure.

"Jesus," I whispered, my legs clenching together as best they could. "If you're gonna put your face down there, at least lick my clit."

"Demanding. I like that," he breathed before kissing my pussy. "You taste good."

I pushed my hips up, basically forcing myself into his mouth.

He laughed against me, and I felt every rumbling sound against my tender skin. His greedy tongue tasted every inch of my pussy. He was unapologetic in its movements, and he went from circling my clit to my opening in less than a second. He ran his tongue around the opening to my pussy, teasing me before pushing it inside me.

His fingers dug into my thighs as he pushed my legs open wider, stretching his tongue farther inside me. I moaned, bucking my hips against him, and fisted the sheets of the bed.

I fucked his mouth—he fucked with me with his tongue.

Until I came, and he covered my pussy with his mouth, swallowing my orgasm.

West trailed his nose up my stomach until he took my nipple in his mouth again. He sucked hard, his teeth grazing it, and he fisted my hair at the nape of my neck.

"Your turn," he said.

I moved to my knees in a post-orgasmic haze as we switched positions. He stayed standing, and I blinked several times to right my vision before I undid his pants and tugged them down his legs. My eyes were in line with his lower stomach and the tight packs of muscle there, not to mention the deep, indented curves that formed the V that dipped beneath his pants.

His pants hit his ankles. I grabbed the sides of his boxers and ran my tongue along the line of that indent as I pulled his underwear away from him. His answering moan was low, barely there, as his cock sprang free and I wrapped my hand around its base.

11

"Sit down," I ordered him.

He did, perching on the end of the bed. I was still holding his cock in my hand, and I licked up the underside of the long, hard shaft. West's entire body twitched as I kissed the head of his cock, licking away the glistening drop of pre-cum.

I hated blow jobs, but I loved the power. It was the only time I did.

I took him in my mouth with hesitation, spitting slightly. My saliva dripped down the sides of his dick, and I moved my hand so I swiftly lubricated his cock before taking him back in my throat. This angle was perfect to suck him fully, and I used it to my advantage.

He was big and thick, but the alcohol had loosened my inhibitions and my reflexes, so he hit my throat before I gagged. His fingers sank into my hair, but I was already moving quickly, feeling the harsh throb of his arousal against my tongue. It felt like his entire body was twitching as I sucked his cock to the point I feared he'd truly come in my mouth. Between the rhythmic strokes of my hand and the hollowing of my cheeks as I gave everything I had, I waited for the salty spurt of pleasure I was sure would come.

It didn't.

He tightened his grip on my hair and tugged my head back, freeing my mouth before he leaned right forward and kissed me. I tasted myself on his tongue, but the kiss was short and harsh, and he released my hair only to throw me over the edge of the bed.

I fucking *ached.* Between the wild pounding of my heart and the intense throbbing between my legs, I was so turned on, so ready, and I bit down on my lip as West leaned over me and grabbed my wrists. He stretched my arms out in front of me, and his cock pressed between my ass cheeks.

His hands stroked down my back as he straightened and moved away from me, I should have been more conscious of the fact that I was bent over the edge of this bed, naked, with my ass in the air, my legs open, and my pussy exposed. But I wasn't—I was too busy waiting as he threw his pants to the side.

I heard the rip echo through the air and took a deep breath. No sooner had I sucked it in than he placed one hand on my left ass cheek and ran two fingers through the wetness between my legs. I moaned, jerking back against his hand in a plea.

I needed more. Desperately.

My fingers wound in the sheet beneath me as West guided his cock to my pussy. The head of it brushed against me, not quite inside me, but the touch was strong enough that it drew a tiny whimper from my mouth. God, I needed it—him. Whatever.

He pushed inside me an inch, his size making me still. He grabbed my hips and pulled me back as he slowly moved forward. "Fuck," he groaned, his fingers digging into my skin. "You're so tight."

I couldn't speak as he buried himself inside me. I turned my face to the side so I could breathe more easily and waited... Waited for him to move. To fuck me properly. To make me lose my mind.

I felt every inch of his cock as he thrust out and back into me. Slowly, he built a rhythm, speeding up so every thrust into me was a little bit harder. Despite his tight grip on me, my body moved every time he slammed into me. My nipples, already sensitive, brushed against the bed. It felt so good, even as he gripped my ass so tight that it hurt.

My orgasm was building. I trembled, my legs shaking with the effort of keeping me in the same position. West's movements were so controlled and strong, each thrust so powerful and determined, that I couldn't have moved if I'd have wanted to. Not as sweat slicked my body and my muscles tensed. Not as pleasure began to rise and he put a foot on the base of the bed, fucking me deeper.

This sex was rough and unapologetic between two strangers.

I loved it.

Loved it even as my orgasm came so harshly that my vision went black and my entire body tightened. My pussy clenched around his dick, and his fingertips dug into me as he thrust for his own orgasm.

And—oh my god.

Shivers accompanied the second orgasm that racked my body. I desperately grasped at the sheets, and my back arched, which lifted my butt back up and against him. I'd never felt pleasure this intense, and I barely breathed as West's relentless pounding drew the orgasm out until he stilled, buried entirely inside me, and dropped his face to my back while groaning.

Holy. Shit.

The man was a sex god.

We stayed that way until my knees finally gave out a couple of minutes later. He pulled out of me and, still wearing the condom, laughed quietly as he took hold of my waist to steady me. "Here," he said quietly, putting me on the bed.

I wiped hair from my face in a daze and searched for his eyes in the semi darkness of my room. I missed them but caught sight of his tight ass as he walked into the bathroom while rolling the condom off his dick. I lazily smiled before a yawn interrupted it midway. I was still feeling the aftereffects of the double orgasm as I halfheartedly scrambled for the sheets.

He would leave now.

No guy who fucked that good ever would stay the night.

I pulled tissues from the box on the nightstand, wiped between my legs, threw the tissue in the trash can, and climbed beneath the sheets. Rude? Maybe, but I was tired, and if I hadn't, I'd have fallen asleep somewhere other than the bed.

I tugged the sheets up to my neck and watched the area by the bathroom for him to come out to say goodbye, but my eyelids felt heavy as the veil of alcohol and orgasms drifted over me.

When I woke up some twelve hours later, he was gone.

THREE WEEKS LATER

I ran my fingers through my hair and looked to the ceiling. I shouldn't have picked up the phone. "No, Mom, I'm not dropping out of the wedding."

"Good." She barely paused before she responded. Her breath crackled down the line. "I told you Darren Costa was a bad idea, Mia. I'd heard things, you know."

The woman was going to be the death of me. I swore that, one day, when I was dead, the inscription on my tombstone would read: *Mia O'Halloran... Death By Insistent Mother.*

"Yes, Mom. I remember you telling me to avoid him." I held the phone between my shoulder and my ear as I opened the fridge.

Where was the freaking cranberry juice? In the pits of Hell, apparently. The exact same place I traveled to every time Mom called.

"And then you agreed I had to make my own mistakes because I'm not a child anymore. Remember that conversation?"

She scoffed as a red carton caught my eye. Holla!

"Yes," she said, "and here is my obligatory call to remind you that, yet again, I

15

was right. Lark, get off the curtains!" she yelled, momentarily distracted by the mischievous family tortoiseshell cat. "Mia, sweetheart, I just wish you'd find a nice man to settle down with."

"I'm twenty-five! All I want to settle down with is a pitcher of margarita and a trashy movie on Netflix."

"I married your father at twenty-two."

"No. You've never mentioned it." I tried not to roll my eyes. I did. Honestly.

"Are you giving me attitude?"

"Yes. Yes, Mom, I am."

She sighed. "I don't know where I went wrong with you."

You keep calling. "Darren was a perfectly nice guy. He was, for all intents and purposes, the guy you settle down with. However, his penis did not want to settle, and that wasn't my fault."

"I warned you," she said again.

I mouthed it as I poured my juice. It had been coming. I'd known it.

"I hear all sorts at the book club, you know. His mom—lovely lady, dear, can't imagine how she raised such a loser of a man—was very annoyed at his womanizing ways the last time she attended."

"What do you mean the last time? We broke up a month ago. Did you know he was cheating on me before I found out?"

Silence.

I knew referring to your mother as a bitch was wrong, but lord almighty, I wanted to.

"I suspected," Mom finally answered. "But I didn't know you were serious."

"Of course you didn't." I put the carton in the door of the fridge, where it belonged, and shut it. "Look, I appreciate the dating help, but I'm on a dating vacay. I don't need it right now."

"As long as you're not dropping out of the wedding." She sniffled. "But you really should find a nice young man."

"I'm not dropping out of my *best friend's* wedding just because he's the best man. That's like saying you're not going to visit your favorite coffee shop anymore because your ex-boyfriend who's rarely there owns it." *Must. Not. Bang. Head. Against. Wall.*

"Hmph."

"Hmph? What is hmph?"

"Your attitude, Mia."

I could picture her running her hand down the side of her face the way she always did when she got frustrated.

"It's very upsetting when you speak to me like that."

I closed my eyes and, pinching the bridge of my nose, counted to three in my head. Three times. It worked—she thought it was when the guilt was setting in when, in reality, it was so I could rein in the attitude and apologize without meaning it.

"Sorry, Mom." Next, the excuse. "I've been working a lot this week and I'm pretty tired."

"That's okay, dear."

I was done with this. "I gotta go. Another call is coming in. Bye, Mom."

"Bye, dear."

I hung up and let out a long, tortured breath before putting my phone on the counter, grabbing the edges of the kitchen counter, and dropping my head. Dear god. The woman was insufferable. As if a degree and a successful career in freelance marketing weren't enough—she wanted me settling down, pregnant and barefoot in the kitchen, making sure dinner was on the table at five p.m. She never failed to mention that she had been married at twenty-two and pregnant with me at twenty-three. It was like a sick form of delight for her. Never mind that the most work she'd done since then, aside from raising me, was browsing Amazon for a new book for the book club.

Not that I was judging. I'd also put in several hours searching Amazon for a new book, but one day, maybe she would understand I held the dubious title of Queen of Dating Disasters, and to settle down, I needed to lose that title.

It wasn't going to happen any time soon.

I straightened, finished my glass of juice, and set the glass in the sink. I'd actually woken up in a good mood this morning, but now... Well. Let's just say I felt like a menstruating Satan. That was the delightful effect Mom had on me.

I could only guess that Dad was playing golf, because she knew better than to call me when he was around. He told her to shut up and give me a break if he caught her ripping me a new one.

And to think she assumed I'd relinquish my duties as maid of honor for Allie's wedding just because Darren cheated on me. We were only seeing each other for six months, and for at least four of those, he was banging his way around town— and the surrounding ones. My friendship with Allie meant a hell of a lot more than that shitstick and his shitty actions.

Besides, I was over it now. Way over it. I was determined that, in two weeks, when she got married, I'd march in like the badass I was, show the dickmonkey what he was missing, then... Well, not walk out, because that wouldn't go down well.

Meanwhile, I'd be convincing her of that fact. I was also pretty sure I'd have to do it every single damn day until she watched me lead my best friend down the aisle.

My phone rang again, and I groaned, reaching for it. Damn it. If this was my mom, I was gonna lose my mind. Luckily, the screen showed that it was my boss's assistant, Emily.

I say luckily. It was a fucking Sunday and my one guaranteed day off.

"Hello?" I buried my hand in my hair, leaning forward on the kitchen side.

"Hi, Mia?" Emily's soft voice traveled down the line. "Michelle wants to know if you can come in to speak with her this afternoon."

"I..." I glanced at the clock that ticked away next to my fridge. "Sure. I can be there by two. Is that good?"

"Perfect. I'll let her know. Thank you." Emily hung up before I could say another word, and a sigh escaped me.

Wonderful.

Even though it was Sunday, I knew I needed to dress professionally. That was the exact reason why the Devil Shoes' heels were clicking their way down the empty hall toward the offices. MM Marketing was my boss, Michelle's, lovechild. The literal equivalent of having a baby in her eyes.

Her second marriage came with her stepson, Jamie, so I guessed she figured her lady bits could do without the torture of childbirth.

That and the woman would never take maternity leave anyway. And she was, well, fifty. So a little on the old side for babies now.

Besides, she had no need to. She'd cemented MM Marketing as the number-one marketing firm to hire in Southern California with grueling hours and determination, but it had been worth it. We rarely had space for last-minute jobs, and she could count any number of Hollywood stars among her friends.

A few had even come into the offices. Not that I'd spoken to them. If I had, I'd have vomited in the nearest trash can. Or on their shoes. Probably the shoes.

After four years, I still wondered how I had been lucky enough to intern here during my senior year and get hired right after graduation. I wasn't going to question it though. Some surprises were worth accepting at face value.

"Hi, Mia." Emily beamed up at me from behind her desk and tucked her honey-blond hair behind her ear. "Michelle's waiting for you in her office. Go right in."

"Thanks, Emily." I returned the smile and swept past her desk. Then I knocked on Michelle's door before pushing it open. "Michelle?"

Her chestnut-brown hair elegantly bounced around her shoulders as she turned away from the window to look at me. There was a distinct and unusual sadness lingering in her dark-brown gaze, and my heart clenched. Her presence was such that, if she felt a certain way, the air changed to reflect it. And the air definitely felt sad today.

"Mia." She smiled her usual stunning smile, but it didn't reach her eyes. "Shut the door and take a seat, doll."

Wordlessly, I closed the door behind me and swept my skirt beneath my thighs as I sat down. The black leather chairs were great until they stuck to your thighs.

I finally spoke when, after a couple of minutes, she hadn't said anything. "Is everything okay?"

She sighed heavily, removed her dark-red glasses, and pinched the bridge of her nose. "We found out this morning that Jamie's mom was in a car crash late last night on her way home from work. She...didn't make it."

Oh no. That poor boy.

"Thankfully," she continued, "he's staying with us this weekend. Alan and Jamie are already driving up to Fresno. I am, of course, going to follow them, but I needed to straighten things out here."

"I'm so sorry." I reached across the table and lightly squeezed her fingers. "I know you were good friends with her."

"In recent years, yes. Jamie, bless his sweet heart, wanted it, so we did it. I'm not sure the news has sunk in for any of us yet."

No kidding. As much of a pain as my mom is, I couldn't imagine losing her at fifteen.

"Anyway." Michelle replaced her glasses and straightened. "I'm going to be out of town for the week, and you can understand this poses a problem for the business, because I was due to fly to Vegas tomorrow to meet with the owner of Rykman and Cruz Enterprises."

I nodded. That was a big. Ass. Contract.

"I want you to go in my place."

I blinked harshly. Did she just—what?

"You...want me to go to Vegas and take over this contract?"

"Yes. It's not one I can reschedule or put off, and I need someone who knows what they're doing. You've been taking on more bars and clubs recently, and very damn well too." She grabbed a red box file from beside her and slid it to me. "Rykman and Cruz Enterprises own several joints in and around the Strip, but their strip clubs are the most profitable, and Mr. Rykman and his business partner, Mr. Cruz, want to maximize on them."

"They need help to market strip clubs. In Vegas." What the hell kinda business were they running? Those things sold themselves, Vegas or not.

"Not necessarily. They want something unique and outside the box. They want to start with the men's club, Rock Solid."

I froze. My tongue flicked out against my lips, and I felt the slight blush that rose on my cheeks. "I, uh... That's where Allie's bachelorette party was."

Michelle smiled again, and this time, it touched her eyes. "Really? So you're familiar?"

A little too familiar. But I wasn't going to tell my boss that. "Yes, and now, I'm really confused. They were packed all night. Why do they need more marketing?"

"Darling, I have no idea. All I know is that, if a good job is done with Rock Solid, they're going to take us on for their other businesses. This contract is huge. Are you up to it?"

No. What if I saw the stripper again? In fact, it was almost guaranteed I'd see him again. But this was an important job. It couldn't slip by the wayside. And if I did it well...

"Sure, I can do it. Will I have to stay in Vegas?"

Michelle nodded. "I have an apartment rented for the next three weeks. I wanted to be completely sure I could be there for as long as they needed. I'll call the owner today and have it transferred to your name, but the payment will stay on the company account."

"Three weeks?" I paused. But that was over the wedding. "Allie gets married in two."

"Come back," she says dismissively. "I'll let them know when I call them to inform them of the change in situation, but you may even be done before she gets married. Don't worry, doll. You won't miss her wedding."

That was a relief. Yet again, I was reminded how lucky I was to have a relatively flexible job. Even if that job was taking me to a place that made me blush on thought.

"Okay, sure. I'll do it. What about my other clients?"

"Emily will contact all upcoming clients and either reschedule or reassign them to someone else. Ongoing ones you can communicate online and work with. Does that sound feasible?"

I looked to the ceiling for a moment and pulled my current work to mind. If I got to it as soon as I got home, I could finish up the Barker project. Then I'd only have the Santiago one, and that was mostly rebranding the restaurant. That could easily be done online, as it didn't really require much of my physical presence.

"I can do that," I confirmed, a small smile on my face.

"Perfect!" Michelle clapped her hands together in front of her, and I knew instantly I'd just taken a huge weight off her shoulders. "This file has all the basic information you need about the clubs. You could easily read it on the plane tomorrow. I'll have Emily call the airline now, and then she'll e-mail you your tickets, the apartment info, and car rental information." The smile that stretched across her face was genuine again, even if it was hiding the sadness that lingered beneath. "Thank you, Mia. You've just made a difficult situation much easier."

"Don't worry." I grabbed the file as I stood. "Three weeks in Vegas to work at a male strip club? Honestly, Mich, it could be worse."

She laughed. "I'm a little jealous, not gonna lie."

"I'll send you pictures. Say it's important, as you're brainstorming with me and you need to know what I'm working with."

"Working with, indeed." Her eyes glittered. "Go on, doll. Go get yourself ready."

I'd spent the last thirty minutes convincing Allie I wouldn't miss the wedding or the rehearsal dinner. The closer the date got, the more Bridezilla she got. It was the strangest thing because Allie was one of the most laid-back people I'd ever known. When most people tore their hair out over moving house, she whipped around like the fucking Flash and had everything packed in a matter of days.

I had known there was a little freak inside her, waiting to come out.

Shame it had to come out on me.

Regardless, she was calm.

"And we have the—oh my god, Mia!" she shrieked, cutting herself off midsentence. "The dress fitting! The final dress fittings are in a week and you're in Vegas!"

Oh, fuck me sideways on a pier. I'd forgotten about that. "I'll come back. It's fine! It's not that far. I can fly down and back in the same day."

"What if there are delays? Oh god. Can you get here by ten a.m.? Are you sure? I can probably make it later. I'm sure they wouldn't mind, but this has been set for months. Oh my god, I'm having a heart attack."

"You're not having a heart attack," I managed to say through the guilt slowly snaking its way through my body. I wasn't a mean person, but I'd honestly forgotten about the dress fitting. "Sorry, Al. I didn't mean to forget. This was a last-minute job." For me, anyway.

"I know, I know." Her voice was small, and I felt even worse. "You're meeting these guys tomorrow, right?"

"Just Mr. Rykman. His partner is out of town for a family event, but yeah. Since they've only spoken with Michelle, I have to meet with him tomorrow and pitch my basic ideas."

"Do you think you can ask about the fitting? I mean... Is that forward?"

Maybe a little, but I had taken this job on unexpectedly and my previous schedule had been worked around wedding obligations. Surely Mr. Rykman had to understand that.

"I can ask. I'm sure it won't be a problem, given the circumstances."

"Thanks, Mi. You're the best."

If that were true, I'd have remembered the dress fitting. Ah... Who wanted to remember a scenario that might tell them they've gained five pounds anyway? Even if it was for my best friend. She knew how forgetful I was.

"You're welcome. I'll call you when I know, okay?"

"Okay. I'm working all day, so text me if I don't answer."

"You got it. Now, go hang out with Joe before he thinks I'm stealing you from hundreds of miles away."

"He's playing the PlayStation."

I could imagine her wrinkling her nose.

"The man's twenty-seven," she said. "Shouldn't he be giving it up?"

"I don't think they ever do." That probably wasn't what she wanted to hear, but oh well. "Did he at least load the dishwasher?"

She paused. "Yes. Oh, I guess he can have ten minutes. I have my Kindle, after all. I'm going to take a bath."

"Atta girl." I grinned even though she couldn't see me. "I'll call you tomorrow, Al. I'm gonna see if I can do some more work here before my meeting."

"Okay. Love you. Thank you. Sorry for freaking out."

"Don't worry about it. I'll fix it. Love you, Bridezilla." I hang up, laughing, but not before she yelled, "Bitch!" down the line. It made me laugh harder as I put my phone on the sofa next to me and reached for my laptop.

As it loaded, I pulled out my plans for the strip club, Rock Solid. I had a handful of ideas that would provide a good basis for conversation. I was sure Michelle had drawn up her own plan, but those ideas were hers, not mine, and she was adamant that we all proposed our ideas.

Despite being business-savvy, she was creative, and she was certain the two mixed. She always told us that you could be the smartest, most driven businessperson in the world, but if you weren't creative, you'd fail at some point, because creativity takes many forms. Paintings, writing, singing, acting—they were all creative acts, and just because you were creative didn't mean you weren't business-savvy.

I hoped that she'd given me this job because she thought I was both of those things. If not, I had to prove it. This job was important to me because I was still the baby of the company, and if I got it right, I felt like I'd prove I had it in me to do this.

I loved my job. I loved marketing—from the branding to the statistics to the plans to get your name out there. I loved helping people realize their potential, maybe because every time I did, a part of me realized my own.

Maybe, if I got through this job and the stops for the wedding, I'd convince myself I was worthy of the opportunity I'd been given four years ago at long last.

My day was going to shit and I'd barely left my goddamn apartment.

If it wasn't the zipper on my favorite skirt breaking, it was the fact that I had to sew a button back on my blouse, and my shoes were rubbing like a sex addict in solitary confinement. I was incredibly fed up, and I muttered to myself in frustration as I got in my car.

I hated this car too. Goddamn sleek, sexy bitch. She was hotter than I was, and I wasn't exactly shit stuck in the sole of someone's shoe. Speaking of shoes—the Devil Shoes were languishing at the bottom of my suitcase thinking about the hell they'd inflicted on my poor, little pinkie toes.

I put the car into gear and pulled out of the apartment parking lot. I was only a few blocks from the Strip, but as I knew Rock Solid had parking spots and I was wearing four-inch heels, I had no intention of walking. I'd have rather dissected a frog than walk that far in the Devil Shoes twopoint-oh.

Okay, these were actually comfortable four-inch heels, but whatever. Heels were heels, and nobody else needed to know they were comfortable.

Vegas was much quieter at this time in the morning. It was barely nine a.m., and the only people out were the locals headed to work or the tourists who hadn't been up all night gambling. That wasn't very many people. It made driving to Rock Solid easy and quick, and I pulled into the small lot five minutes before I was due.

When I'd killed the engine, I looked out the window at the building. I was so familiar with this place thanks to the entire night we'd spent there three weeks ago. I was more than a little disconcerted to be back so soon. I'd honestly never foreseen a circumstance that would say I'd need to come back.

Yet there I was. Waiting. Outside the club.

I glanced one last time at the clock on the dashboard that blinked bright orange and grabbed my purse from the passenger's side, making sure to grab the file beneath it. It was too big to fit inside my beloved royal-blue Michael Kors purse, so it had resorted to being its perch.

I would have strapped the purse in, but maybe that was overkill.

Maybe.

Once I'd gotten out, I locked the car then took a deep breath. With my heels, my white blouse, and my belted pencil skirt with a light blazer to match, I knew I looked professional. Even my lightly curled, auburn hair bouncing around below my shoulders looked professional, but I was nervous. This was by far my biggest assignment since I'd joined MM Marketing, and that wasn't a fact I was going to forget any time soon.

I had to make it count.

Although I knew that it wasn't the sole cause of my nervousness, I had no idea how strip clubs worked. Did the strippers practice at the club during the day? Did they use the poles for fitness? Were they open all day or just in the evening? Would I run into Mr. Multiple Oh-Oh-Oh, as my friends had so courteously dubbed him?

I shook the thoughts off as I approached the front door. There were a few lights on inside, so I hugged the file close to my chest and pushed. The door opened with a slight creak, and I bit the inside of my cheek as I stepped into the club. The sound of a vacuum somewhere in the building filled the air with a gentle buzz, and as I approached the bar, the swishing sounds of the glass dishwasher broke through the vacuum.

I looked around but couldn't see anyone, so I set my things on the bar.

"Hi!" A bubbly, blond woman appeared at the end of the bar.

I jumped, my heart beating hard.

"Oh my gosh! I'm sorry. I didn't mean to startle you. I thought you'd seen me."

"No, but please don't worry." It was hard not to smile at her. "I'm Mia O'Halloran. I'm here on behalf of MM Marketing to meet with Mr. Rykman?"

"Oooh, yes! He told me he was expecting a Ms. O'Halloran around nine." She clapped her hands together, the sound muffled by the towel she was holding, and kicked the door of a small fridge shut. "Give me two seconds and I'll fetch him for you."

"Thank you." I smiled again and perched on one of the seats.

The club looked vastly different during the daylight hours. There were no windows in the building, so the warm, yellow light that flooded the space was artificial, but somehow, it looked just like natural light. Sticky rings still sat on tables, and odd bits of trash still littered the floor, mostly beneath the tables. I guessed whoever was vacuuming would be in there next.

"He said, if you take a seat in the end booth, he'll be right down. He made sure Sally—that's the head cleaner—did that one already. The tables are biggest there. Can I get you something to drink? Coffee? Tea?"

"A coffee would be great, thank you. Just regular, milk but no sugar."

"No problem. I'm Vicky."

"Mia. Obviously." I laughed as I shook her hand over the bar. "Thank you." I got up and headed for the booth she'd indicated. It was several down from the one we'd been in three weeks ago, and she was right. Also the only clean one.

I moved the ashtray to the edge of the table so I had more room and then tucked my purse on the seat next to me. Nerves danced in the pit of my stomach once again, but I managed to fight them long enough to open my file, remove the necessary notebook and pen, and thank Vicky for my coffee.

It smelled so good, and I sighed after taking the first red-hot sip. Yes—I was the freak who could drink coffee the second it was made. A trait I'd gotten from my father, and one I liked. I didn't have to wait as long as everyone else to start the caffeine hit.

A deep, familiar voice rumbled through the air. "Ms. O'Halloran?"

My head snapped up and my gaze landed on the man the voice belonged to.

Dark hair.

Sharp jaw with a five-o'clock shadow.

Plump lips.

Bright. Blue. Eyes.

"Oh shit," I whispered then clapped my hand over my mouth. *Mia! You can't swear in front of clients, even if you've fucked them!* I forced myself to get my shit together and stood, holding my hand out. "Mr. Rykman, I presume?"

His lips curved into a dirty, sexy smirk, and his grip on my hand was firm. "You presume correctly, Ms. O'Halloran. And, if you don't mind my saying so, you make this awful Monday morning a lot brighter."

My cheeks flushed. Damn my blush reflex. "Thank you. Should we get started?"

He was still holding my hand.

Houston, we have a problem. A really fucking big one.

This was bad.

Apparently, my day was determined to really go to shit, because there I was, staring into the eyes of the stripper...who was also the owner. And who, three weeks ago, had fucked the ever-loving shit out of me. And had the most wonderful cock.

Oh god. Why was I thinking about his cock? I shouldn't have been thinking about his cock. What was I thinking?

About his cock, obviously.

Damn it, no! Thinking about his cock was off-limits. Any kind of anything to do with his cock was off-limits.

Why was I thinking *cock* so much?

I had to stop thinking about his...dick.

There. That made a nice change. But I was still thinking about it.

"Are you all right? You look a little dizzy."

I forced myself to stop thinking and focused on the way he was looking at me. With that smirk still firmly in place, there was no doubt it was amusement, pure and simple.

I snatched my hand away from his. "Let's get started, shall we? Michelle didn't tell me anything you'd discussed, as she needed to leave town, so I'm behind on your thoughts."

He motioned for me to take my seat again and sat opposite me. "Actually, I'd like to hear yours."

I swept my hand down my skirt and peered up at him. "I only started work on this yesterday. I don't have very much at all."

"Well, what do you have?"

Was that smirk painted on? Had to be. Either that or he had very resilient facial muscles.

I tightened my jaw but released it before I spoke. I had to keep my cool. Professionalism would be key to getting through this job.

"I think you need to rebrand," I told him.

"As in…a new logo?"

"Maybe an entire new look, but certainly, a new logo. It's not a secret that a new look is the first key to getting attention."

"Is there something wrong with the one we have now?" He slowly raised an eyebrow, still amused.

"Nothing, but it's always my first suggestion. Usually for slow businesses, not ones that are still booming. But, considering the budget I've been given, I'd try it." I tapped my pen against the table. "The next is what you do inside. Have you thought about a theme night? A once-a-week show?"

"No. Great ideas."

"Thank you. And, since your primary audience is women between the ages of twenty-one and forty, you could bring in a mixologist to create a custom cocktail. Keep the ingredients secret, offer it in shots, drinks, and fishbowls."

"I like that. Have you done something like that before?"

"For a client?" I asked.

He nodded.

"Once or twice, but they decided not to keep the ingredients secret, and they had two or three cocktails instead of one."

"So you know someone who could create one."

Not a question. A statement. Man, he was enthusiastic.

"I live two hours outside of L.A. I don't just know someone—I know the best someone." I clicked my pen and scribbled a small note to call Lili. She was the best damn mixologist I'd ever met—and if she couldn't get there, she'd know someone closer who could.

"Great. These all make my ideas look like child's play."

"That's why you hire a professional."

"It is, indeed." His lips moved back to the smirk, and despite the tug it forced between my legs, I couldn't not ask my next question.

"Mr. Rykman—"

He leaned forward, resting his forearms on the table. His white shirt was rolled up to his elbows, and the tightening of the fabric stretched against his muscular arms. "I think you know me well enough to call me West."

"*Mr. Rykman,*" I repeated, looking him right in the eye. "Excuse me for asking, but why have you hired a professional? From what I saw, you don't need any marketing help. Your club is booming. We're usually called into failing businesses who use their last profits to hire us or independent traders or new companies who need to get their name out there."

"We haven't done anything with the club for two years." He doesn't move, and he keeps his bright eyes trained on mine. "We did an initial marketing campaign, got the best male dancers we could, and now, the club runs itself, but it's getting stale. A full club most nights doesn't mean business is growing, Ms. O'Halloran. It's steady, but now, I want more. Strip clubs aren't exactly rare in this city. We have to stand out before someone else does. For all I know, someone's already planning to."

Michelle had been right. He wanted to be unique, get ahead of the game. Beat someone else to the success.

"Do you know what the other clubs around you are doing?" I sipped my coffee then tilted my head to the side.

"I don't make it a habit to go and watch men strip naked," he drawled. "Unless they're being paid by me."

I sighed and sat back. That was his first problem. He had no idea what anyone else was doing. He'd done no market research. This was going to take a long time.

"I need you to go to other clubs and see what they're doing."

Both of his eyebrows shot up. "Excuse me?"

"You can look shocked all you like, Mr. Rykman. This is basic research. For all I know, there's another club rebranding in two weeks, so yours needs to happen before that. Maybe someone else has a custom cocktail. I need to see what's in it to make sure this one doesn't come close. Maybe they have theme nights. What themes? How often? What days? Are they popular?"

"All right. I see your point. And I have to do this?"

"Of course. I don't know what you do on a regular basis here, do I? What's your current marketing plan? How much do you spend on advertising? This is all information Michelle didn't share with me, because you probably discussed it verbally and she didn't write it down." The woman had an eidetic memory, I was sure. "Unless you can provide me with it all in the next six hours, your Monday night will be spent in someon else's strip club."

He looked at me for a long moment before something flashed in his eyes. "Are you coming with me?"

"I didn't plan on it."

"So, you're happy to make me do it, but you're not planning on it yourself?"

"That...sounds one hundred percent accurate."

"What if I go alone and get derailed by a female club?" His lips twitched in amusement. "That'd be far more entertaining for me."

I shrugged a shoulder. "Your business, Mr. Rykman. Not mine."

He craned his neck to look behind the booth at the bar and then slid across the seat to me. Thank god my purse was between us, but he was still too close for comfort. And not because I was creeped out, but because, well, my heart was pounding a little too loudly. I couldn't move because I was sitting on the edge of the seat, but he didn't touch me.

He might as well have been.

My skin burned like he was.

"Ms. O'Halloran...I've hired you. It most definitely is your business."

I turned my face to look at him. Mistake. Big mistake. His eyes were hypnotic, almost, and once I'd looked at him, I couldn't look away.

"Fine. I'll come with you. Three hours, three clubs. But it's completely professional."

"Are you worried it would turn personal?" He quirked an eyebrow. Again.

I hated that—mostly because he looked so damn hot doing it.

I shifted my body so I was facing him, trying to ignore how fucking good he looked. Seriously. It had to be illegal.

"We're victims of circumstance, Mr. Rykman. As far as I'm concerned, our previous...dalliance...never happened."

"Really, angel?" He twirled a lock of my hair around his finger and leaned in so his breath skittered across my skin. "Because, for something that never happened, I can remember all too well how good your tight pussy felt when you came all over my cock. Twice."

I swallowed. So could I. And so could my pussy. She was ready to do it again, right there, right then, the greedy little slut.

I squeezed my thighs together in the hope he wouldn't notice. "That's inappropriate."

"You brought it up."

I... Shit. I did, didn't I? "Then I apologize. I shouldn't have mentioned it."

But it was still inappropriate. So was my throbbing clit. *Fuck.*

His lips quirked to one side. "Apology accepted but unnecessary." He picked my notebook up and ran his tongue over his upper lip as he read.

I knew that it was deliberate, but it didn't stop my gaze from dropping to the slow way it swept over his lip.

I cleared my throat and looked at the stage, which ran down the middle of the club. Completing this contract was going to be harder than I'd thought.

Screwed.

That's what I was. Screwed as fuck.

If Michelle hadn't been in such a shit spot, I'd have called her and gotten out of this, but I couldn't. I was trapped in this situation all because I had decided to make an on-the-spot proposal three weeks ago—one he had taken.

Now look.

I had to work with this man for as long as it took to get his club marketed as something phenomenal. This handsome, powerful, commanding man.

Well, he could dirty-talk me all he liked. He could bring up our night at every turn. I wouldn't give in. I'd made myself the promise to focus on work and nothing else.

I trusted too easily and fell in love too quickly. My love life was one long trail of heartbreaks.

Yes—West Rykman could no doubt seduce the pants off any adult female in the world, but he wouldn't do it me again.

"Ms. O'Halloran?" he asked, interrupting my thoughts, making me turn back to him. "Eight o'clock tonight? They don't get going until then."

I must have been looking at him blankly, because he continued.

"The clubs."

"Oh. Yes. Yes, that sounds fine." I took my notebook from him and set it on the table with the pen. "Write down your e-mail, and when I get back to my apartment, I'll send you an e-mail detailing what we've discussed so you can decide which points you'd like to proceed on."

"All of them." He scribbled his e-mail down anyway. "You have an apartment? You're not staying on the Strip?"

I shook my head and put the pad and the pen back into my box file. "No. My boss has a low tolerance for the Strip, so the apartment she booked is a few blocks away."

He reached into my file and, after tearing a piece of paper out of the back of the notebook, grabbed the pen and put them in front of me. "Write it down. I'll get you tonight."

"I'm perfectly capable of driving myself, thank you." I picked my pen up but pushed the paper back to him.

"I'll get you tonight." He placed two fingers on top of the paper and eased it back toward me, where he held it in place.

"I said—"

"And I said I'll get you. Don't make me follow you back, Mia."

"It's Ms. O'Halloran to you."

"It's Mia. Now, write your address down, because you're testing my patience, sitting there all fiery and gorgeous, and as much as you deny it, you know what happens when it goes."

A bolt of defiance shot through me. Annoyance teased my consciousness, so I scribbled my address down then slammed my pen into the folder and closed it. I grabbed my purse and the folder and stood, smoothing my hand over my skirt.

No sooner had I turned away than I looked at him over my shoulder. He was leaning back in the booth, his gaze hot on me, and he had the scrap of paper between two of his fingers, turning it slowly.

Our gazes met, and this time, all traces of amusement were gone from his blue stare. There was only the dark tinge of lust. He was deadly serious—ironic, consider the game he'd just played.

"Oh, Mr. Rykman? One more thing." I turned my body back to face him and bent forward, resting my hand on the table.

His eyes never left mine. Not even as my lips curved up in a dirty smirk of my own.

"I said that night didn't happen. I never said I didn't remember how I sucked your thick cock right before you bent me over the bed and fucked me senseless."

With that parting shot and a dangerous glimmer in his eyes, I spun and skipped down the steps that led to the main floor and the stage. I swept my hair around one shoulder and walked away without looking back, no matter how badly I wanted to.

Yes—work was my priority, but if he wanted to fuck with me, then I'd fuck with him right back.

I had no doubt his day would be a lot more uncomfortable than mine.

I'd lost my mind. I knew I had.

Going to three strip clubs with a man who was my client, market research or not, was downright insane.

Not that I had any time to contemplate it.

"I can't believe you just ran off to Vegas without informing me or your father."

"I didn't run off, Mom. I'm here to work. Michelle's stepson's mom died, so I'm taking this contract for her."

She scoffed disapprovingly. "You should have told her no. You have a responsibility to be here for Allie!"

"Good grief, woman. She knows I'm here. I called her as soon as I landed. I'm coming back for the dress fitting"—*hopefully*—"and I'll be back in plenty of time for the rehearsal dinner."

Silence rang through the line.

"Oh," she said. "I suppose, if she's okay with it..."

"She is," I said sharply, glancing at the clock.

Five to eight. She still had enough time to bring something else up.

"Why didn't you call her before you left?"

And there it was. "I had to finish up a contract for another client before I could leave. I didn't have time. She understood."

"Your job is too important to you."

That's a matter of opinion, but whatever. It wasn't like I had a cat to fill my time.

"I'm buying you a cat when you come home. You need something else to do."

"I don't want a cat," I groaned.

"Why not?"

"Because. They're assholes." I was asshole enough for my apartment, thank you very much.

"Only when your father trains them."

"Mom, you're killing me here. I don't want a cat. I love my job. Allie doesn't need me to hold her hand through the wedding. She can call me anytime. I'll be home when it matters."

Two knocks sounded at my door, and I stood, making sure the laces of my heels were tied around my ankle.

"Please give me a break. I can't take your neurotic phone calls every ten minutes." I opened the door to West Rykman, who was looking hot as all get-out in a white shirt, his sleeves rolled up yet again, and dark-blue jeans. I motioned for him to come in and tuned back in to Mom's rambling.

"...neurotic is very hurtful, Mia. And why do you have time for Allie's calls but not mine?"

"Because Allie is the one getting married, not you." Guilt trip in three, two, one...

"You'll note that but not that your words have hurt me?"

I rolled my eyes. Right on time. "I'm sorry, Mom. I didn't mean to hurt your feelings. I have to go, okay? I have to work."

"Work? What work could you possibly be doing at eight in the evening in Las Vegas?"

I pursed my lips. I could tell her, but then I'd probably give her a stroke.

"Business dinner," I lied smoothly.

"Isn't that late?"

Not late enough if she could call me. "It was a last-minute addition to my schedule. Everyone was busy before."

West raised an eyebrow as I spun my lie.

"Okay, Mom, my cab is waiting! Bye!" I cut her off before she could finish saying one word.

I closed my eyes and pinched the bridge of my nose. Good. God. There was always something, wasn't there? Anyone would have thought she was the mother of the bride with the way she was going on. I accepted that Allie's mom had been her best friend since they were fifteen, but fuck me. She needed to give me a break.

"That sounded...uncomfortable," West noted, his eyebrow still raised.

"Everything about my mother is uncomfortable," I drawled, grabbing my purse from the kitchen counter. The open-plan living space in this apartment was lovely. "Let's go before she calls again and finds out I'm lying."

His deep laugh follows me out, and I lock the door.

"Why are you lying to her?" he asked.

I sighed and ran my hands through my hair as we stepped into the elevator. "Honestly, if I told her the truth, she'd probably die of horror. On one hand, she wouldn't call me almost every day anymore, but she'd probably guilt-trip me from beyond the grave, and if she did that, she'd probably know I was lying about the apologies too."

"Sounds complicated."

"Complicated, dysfunctional, lunacy... They're all the same, aren't they?"

His lips tugged up in a half smile. "I guess so."

The elevator doors dinged open and we both exited it. I held my hands close to my body to avoid inadvertently touching him. Lord only knew what would happen if I did that.

"Right here," he said, touching my back and guiding me toward a sleek-looking Audi.

There went my no-touching, huh?

He pushed a button on his keys and the lights flashed. Then he opened the passenger's door for me. I paused before I got in, but if he noticed, he didn't say anything.

With Mom over and done with, this was still a bad idea.

Bad, bad idea.

Professionalism. I chanted it over and over. That word was the key to everything and I needed to remember it. Needed to remember that he could look as hot as he wanted and we could throw all the dirty words we wanted around but that was all it ever could be—dirty words. Not dirty touches or anything else.

"That purse looks too small for your notebook," West said after a couple of minutes driving.

"That's because it is. I don't have it."

"Then how are you going to take notes? I assume that's the point of a market research trip."

"Yes, but for starters, this was supposed to be your trip, not mine." I pulled my phone out. "And I'll be taking notes on this. It'll look like I'm texting. If I go into a club with a rival owner and start scribbling in a notebook, it'll look a little suspicious, don't you think?"

"True. But you assume they'll know who I am."

"Is that incorrect?"

"No."

"Well, then. That was a waste of time bringing it up, wasn't it?"

He cut his eyes to me. "You look like you need a drink, angel."

"You'll be the one in need of alcohol if you call me angel again, except it'll be to clean out your wounds."

"Feisty." He flashed me a grin and pulled into the Rock Solid parking lot.

If I had known he'd just park here, I'd have insisted further that I could drive myself. What could I do?

"Come on, *Ms. O'Halloran*."

I pursed my lips as I opened the door and got out of the car. I stunned myself for a moment when my foot hit the floor—I hadn't realized the car was so low—but managed to straighten and shut the door without any further problems. Honestly, I had no idea what model this car was except sexy as hell and low enough that I could hop up on top of the roof and sit there comfortably.

It was very...Vegas, I realized, as I watched West adjust his rolled sleeves to flatten them. He was very Vegas, if there were such a thing. There had to be if I was thinking it. He wasn't flashy—car aside—but he was...put together. His shirts were perfectly pressed, there was never a crease in his pants, and his shoes were always shiny. Even now, the dark-brown shoes he was wearing complemented his well-fitting jeans, and I didn't want to think about how much money that man spent on tailoring.

It had to be borderline unhealthy. Then again, he had the body beneath all the fabric. If I were a guy, I'd want well-tailored clothing to show that shit off too.

"You done staring at me yet, Mia?"

I blinked harshly. "You've got dirt on your shirt."

Lame. Super, super, lame. That's the kinda stuff ten-year-old boys say to ten-year-old girls when they're being tiny idiots.

"Nice try. We need to go or I'm hauling your ass in the back seat."

"Can you try to be professional?" I snapped, stalking around the car. The noise of the Strip carried over, punctuated by the booming music from the building he owned, which was right next to us, but we could talk perfectly clearly. "We have to work together, and I'm not interested in your innuendos."

"Promises."

"What?"

"They're not innuendos. They're promises."

"Again!" I stopped and put my hands on my hips. "This isn't professional, West."

He stopped too and turned back to me. "West. That's the first time you've called me anything but Mr. Rykman since you got here."

"I got here yesterday and saw you for the first time not twelve hours ago!"

"And look how frustrated you are."

Frustrated was an understatement. I was getting downright pissed off with him and his attitude. Fucking hell, why did I always put myself in stupid situations? I should have just agreed to do the research alone.

"I think it's best if I do this alone," I said slowly. "Clearly, this isn't a good idea. I won't be able to concentrate if you're driving me to insanity."

His eyebrow arched, tugging his lips up with it. "A young woman going to various male strip clubs in the middle of Las Vegas all alone? Shit, Mia. Why didn't I think that was a good idea?"

"I'm more than capable of taking care of myself."

"And all it takes is one person who's better at *taking care* of you than you are yourself. You're not doing this alone—and we're not fucking arguing about it. I promise to be professional from now on."

I stared at him, annoyance still swirling low in my stomach, but he looked sincere, and he was right. I couldn't go flouncing around male strip clubs alone. That was asking for trouble, and knowing me, I'd attract it.

"Fine," I half huffed out and walked once more. "But let's get this straight so there are no suspicions about your presence in these clubs. You're a friend of my brother. He's getting married, I'm the maid of honor, and I'm here to find venues for the bachelorette party."

"Nice. And when they ask why you're not going to Rock Solid?"

I sank my teeth into my lower lip as I thought about it. Crap. Why hadn't I thought about that?

"Mia, please stop doing that."

"Doing what?"

"Thank you." He rolled a shoulder. "Well?"

I let the unanswered question go. "My brother is uncomfortable with the idea of it, so you're showing me the other hot joints in town."

He chuckled low and wrapped his arm around my shoulders to pull me out of the way of a cyclist. Stupid idiot should have been on the road.

"Sounds like you've got this all figured out, then," West said, letting me go. "Good timing. We're here."

I looked up at the blazing sign above my head. It flashed neon red: *Sin Ropa.*

"That's Spanish, right?"

"Think so. Ready to go in?"

I shrugged. Didn't matter if I was or not. I was going in regardless.

"Well well, West Rykman. What are you doing here?" the guy behind the counter asked. "Brought a friend? She worked out your place isn't all it's made out to be?"

West smirked. Not the dirty, sexy one I was used to. This one was...condescending.

"Not yet, Ryan. A friend's sister. She's in charge of his fiancée's bachelorette party and he doesn't want it at my place, so I'm showing her around."

Ryan peered around West at me and ran his gaze up and down my body in a leering way. It hovered on my chest for a long moment. "She could show me around."

"I'm sure my tits are happy to hear it, but if you don't mind, I'd like to go inside." I smiled tightly as West covered a laugh with a cough.

Ryan's eyes snapped up to mine, finally, and he nodded.

"Thank you. Although I'd work on your customer service. You're at the bottom of my list and I haven't even seen the other places yet."

I stalked toward the thick curtains—ugh, how cliché—that separated the entrance hall from the club. Even West made an amused grunting sound behind me, but when we entered, it was so dark that I couldn't see him when I turned around.

He immediately took hold of my shoulders and steered me through the crowds of people. There weren't hundreds, but *Sin Ropa* was set up differently than Rock Solid. Instead of one long stage, there were several smaller stages all around the club. It made the tables haphazard as people had clearly moved them to get near the guy they wanted to watch.

We finally got to the bar after dodging an almost-spill by a chick who was overenthusiastically stuffing her dollars into this guy's pants, and West deposited me on a stool, stepping up close to me.

"What do you want to drink?" he yelled into my ear.

"I want to see the cocktail menu."

"Turn around. Plenty of cock there."

I frowned at him, and he frowned right back.

"Cock*tail*," I yelled. "Not cock!" My shout drew the attention of the bartender, who looked at me funny.

Well, we aren't all here for the peen, lady.

"Oh!" He waved to the bartender, who came over after taking a good, long look at him.

Yeah. Didn't blame her. At all.

"What can I getcha, honey?" she approvingly asked him, a Southern twang to her voice.

"Do you have a drinks menu? Cocktails?"

She reached behind the bar and pulled out two different menus. "Drinks," she shouted, putting one in front of him. "Cocktails." She put the other in front of me, her smile bright. "Let me know when y'all're ready to order."

West offered a thumbs-up and grabbed the menu. "She's perky."

"She wants inside your pants," I corrected him, picking the cocktail menu up and looking it over.

Hmm. They were basic. Very basic—all of them could have been found in any bar or restaurant in pretty much the entire country. Classics? Sure. But a girl doesn't always want a classic. Sometimes she wants her mind blown.

"Exactly. Perky." He flashed me a cocky grin and waved her back over. "I might hire her."

I rolled my eyes. Of course he would. Never mind that he was... Well, I had no idea how old he was, but he was a businessman and he was as cocky as an eighteen-year-old guy who just got laid for the first time.

He pointed at my menu. "Drink?"

"Oh, uh, mojito, please." I handed the cocktail menu back to the girl and pulled my phone out of my purse.

West looked at me, amusement dancing across his face. "What are you doing?"

I glanced at the girl mixing my cocktail and leaned up. I rested my hand against his arm to steady myself. "Making a list," I said right into his ear, my voice slightly raised. "What was the name of this place?"

"*Sin Ropa.*"

I typed it into the Notes section of my phone, followed by an abbreviated list of cocktails. I sure hoped I'd remember that LIIT wasn't some fandango slang and translated to Long Island Iced Tea tomorrow.

"Ahhh. You're right. Does look like you're texting."

I grinned and sat back down, dropping my hand from his solid bicep. I saved the note and turned my attention toward one of the stages. The guy on it had a girl in a black, wooden chair that was tipped back. He held it steady with one strong arm as he ground his hips against her, his other hand at the back of his head. I tilted my head to the side as she shamelessly ran her hands all over his body, causing him to move closer. It was...strangely hot, watching it happen to someone else.

"He's gonna drop her soon," West said into my ear.

I jumped at the proximity. I hadn't realized he'd moved so close. "How do you know that?"

"There's only so long you can hold someone's body weight combined with the chair's before you have to either put her down or let her fall."

Ah. That made sense.

True enough, seconds after West had finished talking, the stripper righted the chair onto four legs and grabbed her hands. He pulled her up and spun her, put *her* hands on the back of the chair, and grabbed her hips. My eyes widened as he dry-humped her from behind.

Well, dry-humped was a little crude. He kind of...rolled his hips against her ass. Like a dizzy dry-hump.

West laughed so hard that he coughed on the sip of Pepsi he'd just taken. "You look horrified."

I narrowed my eyes into a frown as I turned my gaze to him. He softened his words with a sexy smile and my drink. I took it from him and sipped hard through the straw.

Hm. It was pretty good.

My gaze traveled across the club. The oddest things were the TV screens around the club. I would have expected them to have music videos or something on, but no. They had a mix of both men and women masturbating. I was both uber creeped out and a little turned on at the very same time.

That definitely wasn't something I needed to be feeling around West Rykman —turned on.

I dragged my attention back from them and focused instead on the rest of the club. They didn't seem to be doing much in the way of marketing. There were no special offers on the posters on the walls or the fliers that littered the bar and undoubtedly the tables. Maybe it was because it was Monday, but there was nothing special.

"Ready to go?" West asked, leaning down to me.

"I..." I looked at my glass. It was empty. I guessed I was drinking on the job. "Sure. Let's go to the next one."

West motioned the bar girl over and handed her his card. He said something I couldn't hear, but she nodded. When she returned two minutes later, she gave back his card with more than one strip of receipt.

He looked through them, chuckled, and put it all in his wallet. I raised an eyebrow, but he didn't say anything as he took my wrist and guided me through and out of the club.

I didn't realize it was so hot in there until even the sticky, humid Vegas air hit me. Or smoky—hell, it was smoky in there.

I took a deep breath of fresh air and turned to West. "What were you laughing about in there?"

He was still half laughing. "The note she slipped me. 'When you're done with her, call me.' Followed by her number."

I had to appreciate her forwardness. That took balls.

"Keeping it classy, I see."

"I could respond to that," he said, "but it'd violate the professional-person line you've drawn."

I hit him with a hard look. *Yeah, but when I hit on you, you were already grinding your erection near my face.*

We made it in and out of the second bar without him being hit on. It was much the same as the first, only without the videos on the TV screens. The screens were present but blank. Boy was I glad of that. I also really needed to make a note to put a drink down once he'd handed it to me, because in there, I'd had two really great cosmos, and I needed to get a glass of cold water in the next club.

The third club we visited, Hot Rod, was busier than the second and first, but not by much. What I did appreciate in this place was that, before we went right in, there was a calendar of sorts, saying what was happening during the weekend. I was allowed to snap a pic to take back to my "future sister-in-law's bridal party," and although I felt a little guilty about the lie—*damn you and your guilt-trips, Mom*—I felt better about using it for good.

Kind of.

It was my job, after all.

I declined West's offer of a fourth drink, instead opting for water. This place was better put together than the previous two, but aside from the sign outside, there was nothing else saying what the plan was. I even flipped through the menu cards and sheets on the table next to me, but there was nothing. I pulled my phone out of my purse and noted it down. *Put promos on every table.*

"All right, darlin'?" A guy wearing ripped jeans and…nothing else…approached my table and grabbed the back of the chair next to me. Dark eyes gleamed down at me. "Here alone?"

"No." I could smell the female lust on him like it was his own personal aftershave.

I bet he wanted to add mine to it. Sucked to be him tonight.

"You look pretty alone." He moved closer to me.

I flexed my ankle. These heels were sharp. "I wouldn't get any closer if I were you."

"Sure? I could keep you company while you wait for your friend."

"I'm wearing four-inch stilettos and my friend is six foot three and probably has twenty pounds on muscle on you. Come on closer, doll." I smiled sweetly and tilted my head to the side.

Two glasses of water appeared on the table next to me, and I felt rather than saw West grip the back of the chair and lean over me.

The guy in front of me took one look at him, snorted, and walked away.

"He bothering you?" West said into my ear. His breath was hot, and I could hear the undercurrent of protectiveness. It was a foreign sound to me.

I shook my head and took a few sips of water. "I think I'm ready to go though."

"Sure. Let's go." He came around and took my hand, looking out at the club.

The people made it impossible, but for the first time, I was truly glad he was with me. If he hadn't been, that guy might not have backed off.

West held my hand the entire way back to the car. "Did you get anything useful?"

"I think so," I said quietly, reluctantly taking my hand back.
His hold had been strong and confident, and despite my words, the guy's insistence had shaken me a little—so had the knowledge that West had probably saved me from having a forced lap dance.

Now that we were away from the main hustle and bustle, in the parking lot, it felt like a different world. Sure, I could hear the music from Rock Solid, but I was tired. I hadn't really thought about it before, but my feet were hurting and I just wanted to crawl into bed and think about this tomorrow.

"You should have come and got me when that prick made you uncomfortable."

I turned to face him. "Are you seriously telling me off?"

We paused as the traffic stopped, and he cut his gaze to me. "I couldn't see you at first. I told you it wasn't safe for you to go alone."

I rolled my eyes. "He was only there for two minutes. I would have stabbed him with my stiletto before he could do anything."

"And I believe you, but it doesn't change the fact that he made you uncomfortable."

We turned a corner.

"I don't want anything to happen to you just because you're determined to do market research."

"Nothing happened to me."

"Mia, it doesn't change the fact that it could've. He only left because I showed up. I watched the entire fucking thing."

"And you only came in at the end? Gee, thanks, West. Knight in fucking shining armor right there, aren't you?" I ran my fingers through my hair and looked away. The light curls were still in place, although they were more of a lazy wave at this point, and I stared at my reflection in the side mirror. "We should probably not do this again."

"On the contrary, I was having fun until the end. I don't have fun much."

"Looking out for me was fun? Yeah, okay."

"I told you," he said, pulling up outside my apartment block, which was really more of a converted three-story house. "I don't want anything to happen to you. I'd feel bad."

"Well, thanks. I'm gonna look over these notes in the morning and I'll e-mail you. Okay?" I paused with my hand on the door and glanced back at him.

He was out of the fucking car.

Why was he out of the fucking car?

"Why are you out of the car?"

He smirked. Damn that smirk. "I'm taking you up."

"Like hell you are." I slammed the door and walked around the sleek Audi to stand right in front of him. I looked up at him and caught his gaze. "I can make it in and out of an elevator."

"I'm sure you can. But I'm still taking you up."

"No. You're not!"

"All right, then." He grabbed my waist and lifted me.

A shriek escaped between my lips as he swung me upward and over his shoulder. I scrambled to keep hold of my purse, but he ignored me as he carried me inside and pushed the elevator button.

"West! Put me down right now!"

He ignored me again and tightened his grip around my thighs when I tried to wriggle down. His strength was crazy. I was stuck there.

"Put me down! Now!"

He shook his head, this time acknowledging my words. But that was it. A fucking head shake.

"This is hardly professional!" I yelled, my voice echoing off walls of the metal box that was the elevator. I couldn't believe he'd slung me over his shoulder like some kind of caveman.

Yo, Wilma, Betty? Fred and Barney escaped. I found one of them.

"West Rykman, I swear to a god I don't believe in that, if you don't put me down right this goddamn second, I'm going to tear your balls off with my bare hands and shove them up your ass!"

The elevators doors opened, and he took the few steps toward my door before finally, slowly, lowering me back down to the ground.

"Ugh!" As soon as my feet hit the floor, I stepped back and glared at him. "How dare you manhandle me?"

He fixed his bright, Caribbean-blue eyes on mine and curved his lips. "I told you I was taking you upstairs. I didn't tell you I was walking you up."

"You're an animal."

"You weren't coming up alone. I was raised a gentleman."

That made me stop rummaging for my keys and raise my eyebrows in disbelief. "You take off your clothes for a living, and the first time we met, you flexed your cock against my face."

He grabbed my waist for a second time tonight and spun me against my door. I dropped my purse in my shock, but I couldn't reach for it because he'd cupped my chin and forced me to look at him.

"And the second time we met," he said in a low voice, "you flexed my cock against the back of your throat. What point are you trying to make, angel?"

"That you're no more a gentleman than I am a lady," I shot back. "Now, let me go so I can go inside and consider how we continue this professional relationship."

West searched my eyes for a long moment before dropping his hand. He took half a step back, and I went to reach for my purse, but he changed his mind.

He smoothly spun back to me, and no sooner had I met the flash of his blue eyes than he had his mouth on mine. I let out a quiet moan when he swept his tongue across the seam of my lips and wrapped one arm around my waist. He pulled our bodies together, my shoulders pressing into the door, and kissed me deeply.

My head swam. I couldn't make head or tails of this, and although it was wrong, so wrong, I couldn't stop.

The kiss was hot—oh god, so hot—and my whole body felt like it was on fire as I wound my fingers in the collar of his shirt and held him closer to me. His fingers twitched against my back as one of his hands slid down and cupped my ass. He squeezed, pulling my hips to his. His erection was obvious, pushing into me, and I whimpered into his mouth.

God, I wanted him.

He pulled away from me as abruptly as he'd kissed me, but he didn't move. His mouth eased its way across my jaw to my ear, and his hot breath skittered across my skin when he paused there.

"I might call you angel, but I have a feeling you're going to be my own personal sin, Mia O'Halloran."

He kissed the tender spot just beneath my ear, making me shiver, and released me. I struggled to control my breathing as I watched him walk away toward the stairwell. He paused at the top, and I sank my teeth into my bottom lip.

He turned.

Dropped his gaze to my mouth.

Met my eyes.

Disappeared.

I sank back against my door. I could still feel his touch. His taste lingered on my lips, and although it wasn't anything incredibly specific, he was there, teasing me without being near me. I brushed hair from my face, picked my purse up, and dug for my key. I found it and let myself into the dark apartment.

I locked the door behind me and walked to my bed. I'd barely undressed and retrieved my phone with its alarm before I buried myself beneath the sheets.

STRIPPED BARE

Shit.

"Thank you." I handed the wallet with my bill and my credit card to the young girl who'd served me my brunch and then turned to look out the window. There was nothing spectacular about this view. I'd checked Google Maps and plugged this address into my rental car's GPS before leaving.

I'd wanted to go somewhere quiet, a little off the beaten track, and this adorable, little twenty-four-hour pancake café had done the job. The stack of pancakes I'd ordered had hit the hunger spot, and I'd been able to pull some things together for West.

I'd actually managed to keep him off my mind for a little while too. Not long, granted, but focusing on the marketing for his club as opposed to his mouth on mine had done me some good. I'd tried to call Allie, but she was already working. Lucie was visiting her parents, and if I called Jaz before noon on her day off, I'd be cursed out of the country.

This had been the best choice in hindsight, even if I was now back to thinking about last night. And not just the kiss—all of it.

He'd said that he didn't have fun much. That was kind of sad. I was a serious person, but even I made enough time to have fun, whether it was vegging out in front of the TV with takeout or hitting a bar with the girls. I wondered if West Rykman was the kind of man who worked, worked, worked, and that was it.

I was wondering about him again.

Did he have family nearby? What did he do when he wasn't working? How old was he? How had he come to get a strip club? What other businesses did he own in Las Vegas? Just clubs, or restaurants too? Maybe a regular bar or two? A casino?

I had no place wondering it, but my curious personality demanded I did. Then again, my curious personality was also the reason for fifty million heartbreaks in my life, so what did it know?

Nothing. That's right. Big, fat nothing. Liar.

I just wanted to complete this contract without a hitch. Was that too much to ask? I didn't want any more kisses or touches or words whispered in my ear. I was tired of it. I wanted to do my job, and that was it, but he was...

Jesus, he was so goddamn irresistible. If I had to compare him, he'd be a hot bath at the end of a long day, fluffy socks in winter, and—no. I had it.

West Rykman was as irresistible as the undeniable, glorious sensation of whipping your bra off when you walk through your front door.

I sighed. Yep. I was screwed if I was comparing him to *that*. I'd compared men to many things—pigs, fuckers, slugs, assholes—but never whipping a bra off.

I had to marvel over the coincidence of this though. Of all the places in the US —in Vegas alone—it had to be his club. I wondered now if he had known that it was me when Michelle had called and told him I'd be there in her stead. If he had, why had he allowed it to happen?

It wasn't for the sex, that was for sure. He'd gotten at least one number last night and all he had done was buy drinks.

I was bugged about that. If he remembered our night so well, surely the name "Mia" would have rung a bell or two. He would have checked his records and seen that I was there that night and that it was me.

I smiled at the girl when she brought my card back. Then I slipped it into my wallet and stuffed it into my purse. There was no use in my going to Rock Solid when I was frustrated. It was the perfect time to work—I needed to work on branding for the club. I loved the design aspect of my job. It wasn't required, but I had the skills, so I utilized them. It saved us having to hire out someone else. I regularly did it for my coworkers too, and maybe that was it.

Design was calming to me. As long as any one of my Adobe products felt like cooperating.

That was my plan. I would work all day, and then tomorrow, when I was calmer, I'd go and talk with West.

—————————— ⟡⟡⟡ ——————————

Turned out working and sleeping on it wasn't the key to calming down.

I was still as pissed as before. Not even drafting three new logos and typing up everything I'd found, not to mention coming up with new ideas, had helped. The idea that he had known who I was and still let me come annoyed me.

It was why I was stalking through the doors of Rock Solid at ten in the morning, dressed in my business best. I hoped that the tight, red skirt and white blouse complete with black heels would draw a line that'd been crossed when I had been wearing jeans and a loose shirt.

"Hi, Ms. O'Halloran. Are you looking for Mr. Rykman?" Vicky looked up from the glass she was polishing, as bubbly and friendly as she had been before.

"Hey, Vicky! Call me Mia, please. And yes—I am. Is he here?"

"I think so." She paused in her cleaning. "I think he's upstairs. Let me call up." She put the glass and the cloth down and turned to get the phone. She punched in a few numbers then held it to her. "Hi, West... Yes, I know, but Mia O'Halloran is here to see you... Yes... Mhmm... Okay... Sure." She hung up and turned to me. "He's not in a great mood, but he said to send you up." She waved over her shoulder as she walked to the door at the end of the bar.

I sneaked around the end of the bar and caught the door before it could swing shut.

"If you go down the hall, you'll find the stairs on your right. The entire floor is an office, so you'll find him right there."

"Perfect. Thank you so much, Vicky."

"You're welcome." She beamed and bounced back through the door to the bar.

Damn. I wanted what she had eaten for breakfast.

I held the handrail as I headed upstairs. This time, I was armed with my laptop as well as a file. If he liked any of the logos or branding but wanted some changes, I'd wanted to be able to do it with him in real time.

It was also heavier to hit him over the back of his cocky head with, but nobody else needed to know that.

When I reached the top, the door was slightly ajar, so I knocked lightly.

"Hello?"

"Mia? Is that you?" West's voice traveled through the air.

It was unnerving how quickly we'd gone from Mr. Rykman and Ms. O'Halloran to West and Mia.

"Yes," I answered. "Vicky sent me up."

"Sure, come in." He opened a door, a phone pressed to his chest with the mouthpiece covered. "I'm just finishing up this call."

I nodded and pushed the door back almost closed as he crossed the room and then dropped into a large leather chair and said, "Sorry, I'm back. Go on."

I held my purse close to me and looked around the room. It was spacious—at least half the size of the club downstairs, and one wall was entirely compromised of desk space. There were numerous cupboards beneath the top, but three chairs were lined up in various places. Large, brand-new computers peeked out from behind the black chairs, and there were noticeboards with all manner of things pinned up and hanging between the windows.

Ahhh. So upstairs had the windows.

I looked to the other side, which was much calmer. A huge sectional sofa faced a television set, and the coffee table in between them had two papers and a dirty coffee mug. I scanned the space for a coffee machine, but I didn't see one. There was a door just up from the sofa, almost directly opposite the one I'd walked through, so I guessed there was a kitchen back there.

"Sorry about that," West said. "I was just talking to Beckett—that's my business partner. He's away on family business and was checking up on next door. That's his baby. He's not very much of a dancer these days."

"Dancer?" I raised an eyebrow. Was that the official name of a stripper? There wasn't much dancing from what I'd seen.

"He's not like me." He flashed me a half grin and motioned toward the sofa. "I wasn't expecting you this morning."

"Well, I meant to e-mail yesterday, but I got caught up working, so I grabbed brunch and headed over here on the off chance I'd catch you." Not entirely a lie. "I have a bunch of stuff I'd like to talk about. Do you have the time?"

"Sure. I'm just doing paperwork, and anything to get out of that." He sat next to me on the sofa. "What do you want to talk about?"

I pulled my laptop from my purse, set it on the coffee table in front of me, and opened it for it to load up. "I actually had a question that's been bugging me."

"Go on."

I peered up at him out of the side of my eye. "When my boss called you and told you I'd be taking over here, did you know who I was?"

"You mean before I walked up to that table and my cock got the shock of its life?"

"Be serious."

"No. I thought it was coincidence." He rolled his shoulders and leaned back on the sofa, stretching one arm out across the top. "Did you know you were coming to me?"

I shook my head and shifted around. "She never told me your first name. Then I would have known. It's not exactly a common name."

His lips twitched. "The club didn't give it away?"

"No. I thought you were just a stripper my best friend had lassoed into giving me a lap dance to pay me back for the one I'd bought her."

"Ah, yes. She was very persistent that it had to be the best and in a private room, much to your other friend's annoyance."

Jaz. Yep. I can imagine that.

"And you offered yourself."

He held his hand out, wearing a cocky grin on his face. "I am the best."

"I'd agree with you, but that's not the purpose of this conversation. I was just curious." I cleared my throat and turned back to my laptop.

It had loaded, so I typed my password and hit Enter. While it finished, I pulled the papers out from the file and grabbed the paper-clipped sheets with the logos. "Before I forget, do you use social media?"

He looked at me blankly. "We have a Facebook page, but I don't think anyone posts on it. Beckett and I certainly don't. We can't exactly post live shots."

"Okay." I scribbled that on the top of another sheet. I'd find it later. I just needed it written down. "We'll come back to that. Anyway, after I'd looked over everything yesterday, I decided that rebranding was the first thing we needed to focus on. Everything else will fall in, so I worked on three logos. They're very different, as you can see." I spread the sheets out in front of him on the table.

West sat up and looked at them. "Talk me through them."

"Well, this one is basic. Just the name, but very bold, very bright," I said about the first, colored in red and yellow. Then I moved to the second. "This one is a midpoint between the three designs. The shot glasses and the pole design show what it is, and the mixture of script and serif fonts, both keeping the purple color, change it up. It's kinda busy, but I didn't know if you'd like it. The third is probably my favorite." I didn't want to admit it, but I'd spent the most amount of time on this one. "The pink-and-green script fonts contrast perfectly, and the silhouette of a muscular man flexing shows it's definitely a ladies club."

"I like it." West took the sheet from the table. "And this? What does it say?" He squinted and leaned in.

"Oh... I played with a tagline. I meant to delete it."

"For your pleasure," he murmured. His bright gaze swung to me, a smile teasing his lush lips. "Rock Solid...for your pleasure."

"Yeah. Like I said. I was supposed to delete that." My cheeks heated up.

He ran the back of one finger across my burning skin and winked. "I love it. Keep it."

"Really? It's cheesy as hell."

"You seen the moves we pull in this place? Take away the music with a heavy baseline and we're just overgrown toddlers trying to aim at the potty."

I covered my hand with my mouth in an attempt to muffle my laughter, but it didn't work. My mind flashed back to some of the awkward moves I'd seen the day before, and I had to admit that he was entirely right. Especially the guy in *Sin Ropa*. If you made the woman a toilet and took his pants down, he would have totally been a potty-training toddler trying to aim.

That was it. I'd never be able to look at strippers in the same way again.

"It's kinda true," he continued, his own laughter sparkling in his eyes.

Seriously—they freaking shone. I couldn't look away, even though I was still giggling into my hand.

"We are rock solid, and it is for your pleasure."

Rock Solid.

For your pleasure.

I'd inadvertently created a double entendre.

And, now that the thought was in my head, my gaze dropped to his pants and I giggled all over again. My stomach hurt, but I couldn't stop, even as I wrapped one arm around my midsection like it'd soothe the clenching pain there.

"Are you all right?" West asked, still holding the paper.

I took a deep breath and slowly let it go. "The name and the slogan. You meant it as your bodies, but now, I'm thinking...other parts of you."

He stilled, his gaze capturing mine once more. He swept his tongue over his top lip as his mouth slowly curved upward into a grin that was oh so delicious. "Dirty girl."

My teeth dragged over my lower lip as I fought my smile. "Couldn't help it. It just...popped up."

"Mia." His voice had dropped, and my name had come out as a husky rasp. "If you keep talking like that..."

I held my hands up as my heart thudded at the implications of what would happened if I did. "Sorry. My bad. Back to the logos. So, the final one?" I swallowed hard and looked away from him.

I couldn't look at him. The battle between restraint and temptation that waged in his gorgeous eyes was intense, and if I looked any longer, I knew I'd make the choice for him. And that was bad, bad, bad.

West cleared his throat and put the sheet next to my laptop. "Can you make the slogan bigger? Not much bigger, just a bit more readable."

I nodded and clicked on the Photoshop icon to load it. I was definitely glad I'd brought my laptop now, because it gave me something to do as his eyes seared a hole into the side of my head. My hair fell from where it had been tucked behind my ear, creating a fiery, auburn curtain between us. Though I would have usually swept it right back, I left it, despite how annoying it was as it tickled my cheek.

Just because I couldn't see his gaze anymore didn't mean I couldn't feel it.

My heartbeat echoed in my ears, the harsh pulsing loud enough to drown out any other sound and impossible to ignore. I didn't want my heart to beat this fast. I didn't want to be attracted to this man in any kind of way, but I was so drawn to him that I couldn't not be.

"Like that?" I asked after bringing up the layered file and editing the text size. I'd had to reposition it slightly, but it almost looked better. No. It did look better.

West reached up and trailed his fingertips across my skin, putting my hair back behind my ear. "Perfect."

I opened my mouth to speak, but the words got stuck in my throat. What I wanted to say was, *Okay, I'll save it.* Or, *Don't do that.* But what I said was nothing, and what I did was turn my face into his touch the tiniest amount.

"I know why you didn't contact me yesterday," he said in that low voice of his, his earlier amusement entirely eradicated. "And, Mia? If I made you uncomfortable by kissing you, I apologize. That wasn't my intention."

"I..." I trailed off and gently sighed. I wasn't uncomfortable was I? No—I was torn. Torn between my own personal wants and my professional needs.

I shifted away from West by an inch, his hand falling back to the sofa. I scanned his body, from his large, rough hands to his broad shoulders and the trim, toned body between them. Even his thick thighs. Until finally my gaze reached his handsome face, meeting his.

He was still as he waited. Didn't push me to speak, which went against everything I knew about him, and that wasn't much. Maybe he really did feel bad for having kissed me. Which he shouldn't have. It was a great kiss, all things considered. Just perhaps super ill-timed.

"You didn't make me uncomfortable," I eventually managed to say to him. "I just... I can't have my personal life get in the way of my professional one. I've worked too hard for a chance at a contract like this, and it fell in my lap by an unfortunate circumstance, but I want to make it work. If we have a personal relationship, all of these lines will blur. If I'm doing a shit job, I want you to be able to tell me without worrying you're hurting my feelings. That can't happen if we're anything more than consultant and client."

He scrutinized my face, his intense and calculating gaze never leaving me.

I didn't want to tell him that I was also really, really bad at personal relationships. I'd been left for another man, for the love of god. Of course, my rational mind knew I hadn't turned him gay, that he had already been gay, but it still stung.

Break up with a girl then come out a week later, yeah?

Let the breakup sink in before you tell her you prefer sausages over tacos.

"Now, tell me the rest," he demanded. Demanded was harsh, maybe, but it was close enough. His voice had a slight edge. "I can see the truth when you look at me. Your emerald eyes are too bright to hide a damn thing."

"I'm shit at personal relationships," I blurted out before I knew what I was doing. "Okay? Like, really bad. I'm the loser they make chick flicks about. I could write a book on dating fails. I have them all. After my last breakup, I said no more. This working relationship solidifies it."

"All right." He turned back to the sheets on the table. "What next?"

I stilled and stared at him. "That's it? You make me spit that out and you say, 'What next?'"

He sighed heavily. Leaning forward and resting his elbows on top of his knees, he turned to me and hit me with his blue eyes. "Mia, angel, I appreciate that. I accept it. But you're as attracted to me as I am you, and sooner or later, you're going to have to give in to it."

"What if I don't want to?"

I knew he was right—there was...something...between us. Something tangible. The tension tingled over my skin every time I was within a hundred meters of him. But that didn't mean I couldn't fight it.

"I don't think want has anything to do with it," he said. "You didn't want me to kiss you last night, but I did, and I bet you went to bed, your pussy wet and aching, wishing I'd never left."

My cheeks flamed. Fuck. I hated that he could make me blush so easily. It was his superpower.

I also hated that he was right.

"Exactly." His lips moved into a smug smirk. "Don't tell me you didn't go to sleep thinking about me and what I could do to you, because you know damn well what I can do."

"Then I won't tell you that." I swallowed. "But that doesn't change the fact that we've veered onto inappropriate territory once again."

West leaned back and lifted one of his feet so it rested on his knee. Even as his bicep flexed as he laid his arm across the back of the sofa again, my gaze was drawn to the obvious bulge pushing against his fitted, black dress pants.

"Mia, when you're in the room, I never leave inappropriate territory. I'm constantly thinking about all the different ways I can make you come all over my cock again."

Oh god. Oh god. My pussy clenched, and I squeezed my thighs together in the hope it would dull the desperate ache that had started in my clit. I was wet—I could feel it—and the inside of my bra was suddenly harsh against my hardened nipples.

I wanted him to throw me back on this sofa, bunch my skirt around my waist, and slip inside me. I didn't even care if we were naked—he could undo his pants and pull his cock out for all I cared. My lust was taking over my consciousness, and I needed to get a handle on it, because it couldn't happen.

I could fight this attraction.

I wouldn't succumb to the temptation that was West Rykman.

"See? I haven't touched you and you're squirming. Are you wet, Mia?"

I refused to answer. I wasn't going to give him the satisfaction of saying yes. He was pushing my buttons, trying to get me to give in.

The dirty, sexy smirk returned to his face. "Am I making you uncomfortable?"

The smug bastard. Cocky, smug, horny bastard.

I could have said yes—ended it. But I didn't. "No. In fact, I think you're making yourself uncomfortable." I looked pointedly at his cock, which was now straining desperately against his pants. A shiver of lust tickled down my spine.

He glanced down and shrugged a shoulder. "It's been three days and I'm already used to it with you." He moved his hand so he could take a lock of my hair. He gently twirled it between his fingers and fixed his eyes on mine. "I don't dance downstairs often," he said, changing the subject. "But I am tonight. It's what I do for fun."

He dropped my hair and wrapped his hand around the back of my neck. He guided my face toward his, pulling me so close that I put a hand out to steady myself, but it landed on his thigh, which immediately tightened beneath my touch. I drew in a sharp breath as our faces came so close that I thought he'd kiss me again.

"And every time I have to touch another woman," he whispered, "and they run their hands over my body and revel in the fact that my cock is hard, they'll be wrong when they think it's for them."

My lips parted when his fingers twitched against my neck. He was going to kiss me—I knew it. Why else was he so close, unless to torture me? His touch was already burning my skin, constricting my lungs. I couldn't breathe easily, and oh god, he—

"I'm going to make coffee. Do you want one?" he asked, letting me go and standing up. He adjusted his pants and raised an eyebrow in question, walking backward toward the door.

Don't look at his dick. Don't look at his dick. Don't look at his dick.

"Yeah. Sure," I answered, looking at his dick.

"Great. My cock will get right on figuring out how to use the coffee machine."

I grabbed my pen and threw it across the room at him. He grinned, catching it in one hand, and then he threw it back onto the sofa.

Dirty, smug, sexy, cocky bastard.

I was playing with fire, and I could already feel the burn.

I'd never been in a strip club alone before. As I remembered back to two nights ago, I knew there was a good reason for it, but I knew that there, in Rock Solid, I was safe.

If West Rykman wanted to fuck with me, to push my buttons and make me squirm until I couldn't cope any longer, I was going to fuck with him right back.

I don't know what made me change my mind. Maybe it was the acceptance that he was right. There was an intense attraction between us, one that defied logic. I would inevitably give in to him. Even if it was just for one more night. The sensation of his lips on mine and the memories of how he played my body were too strong.

Besides, I wanted him. I did. I was human, after all. He was the kind of man who could get you pregnant just by walking in a room and meeting your eyes. Mary, Jesus, and Joseph, move on over. West Rykman was the new giver of immaculate conception.

I wanted to make it as hard for him as he was for me. He was making it almost unbearable. He hands down had the dirtiest mouth I'd ever come across. The fact that he could make me so wet just by talking to me was incomprehensible. It made no sense at all because it shouldn't have been able to happen. He shouldn't have been able to talk about me being wet and then, poof, I was wet.

He wasn't fucking Dynamo with his fancy-ass magic tricks.

He was a stripper who owned a strip club and had tricks of his own—but none of them were magic or even illusions. They were pure skill, and he probably should have been arrested by the CIA to perform sexual torture on women prisoners by now.

Lord knows the filthy fucker was torturing the ever-loving shit outta me.

I was sure that, the moment he walked out onto that stage, the crowds of women gathered around it, waiting for him, would start throwing their panties at him.

That was perhaps an exaggeration, but I'd seen it at concerts, so why would a strip club have been any different? It was actually the more obvious place for a Flying Panty Palooza.

That's why I was sitting at the bar. Far away from any flying panties, but still with an awesome view of the stage.

"Working?" Vicky asked, her long, blond hair now tied into a high ponytail. Apparently, she came in early, got the bar ready, went home, and then came back for the late shift five days a week.

"Hm? Oh, yeah." My gaze flicked back to the stage, where some hunk wearing, well, nothing but tight, red boxer briefs was performing with the pole. When he grabbed it and swung himself around, his arm muscles bulged. I honestly thought I'd orgasm a little—I was that impressed. "I could have a worse job."

I could. Sure, I was there to hopefully torture West, but it wasn't a bad thing. I wanted to see what he wasn't doing in terms of promotion. Aside from fliers that had the names and the pictures of the strippers and the prices for both public and private shows, he was doing nothing. I wrote it in my notebook to rectify it. He needed to get that figured out and quickly.

How he'd been running a successful club until now, I didn't—well, I did know. It was the naked men.

You'd get a lot less store closures if you had hotties like these working at the registers.

"True that. Another drink?" Vicky pointed to my empty glass.

"Uhh..." I hesitated. I shouldn't, but what the hell? "Sure."

She winked with a playful smile as she snatched the cocktail glass up and turned back to the drinks. I was within walking distance of my apartment, I reasoned. Not to mention I'd walked there in the first place.

I had a feeling I'd need something strong inside me if West saw me here.

He'd said that his hard cock would be for me tonight—I was going to make sure of it.

"Waiting for someone?" Vicky's big grin said one word: busted.

"Screw it. When's your boss on? Don't judge me."

She laughed. "Girl, I'm not judging. I've fantasized about him more than once, along with every other woman in the city. He's like the unattainable god around here. Most of these guys?" She waved toward the stage. "They leave with someone. They're the biggest whores. But West? No. I've think I've seen him leave or go meet two, maybe three women in two years after a shift." She held up her hand and went to serve someone a little farther down.

The unattainable god.

I tilted my head to the side and picked my glass up as the guys on stage grabbed their clothes and evacuated it as the music trailed out.

The lights cut out, plunging the club into silent darkness. Several women squealed in excitement, and others in shock.

"Ooooh, here we go," Vicky whispered, grabbing a glass from beneath the bar and settling in on the stool next to me.

I shot her a look.

God knows how she saw it, but she leaned in and whispered, "No one's comin' to the bar. Don't worry."

The low, seductive beat of "High for This" by The Weeknd filled the club. The eerie music echoed around the club in waves until the bass kicked in. At that exact same time, a spotlight flashed in the center of the stage.

On West.

I had a feeling this was his song—the one that set him apart from the others. They all moved to harsh club sounds, but he danced to this erotic melody.

I was right.

He moved his body slowly beneath the only point of light in the entire room. He flexed his hips as he untucked his white shirt from dark, ripped jeans and let it fall over the waistband. The chants of his name were already starting, but compared to the erotic music, it sounded like a low hum.

I was fixated on him as he eased his hands down the center of his body and undid every button of his shirt. He pulled it over his shoulders, and his strong muscles flexed as he whipped the shirt off and threw it into the darkness in a flash of white.

Clad in his jeans, he moved seductively toward the pole. He wrapped his steady hands around it and swung around it in a way I'd only ever seen women do. It was sexy then, but good fucking god—West made it look like foreplay. His arms tightened until every inch of the defined muscle was on show, from his biceps to his triceps. Hell, even his forearms were toned. His veins popped as he moved slowly but certainly.

As his face moved into the light, I caught the look in his eyes. He was smiling too. Loving it. And so he should have been—every woman in this room was lusting after him. Including me.

He released the pole, and that was when I noticed that the music was rolling. The song was lasting longer than it should have, and I'd bet anything it had been remixed to do so. It was flawless anyway, and so was the man walking across the stage.

He stopped and reached down, grabbing the hand of a woman. Her friends all screamed as he motioned for her to go to the end of the stage. As soon as she got there, the light went out, and when it came back on, West swung a chair around in the middle of the stage. He positioned her in front of it and ran his hands down her sides, following the curves of her body. She threw her head back and looked like she was laughing when he sat her down by her hips.

Then he moved. The way he had the night we'd met. His back was to us at the bar, but I could appreciate the view. He gyrated his hips slowly and deliberately, and the girl eagerly ran her hands all over his body until he had his legs on either side of her and was holding on to the back of the chair to stay steady. As he performed deep thrusts, he ran one hand through her hair and tilted her head back.

The chair was low and he was tall, so when her head was back, it was almost as if he were moving in front of her face.

She touched his body again, and a tiny, sick pang of jealously twisted in my gut. I remembered that body, how it felt to have him dancing against me.

West moved back, still dancing, and undid the button of his ripped jeans. He reached behind him and grabbed her hand, encouraging her to pull his pants down. She slid them over his tight ass, and he stepped out of them and kicked them to the side.

Another spotlight hit them, and I saw one thing.

His erection.

Heat pooled between my legs, and I clenched them together as he ran his own hands down his sculpted body and rubbed one over the front of his dick. The light over the chair went out, leaving the girl forgotten, and West palmed himself through the black boxer briefs. His hips moved with the beat of the song, The Weeknd still playing. One hand trailed up his body, his head dropping back.

It was the most erotic thing I'd ever seen. That man, on stage, touching his body as he danced to one of the sexiest songs I'd ever heard.

If he didn't stop soon, I thought I'd orgasm on the spot.

Vicky took my glass from me as I watched him. The light over the chair came back on, and he went back to the girl, dancing for her once more. She tucked dollar after dollar into his briefs, and before I knew it, Vicky had put another drink in my hand.

"Thank you," I whispered.

"You're welcome," she replied with a hint of a giggle. "Damn. He's going for it tonight."

I nodded slowly, transfixed. West Rykman's dancing, even with another woman, was compelling. He was magnetic, and the way his body moved was so goddamn hypnotizing that looking away seemed like a ridiculous notion.

So I watched. And watched. And watched. He danced seemingly without tiring, pleasing the hordes of women who were waving dollars at him, desperate for his attention.

When the song had finally ended after what seemed like forever—a delightful forever—I had a serious buzz as as he made his way around the stage and let all the women tuck dollars into his pants. He stopped halfway around and put his jeans back on, only for the other side to stuff them in his pockets and cop a feel at the same time.

I didn't want to think about how many dollars he'd just had stuffed into his pants.

He bowed at the end, much to the delight of the women, as the normal lighting slowly brightened, and then he disappeared through a door.

"Hey, Vicky?" I grabbed her arm before she went back behind the bar. "There's a restroom upstairs, right?"

She nodded. "Did you need to use it?"

I glanced across the club, which now seemed too bright, at the groups of women heading in the direction of the hall that held the public ones. "Yeah. Pretty badly."

She sucked her lower lip into her mouth and glanced at the bar. It was filling up now that West's show was over. "Shoot. Go quick! West won't mind."

It might have been the alcohol—it was definitely the alcohol—but I was hoping I'd run into him.

I slipped through the door and looked at the stairs. Boy. That was a lot of stairs after a few cocktails and wearing these heels. Still... I gripped the hand rail and managed to get up there without falling. Success!

I paused at the door. What was I doing? This was insanity. I couldn't go up there and attempt to get him. Not after my spiel earlier tonight.

"I can see you there, Mia."

I looked up. The door was shut. How...

I pushed it open and stopped. He was standing by one of the computer screens that was apparently a CCTV feed. Sure as hell, one of them showed the staircase leading up there.

"Sneaky," I said.

West turned, smirked, and threw a stack of dollars down onto the desk. "Now, what could have possibly brought you here tonight?"

"Research." I stepped inside and shut the door behind me, raising an eyebrow. "I didn't exactly dissect your marketing last time I was here."

"And now?" He perched on the edge of the desk and hit me with his bright gaze. His cheeks were slightly flushed, and although I'd barely glanced down, I knew he was still rock hard inside those sexy jeans. "What do you think?"

"You could do with drinks offers. You know, buy two, get one at half price. Buy three shots, get one free. Fifty percent off cocktails between seven and eight, Monday through Thursday. Fliers on each table, ads in local papers and on Facebook."

"Come up to write it down, did you?"

"Yes," I lied. "Absolutely."

"And Vicky let you."

"She thinks I'm using the restroom."

"I see." He didn't look annoyed in the slightest as he pushed off the desk and walked toward me.

No.

Walked was an understatement.

He stalked toward me, his gaze never leaving me, his lips still curved on one side. He stopped right in front of me and cupped my face with both hands. Then he dove his fingers into my loose, fiery curls and pushed them back from my face. He leaned in, ran his nose up my jaw, forcing me to close my eyes, and stepped around my body, making sure my hand brushed against his hard cock.

"I think," he whispered in my hair, sweeping my hair around to one side of my neck. "I think you came here for an entirely different reason, Mia."

His hands burned me through my dress as he ran them up my sides, from my thighs right up to my breasts. His fingers crept around the front of me until he was cupping my breasts and running his thumbs over the exact place my nipples were hardening. Every time he swept across them, pleasure rocketed through my body and my pussy clenched in desperate pleas.

"I think you came here tonight because you knew I'd be hard for you." He pulled me back against him. His cock pressed against my lower back, just teasing my ass. "And I think you came up here to do something about it."

"So arrogant," I breathed.

"Am I?" He dropped one of those large, rough hands to my thighs and hiked my dress up at the front.

My legs parted easily for him to slip two fingers between them. He ran his fingertips along my pussy, covering my clit with my wetness.

"Because..." He pushed one finger inside me then added the other, kissing my neck. "You feel awfully ready for me, angel."

I moaned and bucked against him. My clit rubbed against the heel of his hand, which heightened my pleasure, and as he thrust his fingers inside me, my hips moved against him until I was on the brink of orgasm.

He pulled his hand out of my panties and flattened it against the top of my thigh. "You've been drinking."

"Didn't stop you fucking me with your fingers just now, did it? Which, by the way, thanks. Or not." I shoved his hands from me and stepped away, frustrated with both his quick change of attitude and the orgasm I was hovering at the edge of.

Was there anything worse?

No. I didn't think so.

"Mia."

I ran my fingers through my hair and groaned. "What?"

"How much have you been drinking?" His head edged to one side, and his gaze was contemplative, as if he were deciding if I was drunk or just slightly tipsy.

Slightly tipsy was the answer, for the record. But just drunk enough to let my lust rule my decision making. I was okay with that right now.

I snapped my gaze up to his. "Not enough."

I was standing steady. I wasn't seeing two of him. My words were clear. My mind was only slightly foggy.

He was right.

I would give in.

But I'd be fucked if it was on his terms.

I took the few steps that would close the distance between us, wrapped my arms around his neck, and planted my mouth on his. He paused before wrapping his arms around my waist and kissing me right back. It quickly went from a simple touch to a lust-driven, desperate kiss, and I found myself staggering backward as he pushed me toward the desk.

He swept whatever was on it off onto the floor before grabbing my thighs and sitting me on it. West's hand slid up to cup my ass cheeks and pull my hips forward so his hard cock was pressed against my wetness. I moaned as my clit made contact with his erection and pressed myself against him, but he pushed me back.

The desk was wide, and I could comfortably lie back on it. He leaned over me, allowing my arms to unlock behind his neck and my hands to trail down the sculpted mounds of his chest. My fingers explored every crevice and dip in his taut stomach, and they eventually came to rest at his waistband.

The whole time, he kissed me desperately and deeply, desirably.

I popped his button and slid one hand straight inside his boxers. My fingers immediately made contact with his erection, and my thumb pressed against the bead of pre-cum on the end, swirling it all over the head of his cock. It was the smallest amount but served as just enough lubrication that I could lean up, putting one hand behind me, and work his cock in my fist.

He groaned every time my thumb swept open the top, and I didn't care about kissing him, not anymore.

If this was on my terms, it was fully on my terms.

I pushed him back, sat up, and jumped off the desk. He took two steps back and looked at me, one eyebrow quirked expectantly, like he knew exactly what I was going to do.

I dropped to my knees.

Pulled his pants and his boxers down.

And took his long, thick cock into my mouth.

His groan was loud and obvious, and he twined his fingers in my hair as I swirled my tongue around the head of his dick. The salty taste of his pre-cum lingered there, and I licked until I could taste it anymore. Then I rammed him to the back of my throat. I gagged, my eyes watering, but his grip on my hair tightened, so I held myself there as long as I could before pulling back and doing it all over again.

"Fuck!" he half growled.

I smiled against his cock and wrapped my hand around the base.

He could play with his words all he wanted.

I was playing for real—with my mouth.

His cock throbbed against my tongue as I worked him with my hand and my mouth. The tightening of his hand in my hair coupled with the gentle thrusts of his hips as he pushed himself farther into my mouth spurred me on, moved me faster, and made me take him deeper—until he yanked my head back and looked down into my eyes.

"Up," he demanded, his voice rough and raspy.

I reached back and used the table to help me up as he kept hold of my hair. No sooner was I fully on my feet than West had pulled me toward him, his exhale hot on my mouth.

"Dirty girl." His tone was still deep and rough. "Giving in already?"

"No." I raised my gaze from his plump lips to the sparkling blue gaze that was hot on me. I reached between us and firmly took his cock in my hand. "It's not giving in if I come to you, is it?"

Those lips curved into the smirk I was so familiar with, and he gripped my ass.

so tight that I felt the sting down my thighs. "No, Mia. That's not how it works." He tugged me against him so his cock pressed against my stomach and I had to let him go. "You don't come to me, angel. You give in. And you will give in, and when you do, you'll scream my name so fucking loudly you'll never doubt this attraction ever again."

"Until then? You gonna stand there with a rock-hard cock, are you, West? Gonna pretend you weren't just trying not to come down my throat?"

"Filthy little mouth," he murmured in my ear. He nipped my earlobe. "No, not at all. I'm gonna go lie on that sofa, and you're gonna get undressed so you're in nothing but those heels, and you're gonna come sit your tight, little cunt on my face so I can lick it until you come in my mouth. And then, my dirty angel, you're gonna suck me so hard you choke right before you swallow every last drop of me."

He sharply slapped my ass and let me go. Then he stepped out of the ripped jeans and the tight briefs. He grabbed his cock and held it as he crossed to the giant sectional sofa and lay back on it. He pulled a cushion from beneath his head and looked over at me.

And...fuck.

He lay there, all six foot three of male goodness, his blue eyes burning with lust and his hand wrapped firmly around his cock.

Only insanity would have made me leave.

I grabbed the hem of my dress and pulled it up and over my head. My bra followed, falling on top of the mound of material that was my dress. Then I turned, sank my teeth into my lower lip, and peered back over my shoulder. His hand was moving faster up and down his dick as I hooked my thumbs into the sides of my lace thong and pulled it over my ass.

"Get the fuck over here." It was an order. Short. Sharp. Demanding.

A thrill ran down my spine.

I swept my hair around to one side the way he kept doing and walked to him. Then I bent down over him. I took one long, slow suck of his cock before flattening my hand against his flawless stomach and kissing him. He stroked his hand down my back to my butt and slapped it for the second time.

"On me. Now. Come and sit on my fucking face, Mia."

I swung my leg over his head, looking back to make sure I didn't accidentally hit him—because that was a thing, and I'd done it before. Fortunately, my leg hit the sofa, clear of his head, and he put my knee in the right place next to his head then grabbed my hips.

And pulled me down to his mouth before I could even grab his cock.

He covered my pussy with his mouth and circled my clit with his tongue. It was only instinct that made me take hold of his cock and close my mouth over it. West teased me so expertly with his mouth, and it only took seconds before I was rocking against him, moaning, at the very same time I was drawing him deep back to my throat.

His fingers dug into my skin as he held my hips down, my pussy in his mouth. His strength made it impossible for me to do anything but rock myself back and forth against his deft tongue, and the orgasm built quicker than I'd expected.

I sucked him harder, took him deeper, made him thrust, right as his tongue rubbed over my clit so harshly that my body shuddered and I cried out with my release. I tried to pull away from him as I moaned over his cock, but he clamped one arm around my lower back and kept up the fervent assault, never slowing, never letting my clit breathe.

He worked me again, and again, and again, until I came for a second time.

Two for one.

I drew him deep in my mouth and hollowed my cheeks, sucking, and pulsed my tongue against him. Then I reached my other hand down and cupped his balls. My nails trailed over the tender skin as I literally sucked his orgasm from him. His body tensed, his legs turning into granite, and his cock throbbed repeatedly, his balls tightening, before he sucked hard on my clit.

I came for a third time over his tongue, right as his hot, salty release covered mine. I squeezed my eyes shut as I swallowed it and kept sucking, fighting against every instinct I had to stop and spit it out. My hand worked his cock, and he came for what felt like a second time when I lightly squeezed his balls.

He finally released my clit and dropped his head back. "Jesus fucking Christ, Mia."

"Just doing as I was told," I breathed, half sitting up and running my fingers through my hair to push it out of my eyes. My legs were trembling, so I put my hands in front of me, between his legs, and took several deep breaths.

West pulled his legs from beneath me and sat up. Then, to my surprise, he wrapped his arms around my waist and pulled me back. There was an awkward moment where I didn't know what to do with my legs, but he reached down and tugged my heels off before plastering his front against my back. One of his arms lay over my breasts as the other wound completely around my midsection.

His post-orgasm erection was pressed against my lower back, and I dropped my head back against his shoulder and closed my eyes.

"I shouldn't have come up here, should I?" I whispered.

"Sssh." He raised his hand and pressed his thumb to my lips. It faintly tasted like me, but I didn't care much as he softly stroked my lower lip. "How much did you really have to drink?"

"Not enough," I said, repeating my answer from earlier. "And you know it."

"How do you know?"

"Because you're a persistent fucker, but you're not an ass. Much," I added as an afterthought. "I need to go."

"Do you?"

"Yes." I pushed away and looked into his eyes. "I came up here to pee, West. Not get off three times."

"Three times, huh." His lips twitched to the side, and he dipped one hand down to the apex of my thighs.

I slapped his hand and darted away, grabbing my clothes. "Do you actually have a bathroom up here?"

He nodded toward the door behind me. "No one will see you. Only I'm allowed up here. Usually."

That final word was said pointedly, but not evilly, and I backed toward the door, clutching my clothes to me. I slipped through it and into a kitchenette, and another door, this one open, led to a small bathroom. I locked myself in it, and then I dropped my things on the floor as I sat on the toilet and wondered one thing.

The fuck had I just done?

I was certifiably insane.

No doubt about it.

I cleaned myself up the best I could using toilet paper and dressed. When I returned to the office area, West was nowhere to be seen, but my heels were neatly sitting by the door. Shame flushed my cheeks as I slid them on and walked downstairs to the club.

It was much louder down there, and I paused as my ears adjusted to the noise. Four guys were now sharing the stage and shamelessly dancing with the girls throwing their dollars around.

"Mia!" Vicky touched my arm. "There you are. I have your purse here. Is everything okay?"

"Thanks. Yes, why?" Oh god, did she know?

She leaned in toward me. "West came down looking a little frustrated. I wondered if you'd fought about something."

"Oh...no. Just a slight disagreement about one idea. I'm sure it's because I brought it up late. That's all. Bad timing." I smiled, but my heart wasn't in it. "I'm headed out, okay? I'm sure I'll see you in tomorrow. I'll be back."

"Day off," she answered with a sheepish little tug of her lips. "This weekend though, surely."

"I have to fly back Saturday for... Shit." I hadn't asked him yet. Oh god. It was in three days. "Never mind. I'll figure it out. Thanks for this." I held my purse up and spun on my heel.

All I wanted was to disappear. Get the heck out of this club and away from West Rykman, if only for a whole night.

I stalked through the crowds of people, to the front entrance area. The fresh air that rushed me had me drawing in a deep breath, and I snapped a hairband out of my purse and roughly and loosely tied my hair up in a scruffy topknot. The air was still horribly humid, and I knew I'd barely make it ten steps without my hair sticking to the back of my neck.

"Ms. O'Halloran?" The security guard caught my attention.

"Um, yes?"

He mumbled something into his radio that sounded suspiciously like, "I caught her," and clasped my elbow. My heart thundered as he said, "Come with me," and led me toward a waiting black car.

I felt sick.

Until he leaned in and added, "Mr. Rykman requested we had you sent home in a car, ma'am. He wanted to be assured you arrived home safely."

"Oh. Well, tell Mr. Rykman thank you very much," was all I managed to say before I got in the car and he closed the door behind me.

I dropped my head back and closed my eyes.

How very gentlemanly of him.

hat's wrong with me, Allie?" I slumped forward on the kitchen table, my fingers buried deep in my hair. "I'm a total slut, aren't I?"

My best friend hesitated. "Well, no. A slut would have been sleeping with him on Monday morning. You're like...a baby slut."

"Stop being nice to me. I'm an asshole. I'm so caught up in my own life that I have flights booked for Saturday to come home for the fitting and have no idea if I can even make it because I haven't discussed it with him because he's so fucking hot!"

"Boy, admission for one for the pity party."

"You've got a VIP ticket."

"You're the host, you idiot. Of course I have a VIP ticket," she said fondly. "Why don't you just call Michelle and explain, babe? It's not the end of the world. So you know this guy and you can't stay away."

"Because my life isn't a fucking chick flick?" I turned my face to the side and pinned my phone to the table with my ear so I didn't have to go to the trouble of holding it in place any longer.

"Then...I don't know. Get sick."

"I can't do that. She needs to be around for Jamie right now."

"Then, sissypants, buck the fuck up and get on with it," she finally said. "People are dying around the world and you're worried about getting your panties wet when you have to go to work."

"They're hardly comparable."

"Exactly. So quit bitching and get on with it."

"Geez, Bridezilla," I said slowly. "Who stole your coffee this morning?"

"Nobody. This just isn't the Mia I know. The Mia I know doesn't give a shit how attracted to somebody she is. She gets the hell on with it regardless of the situation."

"Yeah, well, this Mia is screwed because this situation is really fucky. I mean, come on. This situation has a sinfully hot guy with a tongue that could break the world record for the longest vaginal oral sex. He should either be teaching awkward teenaged boys how to do it to save the next generation the horrors we went through or do porn." Probably both. "No, both. He should be doing both of those things."

"That was too much information."

I shrugged though she couldn't see it. I didn't really care. I was in dire straits and her best advice was to get on with it.

"Look, babe, it's not the end of the world. Chances are it wouldn't matter if you knew him already anyway. If you were gonna be this attracted to him, you would be regardless."

"That's the worst thing I've ever heard," I argued. "Got any other predictions up your sleeve, Oh Great Psychic?"

"Not psychic. Common sense. If it's really that bad, then just screw your way through the next couple of weeks. At least then you'll be having fun while you're doing it. And it's not like you're working at an old people's home, is it?"

"Is that supposed to make me feel better? I can't screw my way through the next two weeks."

"Well, it's that or you stop whining about it."

"You have no sympathy for me, do you?" I huffed. Some best friend she was.

"No. You told him yesterday morning you're shit at personal relationships—"

"Because I am."

"—and then, twelve hours later, you were sitting on his face with his dick in your mouth. It doesn't get much more personal than coming on someone's face, Mia."

Like I hadn't already known that. I wasn't going to tell her that I'd done it three

STRIPPED BARE

times, either.

"That doesn't help, Allie."

"I'm not in the mood for helping. You're not helping yourself by moping around on your kitchen table."

"How did you know I was at the kitchen table?"

She sighed. "Because you always mope at the kitchen table."

"Oh, what am I gonna do? I can't go in there right now and act like nothing happened, can I?"

"I don't see that you have much choice," she replied slowly. "You have to finish this off. And him. You finished him off, right?"

"Allie!"

"What? I was wondering. You said about you... Yeah. Never mind." She paused. "You're gonna be attracted to him whatever you do. You may as well just deal with it and go with the flow."

"Jesus Christ, I'm getting schooled by a virgin."

"Ha!" She burst into laughter.

"Do you mind if I just blame you for this? You're the one who booked him for me, after all."

"Yeah, but you're the one who invited him back to your hotel room. I didn't make you do that. This is what you get for taking a virgin to a strip club. The Slut God and Virgin God rain hell upon your greedy vagina."

"You need to lay off the TV," I noted. "But I'm still blaming you. I never would have met him otherwise."

"Yeah, yeah, whatever. If it makes you feel better, blame me. We both know it'll still be your fault. Call him, Mia. At least then he'll be expecting you."

"I'm not calling him."

More laughter. "Call him, and when you get there, try to keep your panties on, okay?"

"No. Gotta go, byeeeeee." I drew the word out and hung up before she could say another word.

True as hell, my phone buzzed with a message from her a few seconds later.

Allie: *CALL WEST!*

No. I damn well wouldn't call him.

Vicky's words about him being frustrated after our supposed chat had rattled around in my head all night. Of course, in typical female fashion, calling him and asking him why would have been too easy. No, I was destined to assume any number of things I'd done wrong.

Could you do something wrong by swallowing a guy's come?

Didn't they like that?

Was he a strange one who didn't?

Was that what I'd done? Had I swallowed it when I was supposed to spit?

Good grief. There's a train of thought I'd never thought I'd have to have.

I slapped myself on the top of the head and sat up, looking out my window. There was no view, just the house across the street, but I stared at it anyway.

I needed to get some self-control. I'd gone freaking looking for an orgasm last night, no doubt about it, and I'd gotten myself three, and a hefty dose of shame to go with it.

Honestly, you'd have thought that self-control was one of my fortes, given the crap I put up with from my mother. Actually, maybe that was it. I used it all up on her, so when it came to West, my control meter was at a big, fat, useless zero.

That would have been a better excuse if I'd spoken to her since Monday. I hadn't.

Was Allie right? Was this attraction really just...too strong?

Sure. Our chemistry was undeniable, but to me, it felt closer to something that would combust rather than simmer along happily.

I had to go to work.

I didn't want to go to work.

I really didn't have a choice. Everything I needed to do involved West or Rock Solid. Once that was done and he'd agreed to let me fly home on Saturday for the dress fitting, I wouldn't have to see him for several days. Because he would agree. He wasn't a horrible person—plus, I'd already called Lili, my mixologist friend, and arranged to meet, try out a few recipes, and get her to Vegas next week.

I sighed as I forced myself to get up from the table and go to my room. There was a pile of clothes on my bed from an earlier attempt at dressing I'd abandoned to call Allie in the hope she'd have something smart to say that would be helpful to me and my current situation.

Obviously, she hadn't, but the call and subsequent thoughts I'd had had given me one good idea.

Don't wear a dress or a skirt or anything that could be easily hiked up around my waist, because despite her oh-so-helpful advice to keep my panties on, I had no doubt West would just slip them to the side and get to work.

I wondered if slipping them to the side was the loophole.

No, I decided, staring at the mess of clothes all tangled. I'd wear light skinny jeans and a white blouse tucked in. Business but casual. Smart but sexy. And a helluva lot harder to get a girl out of.

I dressed quickly and slipped some heels on before running a brush through my knotty hair. It still held the curls of last night, but sleep and the brush had turned them into loose waves that fell softly around my shoulders. They'd do.

I paused after putting mascara on, my gaze catching a bright-red tube of lipstick. I was lucky to have the shade of red hair that could pull it off, and I did always feel good in red... To hell with it. I slicked it on, blotted it on a tissue, and grabbed my stuff before I could change my mind about going to the club.

I hoped he wasn't still angry. I didn't want him to be frustrated, because that would make it even more awkward than I had a feeling it was already going to be. I didn't have a clue what to say to him, which was unfortunate because I had a lot I *needed* to say to him.

I blew out a long breath as I drove. I had an entire list of marketing things I wanted to run by him, but that would be no good unless I got my shit together. I needed a Starbucks or something, because the coffee machine in my apartment wasn't cutting it, but there wasn't one on the way to Rock Solid. And, if I detoured, I'd lose my shit and go home.

I clicked my tongue as I pulled into the parking lot. Immediately, I spotted West's car in the corner, which made me exhale with relief and my stomach twist in nerves. I still had no idea what to say except for, "I want Starbucks," and I didn't think that would be a great conversation starter.

I was struck once again by the difference in the atmosphere of the club during the day. Technically, it wasn't even nine thirty in the morning yet, but the quietness of it was oddly relaxing. If I didn't have to be there during the day to finalize promotion ideas, I doubted I would be.

I pushed the door open and edged inside. The familiar sound of the vacuum cleaner filled the air, except this time, I could see the lady bent over it. She ignored me entirely as I walked past her, and I noticed the buds in her ears. Listening to music instead of the vacuum.

Smart woman.

My heart sank as I caught sight of the bar. Of course, it was Vicky's day off. I liked her. The tall brunette now stacking glasses? The frown on her face told me I probably wouldn't feel the same way about her.

"Hi."

She gave me a cursory glance over her shoulder. "We're closed. Sign on the door says so."

"I'm Mia O'Halloran. I'm working—"

"No marketing calls. Sorry." She turned and slid a business card across the bar to me. "Call this number and leave a message."

"I'm working for MM Marketing with Mr. Rykman." I pushed the card right back.

Well, if she wasn't the cherry on an ice cream fucking sundae delight.

"No marketi—"

"Calm down, Tish," West said, sauntering through the door that connected the bar to the staircase to go upstairs. "Mia's working with me. Something you'd know if you'd read the notes Vicky left you instead of throwing them straight into the trash."

She opened her mouth to speak but swiftly closed it again when he raised an eyebrow in question.

"And check your attitude or I'll send you home and man the bar myself." He turned to me, which silenced her once more. "Mia. I wasn't expecting you this morning."

"I know. Sorry. Are you busy?"

"Just about to head out to the bank." He lifted up a dark-brown leather bag.

"Oh. I-I can come back later." I took a step back, but he gave me a tiny smile.

"No, you're good. Come with me." He rounded the bar and looked at Tish. "Tish, if someone comes in for marketing, you take *their* business card. Got it?"

Her lips thinned. "Yes."

"Good. I'll be back soon." He cupped my elbow and led me toward the doors, away from Miss Grumpalot inside.

When we stepped outside, he let out a long sigh.

"She seems lovely," I said chirpily.

He side-eyed me, dropping my elbow and pulling his keys out of his back pocket. "That's pushing it, don't you think?"

I shrugged. "Just an observation."

"Unfortunately, I can't fire her for being grumpy."

"Well, you could, but you'd have to have enough complaints," I pointed out, getting into the car and putting my purse by my feet.

He got in too. "I'm a couple short." He flashed me a grin and handed me the briefcase right after my belt clicked into place. "Here, hold this."

I stared at it as he started the engine. "Do you often take people to the bank with you?"

"Never, but you can go back in there and keep Tish company if you'd like." He raised an eyebrow before merging with the traffic.

"I'd rather jump into fast-moving traffic in New York City than spend another second alone with her."

West chuckled, the deep sound filling the car. "What can I do for you?"

Everything you shouldn't.

Mind, meet gutter. You'll get along well.

"I wanted to go over the plans for marketing. I spent my time in the bar last night seeing what you apparently aren't doing to promote anything."

"Ouch, angel. Hit me where it hurts."

I rolled my eyes. How dramatic. "You know you're not doing anything. That's why you hired me."

"Yes." He peered over at me. "What are your ideas?"

"Well, the promotions I mentioned..." I paused. There we went. Right into last night. "The promotions I mentioned last night."

"The drinks ones? I liked those." West glossed completely over the mention of last night and turned the wheel. The material of his white shirt stretched so tight across his arm that I wouldn't have been surprised if I heard a rip. "Were you thinking alternate nights?"

"Kind of. If you did a half-price cocktail happy hour Monday through Thursday, you wouldn't want to combine any other offers with it. Or..." My voice trailed off as my mind did. "You could do that Sunday through Wednesday and then an offer for ladies' night on Thursday, one on Friday, one on Saturday... Of course you'd have to look at what you sell most of on what nights and adjust the promotions accordingly... Ooh, you could also do bachelorette party specials. The VIP booths are great, but drinks offers would bring even more in."

"And if all bachelorette parties are like your friend's, then my guys are making a shit-ton of money."

I licked my lips. "Yes. That's the general idea. You want to get them in and keep them in. Cheap drinks just for them is the best way to do it."

West pulled up across the street from the bank and slowly turned to look at me. "Look at that," he said in a low voice, unbuckling his seat belt, before leaning across the car at me. He flattened his hand on top of the briefcase and gripped the back of my seat. "You're more than just a pretty face. And a smart mouth." His eyes lingered on my parted lips for a moment before he pulled the case from between my legs and sat back. "I'll be five minutes."

He got out without another word.

I hated that my heart skipped a beat as I watched him walk away. He drew the attention of everyone as he crossed the street. Women stopped and did a double take, and it was almost as if the men avoided him entirely. He was handsome, no doubt, but it was his presence. He was commanding and *de*manding, and he claimed every inch of space he occupied.

And even the space he didn't occupy belonged to him as long as he was in the room.

Good grief, he had a great ass. It filled those pants out to perfection, just tight and peachy enough...

My mind was in the gutter again, and there wasn't much I could do about it. I sighed and dropped my head back against the headrest. It was getting hotter, and fast, so maybe wearing jeans wasn't my smartest idea—nor was the three-quarter-sleeve blouse. So I turned the air conditioning up and looked out the window at the bank.

Five minutes dragged like hell, and when he finally emerged from the shadows of the doorway and entered the sunlight that drenched the sidewalk, he looked like some kind of modern god.

Hell, he was wearing his uniform of a white shirt with rolled-up sleeves and black pants well today. Really well.

Desire tingled through my veins, but I beat it back down with the equivalent of a baseball bat. Self-control! I possessed it. I needed to use it. I needed to wield it like it was pepper spray.

Pepper spray. Maybe that was the answer to resisting West. Well...pissing him off, sure. I guessed it'd work both ways.

I jolted back to attention when the car door slammed.

"Fuck me. It's like a mobile freezer in here." West shuddered and turned the air down. "You look freezing."

I blinked at him. "I'm good. I was getting hot. I got caught up in my thoughts, I guess."

He raised an eyebrow at me but didn't ask questions.

"Hey! Is there a Starbucks near here?" I turned to him.

"The next block over. Do you want to go?" He paused after starting the engine.

"Do you mind?"

"No. Let's go." He peered in the side mirror and then pulled into the traffic.

It was starting to pick up now, but we made it to Starbucks in a few minutes without speaking. We ordered, West paid—much to my annoyance—and then we moved to the next window.

By the time we made it back to Rock Solid, I'd barely sipped my ice-cold raspberry-acai green tea, and he'd all but finished his hot coffee. I just wanted to get inside and put a little distance between us. If being in a normal car was confining, being in this Audi was something else. It was so small and constricting that it was impossible not to feel him.

I climbed out, clutching my purse and my drink, and walked toward the club. Somehow, although he had gotten out after me, West beat me to the door and pushed it open. His smile made my stomach flip.

I dipped my head and mumbled a, "Thank you," before walking through it.

The air was blowing full force, and I found myself thankful for it. Even in the few minutes between the car and the front door, my temperature felt like it'd rocketed up several degrees. I didn't know it was West or the weather, but I'd bet it was both.

"Do you want to go upstairs and talk?" West dragged my attention back to him with that question.

I swallowed, my mouth drying out. "Um... Maybe it's best to stay down here."

He quirked an eyebrow, amusement shining through the blueness of his eyes.

"I need to see where posters could go." That was the lamest fucking excuse I'd ever given for anything, ever.

He knew it too. His smile grew. "Let's go sit down by the stage. It's bright there and you can see the whole club. For your posters."

I pursed my lips as he walked to the opposite end of the stage from the bar and pulled two chairs from beneath one of the round tables. *All right. Okay.* I followed him down there and sat in one of the chairs, setting my drink in front of me and my purse beside me.

"So," I started, pulling my laptop and my notebook out of my purse. "You're gonna need a lot of fliers in case of drink spills, so we really need to decide what promotions are happening when, and what long-term ones—think the bachelorette deals—will go on the back of those. They'll sit with the drinks menus so everyone will see them every time they get to a table." I opened up my laptop and clicked my pen. "The happy hour one is good and doesn't affect the others too much, but the long-term deals really need to be ironed out so I can start doing at least one side of the fliers tonight."

"Mia."

"And I'm meeting with my mixologist friend, Lili, in San Diego on Saturday, so we could make a bachelorette cocktail where the first one would be on the house for the bride-to-be and the bridal party. Everyone else gets fifty percent off. You price it a buck or two higher than the others on the menu since it's a special and everyone who likes it after the first round will keep buying."

"Mia."

He was staring at me hotly. I could feel myself getting flustered, but self-control, self-control, *self-control*. I whispered it inside my head like it was my mantra and carried on. I had to keep talking. If I stopped, he'd take control and that'd be the end of anything I was trying to do.

"I think, if we could come up with at least three special offers for special occasions like the bachelorettes and milestone birthdays, we could be onto something. There's easily enough space for three offers on the back of an average A5 flier."

"Mia." West grabbed my hand.

I stilled, looking up at him from beneath my lashes.

"You haven't looked at me since we left the bank, and as much as I appreciate your efficiency, I'm already lost."

"Sorry." I tried to scoot my hand out of his grip, but he had it too tight. "I tend to ramble when I get a train of thought."

"Did you say you're going back to San Diego on Saturday?" He leaned forward, his eyes on mine.

"Yeah." I dragged my lower lip between my teeth. "Is that okay? I mean, I have a dress fitting, and I kept forgetting to ask you..."

His lips tugged up on one side. "You don't need to ask me, angel. I've hired you, but you're still freelance. I understand you have commitments you can't change."

"Thank you. Allie was gonna kick my ass." Right after I'd kicked hers.

"I actually have family in Imperial Beach. My grandparents retired there fifteen years ago."

"Oh?" My eyebrows moved up. "I love it there. We spent a lot of time trying and failing to surf as kids. More failing happened than trying, but we gave it a good shot."

"I can't imagine you surfing."

I must have looked affronted, because he laughed, rubbing his hand over his mouth.

"No. I don't mean it like that," he said. "I'm just used to seeing you all dressed up or...not at all. Wearing a bikini seems like a strange middle ground."

My cheeks flushed. I wished they'd stop doing that whenever he said stuff like that.

"Stop trying to make me let go of your hand. You should know by now that I'll let go when I want to let go."

I narrowed my eyes at him. "I need it to type. And one of your staff is right over there." I nodded back to the bar where Ms. Not So Happy was. The cleaning lady had apparently finished and disappeared.

"I own this building. If I want to pick you up, throw you in the middle of the stage, and strip to my boxers to give you a lap dance, I fucking well can."

"West. Inappropriate." I coughed in the hope it'd hide the second heating of my cheeks.

He grinned, finally releasing my hand—only to cup the back of my neck and lean in. I froze as his lips brushed my ear.
"And so was me coming down your throat last night. But I bet, if I teased you enough, you'd do it again right now."

I shook my head. Who the hell was I trying to convince? I had tingles radiating across my skin from where he was touching me, and my lungs burned through the thundering of my heart.

I wouldn't.

Would I?

"See?" His low voice rumbled across my skin, making the hairs on my arms stand on end. "You can't even deny it."

I bit down on my lower lip, dropping my eyes.

He tugged on that lip with his other thumb, cupped my chin, and forced me to look into his eyes. "And, now, I want to kiss you."

I inhaled sharply and looked back down. "You can't."

"I could if we took this upstairs."

Again, I shook my head.

"Anyone would think you're afraid to be alone with me."

I snapped my gaze up to his, and honestly, I answered, "I am."

He held my gaze for a long moment, stroking his thumb against the side of my neck. It tickled, but I dared not laugh. I stayed, captive in the swirling mass of blue eyes that'd hypnotized me so many times before, and tried to remember how to breathe.

It didn't feel like I was.

It felt as though the unconscious action had become all too conscious.

Tish's voice rang out and broke through the moment. "West?"

West dropped his hand to the back of my chair, cutting eye contact off. "Yeah?"

"I'm done setting up. I'll be back at three."

"Come back in a better mood or don't bother," he warned her.

"Yeah, sure."

I turned my head to watch as she grabbed her things and headed for the door.

"Tish? Did Sally leave?" he asked before she'd opened it.

"About five minutes before you got back. Why?"

"Just wondering. Can you lock the door? Ms. O'Halloran and I have a lot to discuss and I'd rather not be interrupted by anyone hoping to get the party started early."

"No problem." She smiled and then disappeared through it.

The click of the lock was deafening.

We were alone.

The thing I was afraid of.

Because I knew—and he knew—that resisting him was virtually futile. Sooner or later, I would have to give in.

Later seemed to be getting sooner and sooner, and I didn't know what to think of it.

est's gaze swung back to me. Laughter danced inside his eyes, and the slow, easy curve of his lips drew my attention. I stared at them as they formed the dirty, sexy smirk I'd come to associate with some filthy stream of words leaving him.

"You look terrified I'm going to jump your bones," he said quietly, his smirk staying firmly in place.

"Experience has shown that to be the usual thing that happens when we're alone." My mouth went dry as his gaze dropped to it and flashed with lust.

"Has it ever ended badly?"

"Every time," I whispered, stilling as he moved closer to me.

He turned in his seat and cupped the side of my neck. His thumb brushed over the tender patch below my ear and down on my jaw and back again. My heart beat a little faster as he leaned in.

"Want me to stop?"

My head shook, answering before I could think about it.

He moved in, his lips barely touching mine, and then stopped. I couldn't move closer to him or away from him. The world melted away as we stayed in a place, not kissing. But we were, and I could taste his coffee on his breath, feel his exhales over my lips, breathe in his very essence.

And then...

"West?" I whispered before taking a deep breath in. "Why do you keep doing this? What do you want from me?"

He sat back, not dropping his arm. A war waged in his eyes, as if he knew what he wanted but didn't know why he wanted it. Neither of those things helped me as I stayed sitting in limbo, still able to lick my lips and taste his breath.

"West? You there?"

This time, he dropped his gaze like I'd burned him. "Beck?" He stood up, his chair squeezing against the floor. "The hell are you doing back?"

"Family reunions, man. They give me hives." A tall, handsome man with dark hair cut a good inch shorter than West's came into my line of sight as I turned. He was a little shorter than West, just as built, and just as freakin' hot.

He'd called him Beck.

This had to be Beckett Cruz, the MIA-until-now business partner.

"I told you to tell your mom you had the flu."

"I tried," he responded. "She clipped me around the back of the head and dragged me through the house by my damn ear."

West and Beckett shared a hug—you know, one of those guy hugs where they beat each other on the back halfway through.

"Come back here. Someone you need to meet."

I bit the inside of my cheek as I stood. I hadn't thought there was anything hotter than having West Rykman walk toward me, but I had been wrong. It was having West Rykman and Beckett Cruz walk toward me.

Speaking of...

Beckett stopped as soon as he laid eyes on me. He appraised me a little too thoroughly, his gaze hovering almost uncomfortably on my eyes. "Red hair. Curves for miles. Emerald-green eyes. I know exactly who you are."

"Uh... You do?"

"Yeah. You're the vixen who had this asshole's head in a spin after that bachelorette party three weeks ago. How'd he find you?"

"I'm sorry?" I looked between West and Beckett.

West looked visibly uncomfortable.

"Yeah. I think he had wet dreams about you for a week like a fucking teenager."

"Beck," West hissed out.

"Actually," I said before he could continue embarrassing us both, "I'm with MM Marketing. Mia O'Halloran."

Beckett's eyes widened. "So, you're... You're not her? Well, shit. This is a bit damn awkward. West, you should've shut me up."

"Well..." I tried to fight the sheepish raise of my shoulders. "I am..." I glanced at West.

"She's also the vixen who had my head in a spin," West ground out. "Thanks for that, by the way."

"Welcome." Beckett slapped him on the shoulder and walked toward me.

I expected him to put his hand out, but no. He grabbed my shoulders and smacked a kiss on each of my cheeks.

"Pleasure to meet you, gorgeous. Beckett Cruz, the brains and beauty behind this guy's... Well, fuck it. I'm the body too. Call me Beck."

"Nice to meet you."

This was awkward. On a scale of one to ten, it was easily five hundred in the best moments. *He talked to his business partner about me.*

"I should get going." I moved back to my things. "I'll probably need the whole weekend to draft these fliers up since I'm not here Saturday, so I'll check in Sunday night and let you know how it's going."

"Nah, gorgeous, don't leave!" Beck clapped his hands together and rolled his sleeves up. Like West, he was wearing a white shirt.

I didn't know if my ovaries would survive this conversation.

"Oh, no, it's okay, really—"

"Stay, Mia. He'll sit on you otherwise." West tugged on a lock of my hair and sat next to me, boxing me in against the stage.

Beck didn't miss it. He raised one eyebrow, but he didn't mention it as he swung a chair around and sat on it backward. "Fill me in. What trouble have you been causin' while I've been contemplating death by plastic fork?"

"He's also a child and a drama queen," West added.

"It was your death, buddy."

"Right back atcha."

They shared a grin.

They'd been friends a long time—I could tell. People like them had a vibe about them, like their friendship had its own airwave. The West I was seeing right then was a West I hadn't seen before. I'd only ever seen serious or sexy West.

Not good-guy West.

This felt a lot like good-guy West.

"Well..." I cleared my throat and pulled my myriad of papers out of my folder. "We've rebranded the logo, which is here..."

"Rock Solid...for your pleasure. Ha!" Beck barked out the most infectious laugh I'd ever heard and smacked his hand against the table. "That's fuckin' genius. Did he tell you that?"

"Close." I couldn't help but smile at him.

"Well, it's fuckin' genius. True too." He put that sheet down. "Go on."

I talked him through everything else we'd done, and between the three of us, three hours and a take-out lunch later, we had a ton of ideas for promotions, more than we'd have gotten between me and West. Beck was a little wild, but he was also incredibly business-minded.

More than that, with him around, West and I had to focus on work—and not each other.

I hoped he'd stay around. We were much more productive with him.

"You staying at a hotel, Mia?" Beck said as I packed my things up.

I shook my head. "My boss doesn't do hotels. She had the apartment she'd booked transferred to me. I'm just a few blocks away."

"What are you doing for dinner tonight? I'm not asking her on a date!" he directed at West. "I was gonna cook at your place. I haven't been to the store yet."

"What makes you think I have?" West asked.

"Nothing. But, if I tell you I'm cookin' at yours, you're gonna go." Beck grinned. "So? Mia?"

My gaze flitted between them, but at West's shrug, I nodded. "All right. Sounds good. Thank you."

"Awesome. Tell me your address and—"

"I'll get her," West interrupted. He swung his bright, blue gaze from me to Beck.

Beck didn't argue.

Neither did I.

I probably should have.

———————◆-◦-◆———————

What do you wear to dinner with a guy you can't stop getting naked with and his business partner, who both technically currently employ you?

I didn't know, either.

That was why I'd ended up wearing the same jeans as earlier, changed into a plain, white tank top, and thrown a black lace kimono over the top. My feet were also killing from wearing heels all day, so I'd put on plain, black flats.

I was about to be even shorter than West. Like five inches weren't enough.

He'd been on my mind ever since I'd left the club. Sometimes with Beck, sometimes without, but every time Beck crept into my consciousness, it was because their friendship was much like one I was already familiar with: mine and Allie's.

It was that happy-go-lucky, easy relationship that silently spoke of undying loyalty and unwavering respect that brought out another side of everyone.

I found it hilarious that I was a bit of a dick alone, but with Allie, I was a lot of a dick.

Alone, West was serious and powerful. With Beck, he seemed like...one of the guys.

A part of me—a bad, bad part of me—wanted to explore that side of him, get to know him better. I had a feeling that the one-of-the-guys West was the best part of him.

Aside from the naked part of him. That won out for sure.

I grabbed my purse when two knocks sounded at my door. My phone rang almost the moment I threw it in, so I yelled, "Two secs!" and fished it back out to check the screen.

Darren.

Why was Darren calling me? He had no reason to call me. I didn't *want* him to call me.

I wanted him to take a long walk off a short pier.

I sent it to voicemail, threw my phone back in, and opened the front door. My line of sight was barely on par with West's shoulders, and my teeth found my lower lip as I peered up at him.

"Maybe I should put some heels on."

He looked down at me, a grin stretching across his handsome face. "I agree. I can wait."

I sighed and turned. I should have known better than to even try. I wasn't even short; that was the worst thing. He was just very tall and very wide. He made me look like a pixie.

I exited my bedroom wearing the same lace-up heels I had been the night we'd explored the strip clubs. His gaze dropped to my feet, his lips twitching, before he looked back up and met my gaze.

I cleared my throat. "Should we go?"

He looked as though he wanted to say no, but he nodded and held the door for me. I scooted past him, fumbling for my keys in my purse, and waited as he closed the door. Something that felt eerily like unsaid words hung in the air between us, lending a hint of awkwardness, as if the permanent tension that buzzed around us hadn't been bad enough.

I locked my door and followed him to the elevator. He ran his hand through his hair and glanced at me several times before sighing.

"What did I do?" I asked, the words coming out so quickly they almost strung together to form one long word instead of a coherent sentence.

"Nothing." He glanced at me, smiling. "But the idea of you spending an entire night in the presence of Beck is, honestly, a little bit terrifying."

"Why? He's not going to do something crazy like propose a threesome, is he? 'Cause don't get me wrong—that's hot in porn—but I'll stick to one hole at a time, thank you."

West stilled, slowly looking at me, then burst out laughing. It echoed around the small space. "Has anyone ever told you that you speak before you think a lot?"

"Who said I didn't think about that?" I raised my eyebrows. "I totally thought about it."

"You didn't think about it, did you?"

I sighed and followed him out of the elevator as the doors opened on the ground floor. "No, not at all."

He laughed again and, wrapping one strong arm around my shoulders, pulled me against his side. I blushed as he tucked me right against his body and kissed the side of my head.

"You're crazy, Mia."

"The evidence does support that theory, yes." I wriggled out of his hold as we reached his car. It was parked right in front of my rental and honestly made mine look like something that needed restoration. "Why are you so scared about me having dinner with you and Beck?"

We got in the car before he spoke.

"So scared is an exaggeration. Apprehensive is a better word." He started the engine. "For the most part, Beck and I are like chalk and cheese. I'm far more serious than he is. Even when we were kids, I was always the one who had to work before I played. He tended to do everything last minute, but luckily for him, he's stupidly fucking smart, so it was never a problem." He laughed low, and I had to smile at the gentle fondness that intertwined with his words. "If I had my way, tonight would be a business dinner, but that stupid dick had to go ahead and do it at my house, where the chance of that happening is nothing. He's likely to tell you every dumb thing we did as kids to embarrass me."

"Won't it embarrass him too?"

He flashed me a half smile. "In our senior year of high school, he was dared to pull his pants down in the middle of the hall. He did it and asked the girls who wanted his phone number."

"He did... Seriously?"

"Yep. He was suspended for a week, but I'm almost certain he slept with a different girl in our year every night that week."

I laughed and tucked my hair behind my ear. "Wow. I think I'm impressed."

"I think, after that, he became a hero to every guy below our year. Even our math teacher was impressed and gave him a high five." He shrugged. "Nothing can embarrass Beck. I've tried."

"You were the one who dared him to pull his pants down, weren't you?"

"Of course not." His eyes sparkled. "I was the one who gave the kid the idea though."

"And you say you're the serious one."

Another shrug. "I am. Most nights, he's by the bar in the club—both Rock Solid and The Landing Strip. The women's club next door," he added. Like I didn't know that. "I'm usually working, making sure they're both running smoothly, while he plays."

"I don't believe you're that serious, West. Nobody who's totally serious strips."

"I told you—that's my fun. I was a stripper before we owned the club. We both were. At Rock Solid before it was Rock Solid."

"What happened? How did you get the club?"

He looked at me when we reached a red light, and a little hesitance glimmered back at me from his eyes. "My parents died in a car crash around the time Beck's grandmother passed away from cancer. Most of her inheritance went to his parents, but she'd left him a good chunk. I don't have any siblings, so I got everything my parents owned. We were twenty-four and realizing we couldn't strip forever. It was good money, sure, but eventually, we'd have to get real jobs. We both had business degrees, so when our boss announced he was selling the club, we invested our inheritances and savings."

"Good choice."

"It was. The club was failing, but between us, within a year, we had it running successfully again."

"And it's been successful ever since."

"Honestly, we almost lost it two years ago," he admitted, his expression darkening. "I made a few stupid choices that almost cost us everything, including some of our other businesses, but my grandparents weren't willing to let us lose what we'd worked so hard for. They lent me money. And charged me interest." He smirked, all traces of darkness disappearing as quickly as they'd appeared.

"Most people wouldn't admit that, you know. Especially not to their marketing consultant."

He laughed. "Yeah, well, your boss drives a hard bargain. You're already paid, angel. She wanted it up front because, apparently, you're very expensive."

"Well, you know. You get what you pay for." I grinned as he turned into what looked like a very wealthy area. I knew nothing about Vegas except for the Strip, but these houses, while they weren't mansions, were definitely bigger than your average property. "Nice."

"It's not bad." He smirked, pulling into one of the driveways.

95

The two-story house was red brick, simple, and the front yard consisted of a stone path and cacti.

"Cacti. In the desert. How original," I teased him, getting out of the car.

Another laugh. *God. I love that sound.*

"Do I look like I garden to you, angel?" He held his arms out. "They look after themselves. Sometimes they even flower. Although I'm pretty sure Mrs. Evans across the street is desperate to come plant some flowers in there. One day, I might just let—oh, fucking hell. Here she comes."

I spun around and saw the classiest-looking older lady I'd ever seen standing on the doorstep of the house opposite West's. Her silver-gray hair was twisted into an elegant updo, and her peach dress fit her perfectly. The pearls around her neck set it off though.

"West, dear! Wait right there," she hollered, turning back into the house. She reemerged five seconds later with a box and sauntered across the street.

"Go with it," he whispered to me.

"You had a delivery this afternoon, darling. I signed for it for you, so here you go." She patted the top of the box with a fond smile and turned soft, hazel eyes on me. "Hello, dear. I'm Patricia Evans. Are you a friend of West's?"

Her eyes sparkled when she said *friend.*

Oh dear. Now I understood his "go with it."

"It's nice to meet you, Mrs. Evans," I said politely, taking her offered hand. "I'm Mia, and I actually work with West. I'm his new marketing consultant."

"Ooh, how lovely." She patted my fingers and turned to him. "Bit late for work, isn't it, dear?"

"Not on the Strip." He smiled at her. "Business dinner."

"Business dinner. Mhmm." She looked back at me. "Well, I'll leave you kids to it. Just wanted to bring this package to you before I forgot."

"Thank you very much. I appreciate it." West bent down and kissed her cheek. "Tell Walter I said hello."

"I will, dear. I will." She took a few steps and looked at his yard. "I do wish you'd let me plant a few flowers in your yard. It'd brighten it right up and attract the ladies, you know."

Because he had such a problem attracting them. I bit my laugh at that back.

"Maybe I'll surprise you in your Christmas card this year," West called after her.

"You do that, darling!" she called right back.

"Quick. Get inside before she drags Walter out to get a look at you," he said in a low voice, gripping my elbow. "Package my ass. She knows I would have seen the card and gone and got it. She heard the car, looked out, and saw you. Nosy old dear."

I laughed into my hand and let him manhandle me into his house. Almost immediately, the rich scent of spaghetti Bolognese attacked my nose, and I inhaled deeply.

"Damn. Is Beck really cooking that?" I asked West.

He nodded. "Isn't a thing he can't do well. Asshole."

"Did Mrs. Evans corner you?" Beck appeared in the doorway to what was, I presumed, the kitchen. "She saw you leave and came over to find out where you were going."

West stared at him. "What did you tell her?"

Beck grinned. "I told her you were going to pick up a lady friend for dinner."

"Jesus, Beck. No wonder she was desperate to get this package to me. I don't even know what it is."

"Oh, it's an empty box."

"Why would she give you an empty box?" I looked at West.

He slid his gaze back to me. "Because Beck kindly told her you were coming and she wanted an excuse to see you. She's shameless, I swear."

"She was one of the most sought-after strippers in the city before she met Walter and married him two weeks later," Beck explained, leaning against the doorframe. "I don't think she knows what shame is."

"Yeah, well, I'm not gonna hear the end of it now, so thanks." West moved past him, package in hand, and dumped it on the side.

Beck winked at me. "Always a pleasure to piss him off."

Oh boy. I had a feeling this was going to be a long evening.

I had been right.

In the last hour, I'd been regaled with tales from both their childhood and teenage years, and almost every one was designed to embarrass the heck out of West. I learned that, when they were eleven, he'd broken his arm climbing a tree to impress a girl. Apparently, he'd never considered that falling was something that might happen to him.

When they were sixteen, he prepared a giant promposal for one of the girls on the cheerleading squad in front of almost their entire high school, but she said no and he refused to go to their prom that year.

And the first time they ever stripped, he fell over, spilled the girl's drink all over her, and almost got himself fired because he inadvertently groped her very intimately as he attempted to clean her up.

To West's credit, he sat there and let Beck get it all out while I giggled my way through both dinner and dessert. Sure, he shot him a few dirty looks and, I suspect, kicked him under the table like a child, but he never told him to stop.

I wondered how many times they'd done this routine before.

"All right, all right," West finally said. "Can we switch to you now? You've done stupider shit than I have."

"You mean like the time I pulled that chick before our sophomore year in college and she ended up being the teaching assistant in one of my classes?" Beck asked. "Because that was a bummer. I was really into her."

"You... You did what?" I put my glass of wine down. "Did you sleep with her again?"

He grinned. "Of course I did. We slept together for six months before she had a pregnancy scare and we decided it was over."

"You mean you decided it was over," West reminded him.

"Was she pregnant?" I questioned.

"No. But she told me she was protected. How many scares do you have if you're sure you're protected?"

"Well..." I paused and thought back. Been there, done that. "I'm protected and

I've had three, but those were less scares and more that I'm *really* bad at remembering dates."

Beck snorted. "See? That's one thing. But she literally had no idea. I wasn't into having kids then. Still ain't. Tell you what though—I used a damn condom every time after that."

"Your condom bill was bigger than your tuition," West said dryly. "You're the only reason we made so much money stripping. They all came to see you again."

"You mean after you'd stopped spilling drinks on the patrons, right?" I teased him, a grin on my face.

He snapped his gaze to me. "I can think of one person I wouldn't mind spilling a drink over."

"You just want an excuse to lick me all over."

Beck roared with laughter as West gave me his dirty smirk. "She's got you fuckin' pegged, pal. How long's she staying?"

"As long as it takes to get your marketing finished," I answered, sipping from my glass and trying to ignore the hot look West was giving me. "And I get a hell of a lot more work done with you around. I've done more work today than we have all week."

"Reeeeeaaaaally." Beck stared at West. "And why's that, West?"

"Not a clue," he answered, still staring at me.

I squirmed under his heated scrutiny of me. Like he really was imagining licking me all over.

Damn it. Now, I was imagining him licking me all over. I didn't need to be imagining that. Not at his house with his bedroom in it.

"Excuse me," I said, looking to West. "Where's your bathroom?"

"Upstairs, straight at the end of the hall."

"Thanks." I got up, feeling his eyes hot on me the entire time, and went upstairs in search of the bathroom. I found myself moving slowly as I looked at the photos that adorned the walls of the staircase.

There were a couple of West and Beck, both younger and recently, judging by the distinct lack of stubble and muscle in the younger photo. One photo had West in the middle of an older man and woman, and the man had a distinct resemblance to him, so I guessed these were his grandparents. Next to that hung a larger photo of a much younger West in a graduation gown and hat, between another man and woman, these two much younger than the other couple. The man was his mirror image, and both he and the woman wore the kind of proud smiles only parents could.

I smiled a little. Another side of West I hadn't known existed. He obviously loved his family very much, and my heart warmed at it.

I found my way into the white-and-ice-blue-decorated bathroom, used the toilet, flushed, and washed my hands. I'd learned more about him and Beck tonight than I'd ever thought I would, and I already knew that resisting West would be even harder now.

He was no longer just a sexy guy who gave killer orgasms and stripped.

He was...a real person. A real guy with feelings and memories, successes and triumphs, low points and mistakes.

That was scary.

Their low voices rumbled through the air as my heels sank into the hallway carpet, and I shouldn't have stopped to listen, but I did.

"Stop beating yourself up," Beck said quietly. "It happened, West. You can't let that one mistake rule the rest of your life. I don't have to be a fucking relationship counselor to see that you like this woman."

I swallowed hard.

"Beck, drop it," West replied firmly. There was a slight pause where the sound of a glass clinking against the table replaced words. "It doesn't dictate my life. And this has nothing to with Mia."

"It has everything to do with her, man. You've been staring at her all night. I've spent the whole time talking to the side of your damn head."

"I don't want to talk about this."

"You have to move on sooner or later."

"There's nothing to move on from because there was nothing to hold on to. Charlotte made sure of that. End of story."

"Whatever you say. I just think—"

I bit my lower lip and stomped on the bottom step a few times. Beck stopped talking, and I wandered back into the dining room, forcing a smile onto my face.

I shouldn't have listened to that conversation. It was obviously private, but now, I had a burning desire to know more about the man I'd spent so much time with this week.

Who was Charlotte, and why was it the end of it?

"Get lost on the way to the bathroom?" West quirked an eyebrow, standing and grabbing my bowl from dessert.

"I got delayed on the stairs, staring at the photos. I'm nosy." I grinned. This time, it was genuine.

"He was an ugly little shit, wasn't he?" Beck threw in. "I've always been the looker."

"You've always been the ego, you mean." West balanced Beck's bowl on top of mine and his and lifted them, looking at me. "Another glass of wine?"

"Sure."

"Beck, beer?"

"Nah, I gotta get going in a minute. You know. For the long walk up the street to my house." He winked at me.

West shook his head, turning his back to us. He'd barely left the room when Beck's gaze on me became too intense to ignore.

"What?" I focused on him.

"Got delayed staring at photos, huh?"

I winced. "I didn't mean to hear. I just kinda...did."

"Good. You were supposed to." He half smiled. "Don't ask me 'cause I won't tell you. Hell, he probably won't tell you yet, either, but I wasn't lying. He can't take his damn eyes offa you."

"It's really not my business, Beck."

His indigo-blue eyes, so dark they could almost pass at black, bored into me. "I think it's more your business than either you or him know."

"I thought you were leaving." West appeared with the bottle of wine. There was just over a glass left, and I'd drunk it all, but I felt completely unaffected by it.

Beck held his hands up. "Going. I'm going." He got up, walked around the table, and kissed the top of my head. "Thanks for a lovely dinner, gorgeous. Much better than being alone with this miserable fuck."

"You're welcome. Thank you for cooking."

"Always my pleasure to cook for a beautiful lady."

"Beck. Get the fuck out." West glared at him, the wine bottle poised to pour me another glass.

"All right, all right." He backed up with his hands up, winking at me right before he left the room.

I smiled and looked down. He was, quite possibly, the most likable person I'd ever met.

West finished pouring my glass and put the bottle in the middle of the table. Then he sat back down. He hadn't drunk all night, but now, he twirled an ice-cold bottle of beer between his finger and his thumb. He was staring at it as it twirled, and an air of awkwardness hung between us.

"We don't have to sit at the table," he finally said after several minutes. "Come sit on the back deck with me."

I nodded and grabbed my glass, following him through the house to the sliding back doors that opened out onto a spacious deck. His backyard was much the same as the front, bare apart from the odd cactus, but the deck held a large sofa, a small table, and a fire pit. There was also a grill at the opposite end, next to an outdoor dining set.

Not to mention the hot tub in the corner by it. I wondered how much time he spent out there—and if he spent it alone.

We both sat on the large, cream sofa, and West put his beer on the table only to grab me by the ankles. I squeaked as his strong grip made me lose balance, but he took my wine before it spilled and put it next to his bottle.

Then, slowly, he unlaced my shoes, pulled them off, and put them on the floor at the end of the sofa.

"They can't be comfortable anymore."

"Not really," I admitted. "Thank you."

He smiled, putting my feet down and kicking his own shoes off. He reached down to peel his socks off and tucked them inside his shoes until we were both barefoot, and then he unbuttoned his shirt, leaving it to fall loosely at his sides.

Did he ever wear anything else?

"So, you heard that, huh?"

$\mathcal{I}$ decided to play dumb and peered across at him. "Heard what?"

"Me and Beck. Talking. In there."

"Oh. Yeah." I bit the inside of my lip. "I guess that means you heard him and me talking."

"Beck's voice tends to carry very well through walls." He kinda smiled. "I bet you're wondering who Charlotte is."

I turned toward him fully, bringing my leg up onto the sofa and hugging it to my chest. "West... It's not my business. Beck said he meant for me to hear, but I shouldn't have listened. Besides, I also heard you say you didn't want to talk about it."

"I don't. But it doesn't mean I can't."

"Then don't talk about it. Talk about something else. Like... How old you are, or what your favorite color is, or the last time you did something other than work on an evening."

"Twenty-nine, green, and tonight."

"You're just saying all that."

He laughed and leaned back, propping his elbow on the back of the sofa. "I really am twenty-nine, I really can't remember the last time I didn't work on an evening, and I didn't have a favorite color until I developed a possibly unhealthy obsession with your eyes."

I pursed my lips. "Stop sweet-talking me. I know you just want inside my pants."

"I do, but is it sweet-talking if I'm honest?"

"Yes."

"Damn it, woman. Shut up and take a compliment."

I rolled my eyes. "All right, all right. Thanks."

He nudged my knee. "I don't believe you mean that."

"I don't."

He smiled, his eyes shining.

I took a sip of wine and rested my chin on my knee. "Do you really work every night? Like, you never take a break?"

"Rarely. Even when I do, I always remember something that needs to be done, or I'm thinking about it, so it's never really time off." He looked away from me, out to the end of the yard, where the now-set sun has painted the sky in shades of golden orange. "Beck pretty much made me do everything earlier and forced me to try to take tonight off."

He was a workaholic—hell, even his idea of fun, when he stripped, was technically still work. That wasn't healthy for anybody. Surely he had to have something else in his life, or was it all so intertwined with the club that there was no line where work ended and fun really began?

I tilted my head to the side, my gaze trailing over his profile. "Are you thinking about work now?"

"Right now?"

"Yes, right now."

West turned his face back toward me, and although his eyes shone through the shadows playing across his features from the setting sun, I saw a hint of rawness glaring at me. It made my mouth go dry, and I forced myself to swallow past the tiny lump in my throat.

"No," he answered quietly, holding my eyes captive with his. "I rarely do when I'm with you. Even when I'm supposed to."

It was still hot out, but shivers trailed down my arms, leaving goose bumps pimpling across my skin.

"Then what are you thinking about?" I asked.

"I'm thinking that, if I don't kiss you soon, I might go crazy."

"So kiss me."

He didn't need a second invitation.

I dropped my knee down as he moved toward me, cupping the back of my neck and pulling me against him. I slid along the sofa with one easy tug from him so our bodies collided at the exact moment our lips did. I shuddered as he entwined my hair around his fingers and wrapped his arm around my back, locking me against him.

My own fingers found the collar of his shirt, and I held it for a moment before one hand fell down to his stomach and the other curved around the side of his neck, my thumb brushing against his stubbly jaw.

My body felt alive—completely and utterly alive. Desire trailed over my skin as we kissed. He licked and nipped at my lower lip until I opened my mouth and flicked my tongue against his. His groan vibrated through my body, and he eased me down until I was on my back and he was leaning over me, my legs wrapped around his waist.

His hard cock pushed against my clit, sending a bolt of desire shooting through my entire body until my blood hummed with need. I gasped when his mouth left mine and trailed up my jaw.

"What else are you thinking?" I breathed, tilting my head back against the sofa cushions.

He was breathing heavily as he nipped my earlobe. "Thinking you're wearing too many clothes." He kissed my neck. "Thinking I'm already fucking crazy." Another kiss, this time on my pulse point. "Thinking you should be naked so I can kiss every inch of you." More kisses, now along my collarbone. "Thinking about licking your clit until you come in my mouth again." Even more kisses, down to the curve of my breasts. "Thinking about pinning you down and fucking you over and over again."

I closed my eyes as he left hot, openmouthed kisses across my chest and reached his hand up to tug the low neck of my tank top down. He did, exposing my bra, and moved his dirty mouth down farther, his fingers moving too, until he pulled the cup of my bra down, popping out my breast, and took my nipple in his mouth.

I inhaled sharply and arched my back, pushing it farther into his mouth, a fact he took advantage of. He sucked so hard that it should have been painful, but all it did was turn me on to the point that my pussy was clenching again and again in desperation.

"Now," I struggled to breathe out, running my fingers up the back of his head and into his thick, dark hair. "Now, what are you thinking?"

He released my nipple and leaned up, positioning his mouth over mine. "Thinking that's exactly what you want me to do. Isn't it, angel?"

I didn't respond for a moment. Lust and common sense warred inside me, but inevitably, as I had known it would, my body's insane desires for him won the battle, and to the beat of my pounding heart, I nodded.

"Say it." He flexed his hips against me, grinding his cock against me.

The seam of my jeans rubbed against my clit, and I moaned. He chuckled, doing it again. And again, so I clutched his hair.

"What's the matter, angel? Can't talk?"

He was using his allure as a stripper on me, and I didn't mind a bit, even if my answer was another moan as he gyrated his hips to a silent melody.

"Don't want me to?" He stilled.

But I couldn't talk, dangerously close to the edge of an orgasm.

He replaced my bra cup with a rough, "Gotcha." Then he let me go, sitting up, and removed my leg from behind him.

He was—what?

No.

No way.

I sat up too, shrugged my kimono off, and threw it to the side. I caught him right before he could stand. I dragged him back by his shirt and sat on top of him before he could move again. I cupped his face and kissed him hard, flicked my tongue across the seam of his lips, and said, "I want you to fuck me, West. Hard. Until I can't breathe. Until I'm screaming your name."

He cupped my ass and stood easily, his crazy strength making it easy to lift me as I crossed my legs at the bottom of his back. "Mia..." he murmured, carrying me into the house. "My dirty little angel. I'll do more than fuck you until you just scream my name. I'll fuck you so hard you'll be screaming my name so loudly the whole damn neighborhood is gonna hear you come all over my cock."

"Dare you," I said against his mouth, grasping the back of his neck. I bit my cheek as the stairs made his cock rock against my clit, which sent more sparks of desire through me.

We reached the top, and he shoved a door halfway along the hall open. He carried me into the room so certainly, so strongly, that it wasn't a surprise when he threw me on the bed so hard that I bounced a couple of times.

He climbed on top of me, pulling my legs around his waist, and kissed me. I lost myself in the magic of his mouth, sliding my hands beneath his shirt and pulling it over his shoulders until he threw it onto the floor. I ran my hands over his body, dipping my fingertips through every muscle ridge and over every inch of his perfect skin.

"Told you you'd come to me," he rasped against my neck, swirling the tip of his tongue in tiny circles. "Despite everything. Knew you'd give in."

"Cocky bastard," I whispered, pressing my hips up to his.

"Confident," he fired back, moving down my body. He pulled me up and lifted my shirt over my head, swiftly making my bra follow it.

"Cocky." It was definitely cocky.

He smiled, flicking his tongue over my nipple a few times before going to the other. Then back to the first, and over to the second again. I moaned, digging my fingertips into his shoulders. His laugh against my skin was deep and melodic, raspy and sexy, and he eased back, kissing down my stomach, until he had his fingers in my belt loops.

He tugged, peeling my jeans over my hips and my butt, right down my legs and over my ankles. He tossed them to the floor, too. Then he stood, undressing himself from his remaining clothes. Harshly, he yanked me down the bed so my ass was on the edge and my knees were hooked over his shoulders. The kisses he peppered along the inside of my thigh made my hips buck as desperation made my clit ache and throb.

West kissed me through the lace of my thong. His probing tongue combined with the roughness of the material rubbing against my clit felt so good, more intense than anything I'd ever felt. He teased me that way, flattening his hand against my lower stomach. Every time I tried to pull away from his mouth, he would tug me right back until he finally moved my underwear to the side and kissed me properly.

His tongue relentlessly explored my pussy, and I went from breathing too quick to barely breathing at all. Sweat slicked my skin as my body took over and moved my hips in a quick rhythm. He stilled, holding me there as I fucked his face, my body pleading for release. I was tight everywhere, desperate for it, begging him for more, and he read it perfectly, sliding one finger inside me and thrusting it until that combined with his tongue against my clit set my body alight with a

EMMA HART

wave of pleasure.

"West..." I gasped, grasping at the sheet and his hair. "God, West."

"I love it when you call me by my proper name: God." He laughed low as he dragged his mouth up my body and kissed me. My orgasm coated his lips, and he slid his hand up the outside of my thigh and gripped my ass. "You mean what you said earlier? You're protected?"

"Yes," I whispered, feeling his cock twitch against my inner thigh. "And... clean."

"Tell me I can fuck you like this," he whispered back, into my ear. He reached between us, wrapped his fingers around his cock, and rubbed the head of it against my sensitive clit. "Tell me I can fuck you and feel you properly."

"You can fuck me like this." I trailed my nails up his back and met his eyes. "I *want* you to fuck me like this."

It was as though my words, whenever I gave him permission to do something, stirred an instinct in him that made him move without hesitation. Within a few seconds, he had my legs around his waist, his cock positioned at my wet pussy. Then he rubbed his fingers down over my clit and dipped them inside me.

Next thing I knew, he'd replaced his fingers with his cock and I had my head thrown back in relief as he was finally inside me.

He grabbed my waist and pushed me up the bed, an action that pulled him out of me. No sooner had I thought it than he'd moved his body over mine and pushed his cock back inside me. His hands slid along my arms until he linked his fingers through mine and pinned my hands above my head.

He wasn't joking about it.

He pounded into me. He hadn't been joking about the hard, either. He fucked me so roughly that my breath caught several times, but I loved every moment. I loved the desperation I felt as he kissed me. Loved the need I felt as he gripped my hands.

Loved the way he fucked me, unapologetically hard, keeping every promise he'd made.

Sweat coated my skin in a thin sheen. Goose bumps covered my arms, and my muscles clenched on and off, my legs tightening around his waist. I wanted to hold him against him, make him push deeper, harder.

I needed it.

I tilted my hips up, and I got it.

"Dirty girl," he said against my mouth, his voice rough and cracking.

My pussy clenched as he thrust hard.

"Squeeze my cock. Go on, Mia. Squeeze my cock so hard you make yourself come. I know you want to. I know you want to feel my cock deep inside you when you do."

I tried to swallow, but I couldn't. His words—oh god, they were sending me over the edge, and I couldn't help but do what he said.

"Fuck, your tight little pussy feels so good," he groaned, breathless.

Surprise flicked through me as he rolled to the side, pulling out of me and pushing me onto my side. He pulled me back against him, lifted my leg, and rammed himself back inside me. He curled one arm beneath my neck and grabbed both my wrists so I couldn't move. Then he slipped his other hand over my hip and pressed two fingers against my clit.

At this angle, he was deeper. Harder. Rougher.

"West..."

"That's it, angel. Come over my cock." He rubbed my clit so hard that I simultaneously tried to push his cock inside me and his hand away from me.

I had no idea how he was fucking me so thoroughly and playing with my clit, but I didn't care, I could only see the end, feel it as it built, breathe through it as he whispered dirty things in my ear about his cock and my pussy, whispered how good it felt around him, how hard he was going to come.

I rode it out as it hit. I had no choice—he was still pressed against my clit, still fucking me, still chasing his own. I moaned and screamed his name, clamping down around him until he finally gave in and slowed, coming so hard that I actually felt his cock emptying inside me.

I dropped my head forward, my hair falling over me and sticking to my face. West released my wrists and wrapped his arms around me, holding me against him. His hot, shallow breaths danced across my skin when he buried his face against the back of my neck, his stubble rubbing against my shoulder.

I didn't care. I'd done what I'd promised myself I wouldn't, but I didn't care about that, either.

West Rykman was addictive; his very touch was an aphrodisiac. His kiss was a deadly drug, and I was afraid I was hooked on him.

EMMA HART

"Mia," he whispered, kissing the curve of my shoulder. He propped himself up on his elbow, his cock pulling out of me, and moved the hair that covered my face. His eyes were heavy lidded as I peered up at him. "What are you doing to me, angel?"

"Probably the same thing you're doing to me," I answered softly before swallowing. I rolled over onto my back and softly stroked my fingers along the curve of his jaw. "And I don't know that, either."

He stared down into my eyes and took my hand in his. He brought it to his lips and kissed my fingers. Then he dropped his mouth to mine and kissed me so tenderly that I forgot I shouldn't want him.

*H*hmphed as yet another pin poked into my side. I'd barely stumbled off my red-eye flight to San Diego when Allie had excitedly squeezed the shit out of me at arrivals, whisked me for a breakfast I could barely eat, and dragged my ass into the fitting.

I still felt as though I needed more sleep, and I did. I planned a long-ass nap in my own bed the moment this was done.

Yesterday, when I'd e-mailed West to ask about one of the promotions, he'd called and acted like nothing had happened on Thursday night and told me to change my flight so I could stay in San Diego tonight. Michelle had approved it and added the charge to the business account. I was undecided whether or not I was bothered about him not addressing what'd happened between us.

I mean, it'd happened before, and it wasn't like I had been expecting him to call me and thank me or send flowers and a card. But it was almost more awkward that it hadn't been mentioned. Of course, I was sure I'd feel that way if he had mentioned it, so it was whatever, but I was driving myself positively insane going over it again and again.

It wasn't doing me any favors.

"Ouch, Jesus! If you have to take it in this much, you don't need to poke me with a needle!" The words exploded out of me as the hundredth pin prodded my hip.

"Sorry, ma'am," the young girl fitting me said. "But there's a lot of material to take in."

I guessed it could have been worse. "Just try to be careful, okay? Those things freakin' hurt."

Jaz snorted next to me—then yelped as she too was prodded.

Allie and Lucie, waiting for their turns on the other side of the room, giggled.

"Talking of being poked," Lucie added, grinning with her eyes on me. "Something to share, Mia?"

I sniffed and looked at her dead on. "A lady never kisses and tells."

"Yeah," Jaz input, "But you ain't no lady, and it's not kissing and telling if you're screwing the guy."

"I'm not screwing anyone." And I wasn't comfortable having this conversation in front of anyone else, for what that was worth. Not that these bitches cared.

"Noooo, you're only screwing the stripper." Allie clapped her hands together.

"Screwed," I corrected her as my fitting girl fought a laugh. "I screwed him. Screwing would imply I'm doing it right now or that it's a long-term thing."

"Is it a long-term thing?" Lucie asked.

"Well...no."

"You don't sound so sure."

"Stop asking me hard questions. I was at the airport at five a.m. Lay off."

"Oh god," Jaz groaned, turning to look at me. "Are you doing a Mia?"

"What the hell is doing a Mia?"

"Falling too fast and too hard," Allie explained. "It's what you usually do."

"I'm not falling anywhere. Fast or hard!" I sputtered.

Lucie shrieked a laugh. "No. You're just getting fucked like it!"

"Oh my god!" My cheeks blazed. "Why don't you get a speakerphone and announce it to the world? Holy crap!"

"Please tell me you're bringing him to the wedding!" Jaz clapped her hands, much to the annoyance of her fitting girl. "Oh my god. Are you bringing him to the wedding?"

"I'm not bringing him anywhere!"

"Except to bed."

"Jaz, I swear to fucking god I will come over there and beat you with my bare fists."

"Is that what you say to him in bed?"

I moved as if I were going to whack her one, and Allie jumped up.

"Okay, okay!" She held her arms up. "No more ribbing on Mia. She's having a really hard time."

"I bet she is," Lucie snorted. "Super, super *hard*."

"Lucie Mayer, I will kill you in your sleep," I snapped, my cheeks flushed.

Damn. Why couldn't I have nice friends? Why did they all have to be asses?

Oh, that's right. Because they were just like me. An ass. Nobody else would have us.

"Please drop it now. I don't want to talk about West or anything else, okay?" I let out a heavy sigh. "Let's move on."

"Ma'am? You're done," my fitter said to me. She unzipped the back of my dress.

I quickly stepped out of it and grabbed the sundress I'd thrown on before going to the airport.

"I just have one more question." Jaz held her finger up. "Have you actually spoken to him since?"

I nodded.

"About what happened?"

I didn't say anything.

"Mia!" Allie pulled her shirt over her head and climbed onto the mini box thing I'd just been standing on. For a virgin, the girl was shameless in her neon-pink bra and thong. "Why not?"

"What am I supposed to do? Break into the middle of a work chat and be like, 'Hey, West, thanks for that shit-hot orgasm, by the way! You gave me the fuck of my life'?" I slapped my hand against my forehead and slumped down the sofa. "No, Al. I can't just do that, can I?"

"I've done it," Jaz chirped up, sitting next to me while Lucie took her place.

"But that's you, and you're special." I patted her knee. "I don't need to talk about it with him, okay? I'm not insecure about my...skills...in the bedroom. I literally don't need to thank the guy."

We all paused as the girl buttoned Allie's dress. Her hair might have been in a messy bun, piled on top of her head, and her makeup next to nothing, but damn. In that figure-hugging, lacy gown that elegantly flared out at her feet, I knew one thing for certain: I had the most beautiful best friend in the world.

Who currently had her finger pointed at my face.

"Don't you dare cry, Mia O'Halloran! If you cry, I'm gonna cry. Then we're all gonna cry, and then we're all in trouble."

I smiled, fighting the fond bubble of emotion back. What was it about wedding dresses, huh?

"You look gorgeous, Al. If I didn't think Joe would put up a fight, I'd marry you myself."

"So, you'll marry your best friend but not discuss mind-blowing sex with a man who makes the guys in Magic Mike look like drunk amateurs?" Lucie raised her eyebrows.

I sighed and looked at her. "You just had to ruin the moment, didn't you, Luce?"

"I was just—ow! That hurt!" She jerked away from the fitter and almost fell off the raised block. "You weren't kidding, Mia."

"Told you," I muttered, sinking down the sofa and petulantly crossing my arms.

Seriously, they needed to give the sex a rest. I never should have told them.

I had no idea why I'd told them. I had known what I'd be getting myself into if I did.

I really, really needed a nap.

Alas, I knew I wouldn't be that lucky because I still had to see my mother. That would be the biggest test of my life as I knew it. I was sure to be in for an ass-whooping for my impromptu trip to Vegas—for work or not—and questioned about who, if anyone, I would be taking to the wedding.

If only I'd had any idea what I was getting myself into, I would have skipped it all and gone back to Vegas.

<hr>

I knocked three times at the door of my childhood home, narrowly avoiding an attack by a rogue rosebush branch, and pushed the door open. "Mom? Dad?"

Lark, the temperamental, pissy little feline my mom both loved to hate and hated to love, opened one eye from his perch on the side table. Sun streamed in through the glass windows that surrounded the door, right over him.

"Hey, Lark." I scratched the top of his head with my nails, and he closed his judgmental little eye and purred loudly.

Sure, he was an uptight little shit, but I didn't see my mom's huge problem with him.

"Mom? Dad?" I called again. "Have you suddenly developed a desire to ignore me?"

Please say yes. Please, please, please.

"Don't be overdramatic, Mia." Mom walked down the stairs, drying her hands on a perfectly white, fluffy towel. "I was cleaning the toilet and had to wash my hands."

"Hello to you too." I shut the door behind me. "Where's Dad?"

She leveled her steady, calculating, green-gray gaze on me and pointed one perfectly manicured finger toward the backyard. "Tinkering."

"Ah. What's he building this time?"

"A go-kart for the neighbor's boy. Although, to the boy's credit, he's working with him on it."

"That's good. He might learn something."

"Such is your father's life mission: to teach the younger generation how to make shit things stunning. Come get some tea."

I flattened my lips together. Oh boy. She was in a delightful mood, wasn't she? She made West's bar girl, Tish, look like a baby bunny or something.

"How have you been, Mom?"

"You'd know if you called more often."

"We speak three times a week. How many more times do we need to call each other?"

"Called by, Mia. Not on the phone." She shook her head as she poured boiling water into a white-and-blue china teapot.

Excellent. We were having tea in her nice set. Even more things to hate about tea.

"I work a lot, Mom. It's not that simple."

"Yes, yes, I know. You work too much. I keep telling you to stop messing around with careless, young men and find yourself a nice, steady gentleman to take care of you."

I stared at her as she set the tea tray in the middle of the kitchen table and motioned for me to sit. "I don't need a nice, steady gentleman to take care of me. I can take care of myself."

"Then to keep you company."

"I have my friends to keep me company."

"It's not the same, Mia." She poured the hot tea into her teacup, holding the lid of the pot in place. "You're twenty-five."

"Precisely. Not forty-five. There's time left in the old, ticking egg bombs yet." I politely refused the tea. I couldn't deal with two of my least favorite things in one hit, given the mood she was in.

She *hmm*ed as she sipped from her teacup. "That reminds me. Darren called for you yesterday."

I frowned. Twice in two days? "Did he say what he wanted?"

"No. He seemed insistent upon talking with you though." Her teacup clinked against the saucer. "Has the dirty dog called you?"

Dirty dog. That was something I'd never heard her say.

"Yep. I sent him straight to voicemail."

"Good. Although I do want you to find out what he wants so he stops bothering me."

I wouldn't have said one visit was a bother, but then again, this was my mom. "Sure."

She looked up, piercing me with her gaze.

"I'll just go call him right now..." I plucked my phone from my purse and walked into the front room. I took a deep breath before I unlocked my phone.

Lord, the woman sucked all the oxygen out of the room, didn't she? Or maybe she just sucked my oxygen out. It was no secret she was trying to kill me.

At least it felt that way.

I tapped in the passcode for my phone and frowned. One new message from West.

West: *Can you talk?*

I hit Reply.

Me: *No. My mother is making me call my ex-boyfriend.*

I waited for a moment for his response, but when it didn't come, I opened my contacts, scrolled down to DoucheNozzle, and hit Call. I wasn't surprised in the slightest that Darren answered immediately.

"Hey. I thought you weren't going to call me back."

"I wasn't going to," I confirmed. "Then you bugged my mom and she bugged me. Don't think I'm calling because I want to be."

He was silent for a few seconds. "Mia, I just want to talk to you."

"I can honestly say this feeling isn't mutual."

"Can you listen for five minutes? We need to at least be civil for the wedding next weekend."

"You should have thought about that before you parked your car in some other chick's garage, shouldn't you?" I snorted. "We don't have to be anything, Darren. You have to escort me down the aisle, take a few photos with me, and then that's it. We don't have to speak at all."

"Be reasonable, babe."

"Call me babe once more and I'm gonna march over to your house and file off your balls."

"Be reasonable."

"I forgot how to the moment I walked into your house and found you screwing another woman over your kitchen table."

More silence. "That was an accident. A mistake."

"Penises don't slip and fall into other people's vaginas, Darren. Especially when there are usually clothes covering said penises and vaginas. Unless they happened to fall off too."

"Yes, well." He coughed. "I miss you."

"Good. I'd miss me too. I'm freakin' awesome." Nothing like blowing your own horn. *Toot toot, motherfucker.*

"You...don't miss me?"

"Am I supposed to?"

"Well, no. Guess not. I fucked up," he said quietly.

"Yup."

"I just thought you'd be ready to talk. I was kind of hoping to work things out."

"Nope." I smacked my lips together.

Was he drunk? I hoped he was drunk. He better have been drunk.

"We're supposed to be going to the wedding together, Mia."

"No, we're not. Allie added two plus-ones the day we broke up."

"Why did she do that?"

I grinned. "I asked her to."

"Oh. And you're taking someone?"

Truth? Lie? Truth? Lie?

Ah, fuck it. I'd open my mouth and see what came out.

"Yep. I have a date." That wasn't what I had been hoping for, but it was an answer all the same.

"Right. Never mind, then." He hung up.

I stared down at my phone. Well, that had been a little awkward. But was that really it? Did he really—the sneaky little fucker.

He had to have known we'd had our plus-ones added. He was the freakin' best man. Of course he had. He'd just been feeling me out like the dirty little snake he was.

Ugh.

Now, I had to find someone to go with me.

The handsome face of a certain stripper flashed in my mind. I swayed on the spot. Man, that would be sweet. I could imagine it—I knew Darren. He'd have the hottest girl he could find as his date, and I'd show up with West...

No.

No, Mia.

That's not a good idea. Not even close *to a good idea.*

Especially since my phone was telling me he'd texted me back.

West: *No problem. Can you talk later?*

Me: *Around eight. I'm at my mom's then having dinner with friends. Is something wrong?*

West: *No. I'm just imagining you naked.*

Me: *Umm. I wasn't expecting that.*

West: *So I'm also really fucking hard and wondering what my chances of phone sex are.*

I stared at my screen. Was it inappropriate to ask for a dick pic in this situation? I mean...he'd started it.

Me: *I kind of want to ask you for a dick pic.*

That had been brave. I felt...well, more empowered than I did when I logged onto Facebook and had delightful messages from strange men accompanied by pics of their peckers, that was for sure.

"Mia? Are you done?"

I turned to look at Mom. "Yeah, sorry."

"What did he want?" She led me back toward the kitchen. She'd finished her tea and was in the process of cleaning it up.

I put my phone on the table and leaned against it. "To sort things out with us."

"I hope you told him no."

"Yes, Mom. I told him no. I'm not stupid."

"Well, I do wonder."

I rolled my eyes just as my phone lit up with another message on the table. "I'm perfectly capable of making my own decisions, you know." I tapped in my passcode and opened West's text message. My cheeks were already a little flushed from what his response might—

Oh my god.

Oh. My. God.

"Mia? What on Earth is that?" Mom leaned forward.

Toward my phone.

I slapped my hand over it and scooped it up at the same time, almost dropping it in the process. "Nothing. I gotta go. Tell Dad I love him and I'll see him next week at the rehearsal dinner." I snatched my purse up and turned, heading for the door before she could say anything else.

I didn't breathe again until I was in my car, with my doors locked and my air conditioning on. I'd barely glanced at the screen, but what I'd seen had been enough to fluster me.

Apparently, I'd missed the warning message of, *Ready?*

Slowly, I lowered my phone from where it'd stayed plastered against my chest and unlocked it once more.

Sure as shit, my screen filled with cock.

Not just any cock.

West's cock.

West's *hard* cock.

He was sitting down, his pants undone and his boxers pulled down, and his shirt unbuttoned and his abs on show. His lick-me lines, the V that was so deeply indented by the perfect muscle there, lean down right toward his cock, and I understood then why I called them lick-me lines.

I'd never wanted to lick a man so badly in my entire life.

West: *Does that solve the problem whether or not to ask?*

I swallowed. Hard. His hand was wrapped around the base of his erection, and now, I had an imaginary movie playing in my head. I imagined him moving his hand up and down, getting himself off as he thought of me naked, just like he'd said he was.

My pussy ached.

Me: *Yes. Thank you. But just so you know, there's every chance my mother just* *saw your cock.*

If that didn't kill an erection, nothing would.

———◆◆◆———

West hadn't responded to my message about my mom possibly having seen his penis. I didn't blame him. If I'd sent him a vagina shot and someone else had possibly seen it, I'd probably be trying to leave the country. Quickly.

Of course, my next question was what he was doing in the middle of the afternoon with an erection. Even for a stripper-slash-strip-club-owner, it was eccentric. It wasn't like he just walked into the kitchen, pictured me naked, and gotten a hard-on, was it?

Well. Maybe.

The guy was insistent, and from what I knew alone, his sex drive was a force to be reckoned with.

I guessed I'd assumed that would have stopped when he'd gotten what he wanted—me. But it hadn't. Not if he'd had an erection that hard in the middle of the afternoon when we weren't in the same city, let alone the same state.

I couldn't lie. I was kinda impressed. Usually, it took a bit of going to get a dick that hard.

I slumped back onto my sofa at five to eight and swiftly fell to lying down. Dinner with my friends had been exhausting. I'd thought ahead and decided that informing them about West's picture wasn't a good idea, but the entire time, I had been stuck.

What was the appropriate etiquette for responding to a wanted dick pic? Was it a tit shot? Underwear nude? Pussy snap? Nobody had taught me this, and for all of its smarts, Google didn't have a fucking clue, either.

I basically wanted to address my next thought to my high school: Algebra didn't help me in this situation, did it? No. Algebra rarely helped in real-life situations. Rarely helped in any situation, if I was honest.

I was so hung up on the etiquette of responding to wanted dick pics that I didn't notice the time passing until my phone rang on the coffee table. I forced myself to sit up and grab it, unable to help the groan that escaped me.

West.

"Hi," I said into the phone. "What's up?"

"Me," he rumbled back. "I'm pretty sure I've been hard all fucking day."

I swallowed. Was this phone sex? I'd never done phone sex before.

"West?"

"Yeah?"

"Are we going to have phone sex?"

He paused. "Do you want to have phone sex?"

"Are you hard?"

"I'm always hard when I think about you."

I felt like I needed to preen a little. "I've never had phone sex before."

"What kind of assholes have you been dating?"

"You really don't want to go there. We'll be here all night. I mean, seriously. I bore myself at this point."

"You're rambling. Are you drunk?"

"I wish," I mumbled. I needed to be drunk to phone-sex, didn't I?

Yes, I decided, blankly staring at my TV. I did. And not just any kind of drunk. I needed to be absolutely hammered.

"You didn't answer the question, Mia," he said softly.

Oh. Right. Did I want to. Well, I had looked at that picture several times...

"Yes. I want to." I was officially crazy. I'd lost my mind. No doubt about it.

"Where are you right now?"

Through the phone, I heard a door shut.

"Are you in bed?" he asked.

"No."

"Get into bed. Take your clothes off first."

His tone was commanding and strong, and before I could think it through, I was in my room, my phone was on the bed, and I was stripping down to my underwear.

I picked the phone up and climbed in bed. "I'm in bed."

"Good." His voice was a little gruff. "What are you wearing?"

I bit down on my lower lip and glanced at the scarlet-red underwear set I had on. "Hold on." I brought up the camera on my phone, kicked the sheets to the side, and took a photo of myself using the front camera. It was good enough, so I texted it to him. "Check your messages."

He was silent for a good few seconds. Then there was, "Jesus, Mia. Fucking hell."

"Do you...like it?"

"Like it? You look sexy as fuck. If I were with you right now, I'd rip those fucking panties off you."

"And do what?" *Look at me go.*

He laughed slightly. "Kiss you," he answered roughly, all traces of laughter from his voice quickly gone. "I'd run my hands up your body as you wrap your legs around my waist."

I swallowed, my clit aching as the low tone of his voice mixed with his words turned me on.

"I'd kiss down your neck and unclasp your bra so I could touch your gorgeous tits."

My hand hovered as I contemplated doing it—and then I did it. One quick fiddle with the clasp between them and my bra cups fell to my side. My nipples were hard, and I cupped my right breast, my thumb ghosting over my nipple.

"I'd take them in my mouth. Roll my tongue over your hard nipples until you moan beneath me and beg me for more."

My eyes closed.

"And then I'd kiss my way down your stomach to those tiny, red panties."

My hand took on a life of its own as it followed his words. My fingertips trailed down the center of my stomach until they brushed the waistband of the red lace thong.

"Then what?" I asked.

"Then I'd peel them down your legs and, once they were off, open your legs so I could see your wet little pussy." He exhaled. "Are you naked?"

"Yes," I replied softly.

"I want to see you."

"Will you send one back?"

"Yes."

"Okay," I whispered. Then I awkwardly took a picture.

Luckily it wasn't blurred, and no sooner had I sent it to him than one came right back. No face, just like mine, and my eyes skipped right over the hot body to where he looked like he had a tight grip on his cock.

I struggled to right my breathing. I was even more turned on now, seeing that he was too.

"Fuck, Mia. I'm so hard for you."

I swallowed. "Are you touching yourself?"

"Yes. But, if you send me another picture like that, I won't need to." He paused. "Are you touching yourself?"

"Not yet."

"Touch yourself. Now. Open your legs and slide your fingers over your clit." The demanding tone was back, and I loved the thrill that danced down my spine on a shiver. "Rub it and put a finger inside your pussy. I want to know how you feel when you fuck your own tight pussy."

My heart pounded in my chest as I did what he'd said. I slid my hand down between my legs, ghosted a fingertip over my clit, and bit down on my lower lip as I pushed my middle finger inside myself.

"Move it," he ordered me, his voice gruff. "Rub your thumb against your clit. Fuck your own hand, Mia, and imagine it's mine. Imagine I'm there watching you finger yourself and get off."

My breath caught in my throat. I was good at following instructions, and I was all ready to demand something right back, but when I opened my mouth, a moan came out instead of words.

I was turned the fuck on and I couldn't say a damn word.

"Imagine I'm watching you, naked, and stroking my cock. Close your eyes and picture it. Picture yourself watching me watch you get off. I bet you look so fucking sexy with your fingers deep inside your wet pussy."

More moaning. It was all I could do as my veins thrummed with pleasure. Adrenaline pounded around my body until my heartbeat echoed in my ears.

"I'm so damn hard for you. If you were here right now I'd have you on your knees, your face buried in the sheets, and I'd fuck you from behind. Fuck," he finished on a tight mutter.

"Keep talking," I breathed, pulling my fingers out of my pussy and moving them to my clit.

God, I wanted him to keep talking. I could feel the orgasm building deep within me, coiling my muscles, buzzing through my blood, and I wanted—no, needed—more. All of it. I needed the release.

"Think of it," West said, almost as breathless as I was. "Think about how fucking good it feels when I'm inside you. When your greedy little cunt is hugging my cock. When you're scratching up my back and screaming my name. Think about how goddamn good it feels to have my cock buried inside you and pounding into you."

Oh god. Oh god. Oh god.

"Think about how fucking amazing it feels when your tight pussy comes all over my dick, Mia. When you collapse and I'm still inside you. Think about it."

"I—oh god, West," I moaned. *Why is this so freakin' hot? Am I really about to come on the phone with him?*

"Yes," he half hissed, half growled. "Fuck yes, Mia. Think about it. Think about how you felt when I came inside you."

I did.

I thought about it.

And I came, my entire body trembling. I almost dropped the phone, but my clenching muscles kept it pinned to my ear as West's deep groan of his own release vibrated down the line. I was breathing crazily, thanks to the most intense orgasm I'd ever had courtesy of myself.

I couldn't believe I'd just done that.

A few minutes of silence passed between us. I was thankful for it. I was able to catch my breath and calm my heart in that quiet time, and I assumed he was doing the same.

"What time do you get back here tomorrow?" West finally asked.

"Around half past twelve...I think. It's definitely around noon." I sat up in bed, pulled a handful of tissues from the box on my nightstand, and awkwardly wiped my fingers. It'd do until I could shower in a few minutes.

"You have plans after?"

"No. None. I was going to work."

I swore I could hear his smirk.

Then he said, "I'll be waiting outside your apartment."

*W*est pulled out of me and collapsed onto my bed next to me.

He had been waiting just like he'd said he'd be, and the moment we'd gotten into my apartment, he'd thrown my bags to the side and we'd magically found our way to the bedroom, our lips locked.

Any hesitance about a sexual relationship with him had disappeared.

Unfortunately for me, the feelings that had replaced it would be a problem.

They weren't crazy, but when I looked over at the man lying next to me—sweat beading on his forehead, a tiny smile curving his lush lips—I knew that maybe there was...more. I couldn't focus on it though. I couldn't give it brain time or more would become *more*, and there were way too many issues between us to think about that.

Like the fact that he was my client, I lived in San Diego, and who was Charlotte?

I'd lied when I'd said that I didn't want to know. I wanted to know. It was clawing away at my female curiosity. Who was she, and why was she so important she needed to be brought up? It was obviously a huge part of his life he didn't want to acknowledge, but Beck had made him.

And me. He'd made me too, the moment he'd known I'd hear the conversation.

West rolled onto his side and hit me with his gorgeous, bright-blue eyes. They searched my face, flitting this way and that, and slowly, he smiled.

"Wanna get lunch?" he asked.

I turned my head toward him, tugging the sheets up over myself, and raised my eyebrows. "Really?"

"Yeah. I'm hungry." He flicked some hair out of my eye. "And then you can work."

"Because that plan is working so well already."

He laughed and threw himself on top of me. I faked an *oomph* and stared up at him, wrapping my arms around his neck. His grin was infectious, wide and bright, as he spoke.

"I promise. Food then work. Beck will be at the club to make sure it actually happens."

"What is he? Your own personal cockblock?"

"My voice of reason." He grinned even wider and touched his nose to mine. "Thank god I can get rid of him sometimes and do crazy shit like this."

"Having sex with me is crazy shit?"

He rolled us both over so he was on his back and I was on top of him, and I squealed.

"Yeah," he said, "having sex with you is crazy shit. Inviting you for lunch is even crazier. As a rule, I don't mix business and pleasure, angel, but you make me want to sin."

I touched my forehead against his. "So sin."

He ran one hand up my back and fisted my hair. "I already am. Every fucking time I look in your eyes." He pushed my face down to his and kissed me hard. "Come on. Let's clean up, get dressed, and get food."

So we did. I locked the bathroom door while I showered so he couldn't get in, much to his annoyance. He, however, left it open, almost expectantly.

I didn't know what he was waiting for—clearly, he'd never been with a woman who had thick hair and lots of it. It took me thirty minutes to get my hair to an acceptable dryness, and that was after it'd sat in my towel turban for twenty minutes while I'd dried off, dressed, and applied my makeup.

Regardless, we left my apartment and reached a restaurant at a time too late for lunch but too early for dinner. I had no idea what I wanted to eat, even as I'd looked at a menu and ordered.

We were heading into awkward territory very quickly, and I didn't know how to slow it down. It was plainly obvious that Beck really was a cockblock, and the exact kind of one we needed. He all but made us talk about work, and now he wasn't here to do so, I was wondering what to say.

Which was exactly why the one thing I didn't want to say vomited itself out of my mouth.

"Who's Charlotte?"

West's gazed snapped to me from where he'd been looking out the window. "That's...abrupt. And very random."

I clapped my hand over my mouth. "I'm sorry. That was rude of me. It doesn't matter."

His lips twitched to one side. "It's not a secret, Mia. Just a part of my life I prefer not to discuss, but since Beck forced it up..."

"It really doesn't matter." Damn. Why had I had to ask that? And why was I saying it didn't matter? It did. It shouldn't have. But it did. "Just...forget I asked, okay? I don't really care. Not that I don't care. I mean... I don't need to know. It's not my business. Damn, West, why can't you stop me talking?"

He laughed low and reached across the table, putting his hand over my mouth. "There. Does that help?"

I nodded, and he dropped his hand.

"Yes. Thank you."

"Mia... If you want to know, I don't mind telling you."

I shook my head and looked away. "It's not my business. I'm going to junk-punch Beck for making me hear about her."

"Honestly..."

"West." I met his eyes. "It doesn't matter. I don't need to know about her. It's not like what we have going on here is going to last once Rock Solid's marketing is in place and I'm back home, is it?"

He said nothing.

He just...stared at me. Even as he picked up his glass of water and sipped, his stunningly bright eyes stayed fixed on me, indiscernible emotion warring in them.

I dropped my gaze to my lap and swallowed hard. That was it, wasn't it? This would end. Once real life took over, once this job was over, this sexual relationship would be too.

I was equal parts looking forward to it and dreading it.

Our food was brought out then, which momentarily sliced through the awkwardness. Only momentarily, mind you. The second our server left us, the awkwardness descended once again.

I couldn't believe I'd asked him. God, what kind of idiot was I? A prize one. Olympic gold medalist at stupidity. I had to be.

It wasn't my business. I chanted that inside my head as we ate in silence. This...relationship...was temporary. There was no room for personal feelings or stories. We were sex, born of irresistible desire. Nothing more, nothing less.

Why couldn't I understand that?

Why did my heart clench when I told myself that?

"Charlotte's my ex-wife."

I snapped my head up so fast that I gave myself whiplash. "Your...ex-wife," I repeated dumbly.

West nodded once and waved for the check. It came in moments, so he slipped some cash inside and then stood, his hand held out for me.

I didn't hesitate before I took it. We made our way outside, his grip on my fingers never wavering. I didn't try to pull away as we walked down the street. Fluffy, white clouds drifted in front of the sun now and then, lessening its heat a little.

His ex-wife.

"Your ex-wife, huh?" I said quietly, looking forward. I should have brought my sunglasses.

He glanced down at me. "She's the single biggest mistake I've ever made."

Ouch.

"We were young. We'd just bought the club. She worked behind the bar. I hired her, believe it or not It didn't take her long to pull the claws out. Beck warned me, but I didn't see her for what she was back then." He ran his other hand through his hair as he lightly squeezed my fingers. "She looked at me and saw money. I fell for it."

I didn't know what to say. What did you say?

We darted to avoid two young women laughing. They both stopped in the middle of the path and looked at West as they passed us. He ignored them completely.

"We got married pretty quick. I thought I was in love." He snorted. "Not even a year later, I found her banging one of the strippers in the back room. She still took me for almost everything I had."

"Even though she'd cheated?"

"I was stupid, Mia. Not long after we separated, I hooked up with a woman I later found out to be a hooker. The court wouldn't tell you, but Charlotte hired her and they collaborated to make it seem as though I was the cheat." He half shrugged. "I didn't have the strength to fight. As long as I held on to the club, I didn't care what she took. I lost my house, my car, and everything but Rock Solid. I almost sold out to Beck just so she couldn't have it."

"Wow. She sounds like an epic bitch."

"She was, but I was an epic idiot. That was when my grandparents bailed me out. They waited until the settlement was in place and the papers were signed. Seemed everyone had seen her for what she was except me."

"Do you feel mad?" I asked quietly, looking at him. "That they didn't try harder?"

"They did. I was twenty-six and stupid. I didn't want to hear it."

Hottie was preaching to the goddamn choir. I was twenty-five and dumb as fuck.

Mind you, I hadn't married an idiot yet, so maybe I was smarter than I gave myself credit for.

"I'm sorry." I ran my teeth over my lower lip. "That's pretty shitty."

West looked down at me, a smirk on his face. "I'm over it, angel. Beck has this crazy idea that I let it influence my life. Perhaps I do, to an extent, but it's unintentional. More...a preservative action."

"Because you have a successful business and a thriving career, and whenever someone comes to you, you automatically assume they're more interested in that than you?"

"That pretty much sums it up."

I shrugged a shoulder. "I get it. I got my job right after graduating, one of the lucky ones, but I've kept it by working hard. Michelle could have sent any number of more qualified staff members to do this, but she sent me. Most of the guys I meet don't earn as much money as I do and probably never will."

West side-eyed me. "How do you tell them apart?"

"I'll let you know when I work it out," I muttered. "Besides, their 'forgetting' their wallet on your first date so you have a pay is generally a pretty big indicator."

"Someone did that to you?"

"Yep. I took the check, and when I got home, I sent him an invoice for his half."

West stopped in the middle of the pavement, yanking me to a stop too. "You sent a man an invoice after he made you pay for a date?"

"Yes." I looked up at him earnestly. "The arrangement he'd suggested was that he was treating me to dinner. He voided it when he made me pay, so I charged him."

"Did he pay it?"

"I sent him three reminders, and in the end, yes."

He tilted his head to the side a little, and his lips pulled into a smile. "I'm...impressed and terrified at the same time."

"Why? It's no different than you and Beck going to, say, a bar, and agreeing to get two rounds each, but he only buys one and you get three. The next time you went, you'd make him buy three rounds so you'd be even."

"It is a little," he said, walking again. "I'd just do it to piss him off."

"Right. So you'd make a friend pay you back, but an almost-stranger is crazy?"

"Point well made, angel."

Obviously. I knew that. I wouldn't have made it if I hadn't thought I could make it well.

We'd turned around at some point, and now, we were back to the restaurant and by West's car. My purse was snug in the passenger's seat with my work files and my laptop.

"I love that your grandparents helped you," I said once we were in. "Not many people would have done it."

West shrugged. "They're all I've had for a long time. Although there were some...issues...about my career choice, my granddad ultimately convinced my nan to do it."

"Issues? Oh, right. That speaks for itself."

"When they found out I was a stripper and had bought a strip club, Nan almost fainted, while Granddad whooped, punched the air, and asked me if I'd teach him how to dance."

I laughed. "He sounds like a character."

"He's pretty special." West's eyes twinkled as he spoke about them. "It was when we bought The Landing Strip that he really got excited. He's eighty next month and keeps asking me if I'll host his party there and bring the best ladies in for him."

"Seriously?"

"Oh, yeah. He doesn't even want a lap dance. He just thinks it'd be fun getting all his buddies up here and watching them. He's something else."

That was crazy.

"And he retired to Imperial Beach," I said.

"Yeah. I think the peace is getting to him. He likes to get a little crazy, even if it'll throw his back out. Which has happened more than once," he added almost as an afterthought. "He's now banned from doing the limbo."

"I can't imagine any situation in which a man who's almost eighty would need to do the limbo."

"My uncle's fiftieth birthday party. It was set up for the kids, but in my family, that doesn't mean people under the age of eighteen. It's more mental age." He pulled into the parking lot of Rock Solid and got out before I could reply.

I jumped out and grabbed my things. "Yet you're so serious," I mused, closing the door before following him into the club. "How does that work?"

"I'm not that serious." He leaned in toward me. "If I were, I wouldn't be thinking about fucking you again."

My cheeks flared, and I cleared my throat. "Inappropriate, West."

"So was what I did to you an hour and a half ago, but you enjoyed that."

I slapped his arm with the back of my hand. "Stop it."

He grinned, taking my things from me and setting them on the edge of the stage. We were the only people in the club, judging by the empty bar and the eerie silence, but even still, I squealed when he grabbed me and sat me on the edge of the stage.

He laughed, grabbing my knees and pushing my legs open. He slipped between them before I could close them and locked his hands at the base of my back. My heart thudded against my ribs a little too loudly as he met my eyes and fully held my attention.

All I saw was a blue sea of mingled emotions, from hesitance to desire to amusement, and maybe I was crazy, but I wanted to swim in it.

I wanted to drown in his eyes.

He didn't move, so neither did I. He stood with his arms wrapped around me, and I had my fingers lightly clutching his shirt, both of us just breathing. Just...being.

It felt all kinds of wrong but completely right at the same time. So many of our interactions had been sexual, rooted from desire, but this... This wasn't.

This was sweet. Gentle. This was...this. Natural, almost.

It was how he was looking at me though. The amusement and desire faded from his eyes, and in its place, I saw a hint of confusion, a flicker of warmth, something almost hope-like.

He looked at me as though I mattered to him. As though I were important. As though the thought of not looking at me were ridiculous.

He looked at me as though he wanted me. Truly wanted me—all of me.

And it hurt.

It was, perhaps, the way I'd wanted to be looked at my whole life, but now that I was, I didn't want it. Because West Rykman was not the man who could have all of me.

He knew it.

I knew it.

This wasn't destined to last.

I slid my hands up his body, cupped his cheeks, and touched my mouth to his. His fingers dug into my back as he tightened his grip on me, responding to the kiss. It was slow, easy, the kind that would take your breath away if you'd let it.

Just like he would.

And that was the problem, wasn't it? West Rykman could easily steal my breath. Hell, he did it every time he walked into a room I was in, or every time he spoke, smiled, or looked at me. Getting it back? That was a whole other ball game. I didn't know how I was supposed to make it through the next few days until I could go home again.

I'd never really been in this position before, of wanting someone I couldn't have.

And I did.

I wanted West Rykman. I wanted him desperately, more than I'd ever thought I could want someone. But I couldn't have him.

It wasn't how this worked. I didn't know how it worked, just that it didn't work the way I wanted it to.

I could never have him, and he could never have me.

My heart clenched as I broke the kiss. "I have a question," I said before I lost my bravado.

"Mm?" West met my gaze. "Which is?"

"I…kind of need a date for Allie's wedding on Saturday."

He stepped back and rested his hands on my thighs, his lips curving to one side. "Mia, are you asking me on a date?"

"No. I was going to ask if you think Beck would go with me."

He grabbed the back of my neck and tugged my mouth down to his. The forceful kiss sent tingles through my body, and I couldn't help but bite my lip and smile when he released me.

"Kidding." I straightened his collar, as it'd gone crooked when he'd kissed me. "And…yes, I guess I kind of am. I wouldn't ask, except my ex tried to get back with me, and I kind of already told him I had a date, except I don't have a date, so I need a date."

He looked at me for a long moment, before his lips slowly tugged up into his dirty, sexy smirk. "Do you know you ramble when you're nervous?"

"I'm not nervous," I lied right as the nerves tap-danced through my belly.

"Angel," he said in a low voice, taking my chin in his strong hand. "You are so nervous, and it's the most fucking adorable thing I've ever seen."

"Okay. Fine. I'm nervous." I exhaled, partially huffing, and dropped my hands from his shirt. "I'm not used to asking people on a date."

"I seem to remember very vividly that you had no problem informing me that you swallow when you suck cock, but asking me to accompany you to your best friend's wedding is scary?"

I glared at him. "I was drunk."

"There's a bar right over there."

EMMA HART

"I'm sure you'd love it if I got drunk."

"Only if you promise to offer to suck my dick and swallow my come again."

"Whoa!" Beck's voice echoed through the club before I could answer. "Should I come back in a few minutes?"

"Oh my god!" I shoved West away from me, my cheeks flaming, and slammed my legs shut. My hands came up to cover my face and I bent forward while the bastard just laughed his ass off.

"I probably should have said that a little quieter," he managed to eke out through each deep chuckle.

"You think?" I half shrieked at him. "I've never been so embarrassed in my life, West!"

Beck came into my line of sight, a mad grin on his face. "Enthusiasm in the bedroom. I have a lot of time for that. Especially when a woman's as enthusiastic on her knees as she is on my face."

Oh. My. God.

I'd been unwittingly dragged into the lair of two sex-mad men who had no problem embarrassing every woman nearby.

"Sorry," Beck said. "We're used to shameless hussies trying to pull our pants down. This blushing thing is new." He reached forward and lightly poked my flaming cheek. "How does it stop? Is there a button?"

I hit his fingers away and buried my face in my hands.

"Aw, damn. You looked cute as fuck."

I kicked my leg out at him and connected with his shin.

West laughed as Beck let out a small stream of curses. "Leave her alone. She's had a long day."

"A long....*enthusiastic* day?" he asked.

I dropped my hands and glared at them both. "You want me to kick you again, Beck? I'll show you enthusiasm."

He leapt backward and held his hands out. "I'm good, gorgeous. Just teasing. It's his fault." He cocked his thumb toward West. "Now, I've got ideas and shit."

"Yeah, well, keep your 'ideas and shit' to yourself." West moved back toward me and grabbed my waist, pulling me down from the stage. It wasn't particularly high, but whatever. He could do what he wanted, and he would. "Mia doesn't

136

need to hear about them."

"Because you've already shared yours with her?" Beck retorted, his eyebrows raised.

"Do you want me to kick him again?" I asked West innocently, turning to face him.

He smiled at me, his eyes sparkling.

"I like her," Beck announced, looking from me to West. "She's feisty. Can we keep her?"

"Can you keep me?" My eyebrows shot up. "The hell am I? A puppy?"

"Don't you have work to do?" West interjected, looking at him. "We need to get the month's books to the accountant so everyone can be paid and I haven't seen The Landing Strip's."

"Sheesh, Dad. I dropped it off to her this morning."

"Her?"

"Yeah. Robert's assistant. Nice girl." Beck's smile turned devilish. "I'll find out how nice this week at dinner."

West rolled his eyes then ran his hand down his face. "All right. Fine. I should have guessed that was the case. Do you have work to do or not?"

Beck's gaze flitted to me. "Are you going to work?"

Jesus. It was like being in the middle of a childish argument.

"Yes," West said tightly. "Fliers for the promotions. I want them here in a few days."

"What about tonight? Are you working?"

"No. Tomorrow. That strange Monday night bachelorette party." West ran his fingers through his hair. "Requested me, apparently."

Lucky bitches.

But who had a bachelorette party on a Monday? That was the strangest thing I'd ever heard.

"Oh, and by the way, Beck," West added, calling after him. "You'll need to take over my shift here on Saturday night."

"Why?" he frowned.

West looked at me, half smiling. "Someone's taking me as a date to their best friend's wedding."

"You know he's boring, right?" Beck asked me, pointing at him. "I'm the one you want to take to a wedding, not him."

"Beck. Get out," West ordered him. "Now."

Beck walked to me and dropped a kiss on my cheek, watching West as his eyes narrowed. Then he disappeared without another word.

I stared at West. He was watching Beck go, and when the sound of the door shutting filled the air, he looked back to me. There was a small glint of possessiveness in his eyes, and I didn't know what to make of it.

He dropped his head and put my things on the table. "Bastard's doing it deliberately," he muttered—mostly to himself.

"Doing what?"

"Flirting with you. Getting under my skin."

"Oh. Right." I sat at the table and opened my laptop. "Why is he doing that? I mean, I get the whole guy thing, but... Never mind. I'm rambling again."

"He's doing it to push me," he said quietly, looking up and meeting my eyes. "Because he knows eventually I'll give in."

I was almost afraid to ask. "To what?"

"You'll know if it happens."

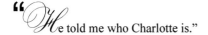 told me who Charlotte is."

Beck raised an eyebrow and slid the bottle of ketchup toward me when I eyed it. "I'm surprised. Did you have to bribe him? Offer sexual favors?"

"Thank you. Don't be ridiculous." I dipped a long fry into my ketchup, sighed, and set it onto my plate. I didn't even feel hungry. Ever since Beck had left the club yesterday and West had said that I'd know if it happened, I'd been in a world of my own.

What might happen?

How would I know?

He wouldn't elaborate. Refused to, actually. The carefree atmosphere that had formed around us since he'd slammed my apartment door behind us had descended into a tight, tense buzz of air that'd hummed with unsaid words.

"I just asked him." I looked at the handsome guy sitting across from me. "Accidentally, obviously."

"Obviously."

"Was it really that bad?"

Beck's mouth twisted to one side before he shrugged. "He's stubborn, Mia. He didn't listen to any of us back then. He was still getting over his parents dying, and I think she gave him comfort he thought he needed."

"But to get married? Isn't that overkill?"

"He thought she loved him. Hell, he thought he loved her, but all he loved was probably how she looked on her back."

"Classy. You're so eloquent when you talk about women."

He grinned. "Hey, if they're gonna treat me like a piece of meat, I'm gonna do it right back. When they respect me as a human being, I'll respect them too. Like you."

"Really? Your games yesterday were you respecting me?"

"No, those were me pissing West off. I know they're easy to confuse, but you'll get used to them."

"Cute." I bit the end of the fry I'd dipped into ketchup, chewed, then swallowed before putting it back down. "There's no point me getting used to anything. We're all steaming through this marketing. There isn't much left to do. At this rate, when I fly home on Friday, I'll be staying at home."

"Then I order you to take a day or two off."

"You order me. Really?"

His smile was the typical infectious one I'd become relatively familiar with. "Yes, I order you. I demand you put your shit away and relax. You've worked ever since I met you. I bet you even work when you're not with us."

"Well..."

"Then it's settled. You're not allowed to work for the rest of the day. Or tomorrow."

"I need to order fliers. And my friend is coming up from San Diego tomorrow to mix cocktails."

"Is she hot?"

"Yes."

She was also definitely not into men, but I wasn't about to tell him that.

"Then work tomorrow when she's here. Otherwise...chill a little. We've got it handled. Fliers don't take long to order." He took a big bite of his burger. "Plus, it'll really piss West off when he sees you hanging out with me at the bar tonight and he might stop being such a wet fish."

"What is it with men and not saying what they mean? First West, now you. I give up talking to you."

Beck rolled his eyes and dropped the burger onto the plate and grabbed a napkin. He wiped both his hands and his mouth before resting his forearms on the table. He leaned forward, looking me right in the eye.

"He'll be thirty next year, but he's as afraid of fucking up as anyone. He did it once before, and no matter what he says, the situation with Charlotte has scarred him. He refuses to get close to anyone. I asked you to dinner last week because he should have said no. He's done it before, but he didn't this time. He damn well *brought* you to dinner, gorgeous."

"Because it would have been awkward to say no. Stop dressing this into something it isn't. You can't put a rabbit in a tutu and call it a freakin' ballerina."

He paused. "I've never heard that one before."

I carelessly shrugged a shoulder.

"Mia... I know him better than anyone. We've been friends our entire lives. I also know when he needs a boot up his asshole to get him to admit things."

I shook my head but didn't say anything. I was starting to get the feeling that beneath the jokes and silliness, Beck was a romantic at heart.

"Trust me. He's afraid of fucking up again. He won't listen to me though, which means I have to piss him off until he realizes what's in front of him."

"Beck. We're sleeping with each other. It's circumstantial. When this job is done, I'm going home to San Diego, back to my regular job, my crazy best friends, and my overbearing mother. I appreciate your efforts, but you're leading your own little army into a battle you'll lose."

"So, you shouldn't fight just because you think you'll lose?"

"One, I know it's a losing battle, and two, there's nothing to fight for." I impatiently jabbed at a few fries.

"Is that why you're getting angry with me?"

"I'm not..." I stopped when I realized my voice was a little too loud. "I'm not angry. Okay? Can we talk about something else?"

He nodded, but I only managed to eat two fries before he spoke.

"You got feelings for him?"

I ran my hand through my hair and looked away. Two days ago? I might have said no. Probably would have. Now? Now, I didn't want to talk about it.

"I don't want to talk about it."

"Funny," he mused, picking his burger up again and staring at me hotly. "That was his response when I asked him the same question this morning."

"Beck?"

"Yeah?"

"Shut the fuck up."

———◆◆◆———

I didn't want to admit how many times I'd changed my clothes. I'd gone from a trusty little black dress to jeans to a skirt and back to a dress. I had a discarded pile of clothes on the floor of my bedroom, staring at me in annoyance.

Yeah, yeah, whatever. So I'd brought too many with me. It was what it was.

I was trying to reconcile the dirty-mouthed, cocky West with the one Beck had revealed to me earlier and, indeed, the one West himself was slowly revealing to me. It seemed incomprehensible that the demanding alpha male I'd come to know so well had such a soft, reluctant side.

More importantly, why was it coming out with me? Why, two years after his divorce and apparently several women, was I the one he was showing it to?

It didn't make any sense. Mostly because I was the one he shouldn't have been showing it to.

I was nothing special, but then I wasn't not special, either. I was average, as far as a woman in her mid-twenties went. Sure, I probably could have stood to lose a few pounds and might or might not have always remembered to brush my hair, but it could have been worse.

I was honestly torn, and the more I thought about it, the more I realized it was stupid. I knew nothing about West. Sure, I knew how he'd come to own the strip club, he was divorced, and he had a kooky family, but that was it. I didn't know anything about the man inside, not really.

So how was it possible that I was slowly falling for the man?

I dropped onto my bed and huffed. Was I really going to do this? Go out for the night with Beck? Even if our first, last, and only destination was Rock Solid, it wasn't the point. It was insanity. I was already too involved with these two men. My projects didn't usually plan for me to get so up close and personal with my clients. Usually, the most intimate it got wass a business meeting with food.

But...damn it, Beck felt like a friend, and West felt like...West.

I didn't want to think about what he felt like to me.

I sighed and looked at my pile of clothes. I didn't feel like getting dressed up. I felt like climbing into bed and sleeping, if I had to take time off. Still, I didn't think Beck would appreciate it if I was still in my underwear when he showed up.

Or maybe he would. He probably would.

I forced myself to get dressed into black jeans, a black tank, a white kimono, and nude heels. I felt like my hair was a mess, but I honestly couldn't be bothered to brush it, so I ran my fingers through the flame-colored strands a few times until I'd gone from mess to messy-sexy.

It was still a mess, but I was telling myself otherwise.

By the time Beck knocked at my door, I was ready. Kind of. I didn't know what I was ready for, but I did know I'd barely spoken to West that day, if a couple of text message exchanges counted as speaking, and I wasn't sure they really did.

"Cheer up, buttercup." Beck chucked me beneath the chin before he pulled away from the curb. "If he's still bothering you, don't worry. He's been a grumpy bastard all day."

I was probably the reason why. "I just don't know if this is a good idea."

"I'm taking you for a couple of drinks, Mia. You've been working hard and you need to unwind. Unwinding with West only complicates the situation further because I know his kind of unwinding."

"It's pretty unnerving that you know all this stuff."

He shrugged. "I might be the joker out of the two of us, but I notice just as much stuff as he does. Like I notice how you look at him when you think I'm not paying attention."

"Well, he's hot. I'm female. Sue me for staring."

"I notice how he looks at you when he thinks neither of us will realize."

"I don't have an answer for that."

"Of course you don't."

I caught his grin out of the corner of my eye.

"There isn't an answer for it you can give."

I looked away and just managed to resist the powerful urge to roll my eyes. I didn't want to think about answers or questions. I still wanted to go home and go to bed, but as Beck pulled into the parking lot of Rock Solid, next to West's Audi,

I sighed with resignation.

I was going in there whether I liked it or not.

"Hey, Beck, who's working the bar tonight?"

He frowned as he locked the car. "Vicky. Why?"

"Oh thank god. If it was Tish, I'd consider clawing my eyeballs out with a plastic straw."

"Wow. I know she's not exactly Little Miss Sunshine, but that's drastic."

I briefly recapped our first meeting for him.

He fist-bumped the security guys and held the door open for me. "Okay, I get it," he said loudly as the thumping music pounded through the air.

It was already busy in there, even for a Monday night, and again, I found myself wondering why they'd hired me. It'd been on Michelle's schedule for a long time, so I knew that it was coincidence, but still.

Maybe I was overthinking it. Maybe it really was just a refresher thing.

I followed Beck to the bar and plopped my butt down onto a stool. Vicky was bouncing at the end of the bar, grinning as she served a group of giggling girls. She was good as she played up to them, pouring their shots like a pro. Beck watched with a grin.

I nudged him. "Behave."

He smirked at me. "No screwing the staff. But seriously, watch her. You know why she's so good?"

I shook my head.

"She flirts with the women as well as she does men. And, whether or not women realize it, they like to be flirted with, even by another woman." He pointed to her, and my gaze followed.

He was right. Vicky was leaning across the bar, smiling, giving the girls her undivided attention.

"They'll come back to the bar, spend more money, and then, at the end of the night, give her a giant tip. We're happy because a group of...two, four...seven will spend a lot, and she'll be happy because that tip will be worth all the hard work."

"Sounds like you've spent a lot of time figuring it out."

"I told you—just because I'm not serious like your lover boy doesn't mean I don't notice stuff. I'm the friendly, happy guy, and West is the grumpy, miserable fuck."

"He's not my lover boy. And he's not miserable. He's about to strip off his clothes for a bachelorette party, and miserable people don't get naked and grind their penises in the faces of random women."

"Ooh, defensive." He grinned again as Vicky approached us.

"Mia! Beckett. I didn't know you were coming tonight. West didn't mention it." She flicked her blond ponytail over her shoulder and blew some hair out of her eyes. She paused when Beck's smile didn't drop. "You didn't tell him you were coming, did you?"

"I don't need to tell him. I own half of this place." He leaned forward, his arms bulging against his black, button-down shirt.

When that combined with the guys stripping on the stage... Well, if West walked out in the next two minutes, there was a high chance my ovaries would combust.

Actually, screw the high chance. It was downright certain.

"Mia. What do you want to drink?" Beck waved his hand in front of my face.

"Oh... Surprise me," I said to Vicky, flashing her a quick smile before returning to my perusal of the club.

"Up there." Beck pointed to the same table we'd once occupied for Allie's bachelorette party.

My gaze landed on the giggling girls who'd been at the bar not so long ago. They were all hot. Ugh, why were they always hot?

"Dunno. Probably the universe thanking us for our service to vaginas everywhere."

"What?" I blinked at Beck.

"You asked me why they're always hot." His mouth pulled up on one side. "I answered."

"Shit. I didn't mean to ask that. Not out loud."

"I guessed. I answered anyway because I'm helpful like that."

"I noticed," I muttered under my breath as Vicky placed a cocktail glass filled with a bright-blue liquid in front of me. I sipped it. "I'm going to need another ten of these," I yelled at her, glaring at Beck.

She laughed, and he did too when he caught me glaring.

Asshole.

"What are you doing?" he asked when I reached inside my purse.

"Paying for my drink," I replied, slowly looking back up at him.

"No, you're not."

"Yes, I am."

"No. You're. Not. You're drinking alcohol from the half of the bar I own, and I'm not charging you."

I glared at him again.

Beck laughed and leaned down. "Glare all you like, Mia, you're not paying for it. You need to unwind."

I could unwind and pay for my own drink, but I could see that it was a losing battle.

Instead of fighting him, I thanked him and gave my best attempt at not watching the bachelorette party table.

I failed. Miserably.

"I'd go use the bathroom if I were you," Beck said as West came into view. "You look like you're about to shank somebody and I don't want to call the cops on you."

I pursed my lips and hit him with a hard look. Now, he was just being ridiculous. I wasn't that bad at all. So what if my gaze snapped back to West as though it were connected to him by elastic? So what if I stared at him as he approached the girls with a devastatingly sexy smile on his face and leaned down to whisper in one of their ears?

So what if he untucked his shirt and spun her around in the booth so she was facing outward—and him?

So what if my heart clenched and my stomach uncoiled as he danced, his shirt came off, and she ran her hands over his muscular body?

What could I do? It didn't matter. It was West's job. He enjoyed it. It wasn't my place to be pissed off that he was going to dance all over some other fucking woman, was it?

No. No, it wasn't.

It wasn't my place to be pissed off about her wandering hands, either. He didn't belong to me. He wasn't even close. She could give him a blow job if he wanted and it wouldn't matter.

I had no claim to man who'd given me more orgasms in a week than I'd had in a month with previous partners. I had no say over how he moved his hips and flexed his cock against some other woman and touched her breasts and turned her on.

Nope.

No say at all.

That was exactly why I wanted to climb over every person between us and claw her eyes out with my nails.

Especially as he whipped a chair around from a table close by, set her on it, and then straddled on her.

Last time, I had been turned on.

This time...I had to swallow back a nauseating lump in my throat and pretend I didn't care.

This time, I had to watch with the knowledge that I did care, although I had no right to.

"Mia?" Beck moved closer to me and flattened his hand against my cheek. He forced my face to turn away from where West was finishing up dancing and made me look at him. "Don't."

I swallowed hard and shook his hand off, grabbing my glass. "I'm fine."

"You don't look fine."

"I said I'm fine."

"She's not fine. Fine is woman code for fuck off," Vicky yelled helpfully, sliding another blue drink in front of me.

I had no idea what she was feeding me, but it was damn good.

She leaned right over the bar. "He's seen you. He's headed over here."

My stomach twisted once again. I downed the last of the first glass and slid it back to her. "Good timing on this, then," I said, picking the new glass up.

Beck raised one eyebrow at me as I took a drink and ran my fingers through my hair.

I wanted to get drunk.

Stupid idea, but it seemed pretty good all the same. Maybe I'd be able to drink enough of these blue things that I'd forget how it had looked when he'd thrusted his hips all over that bride-to-be. Maybe, maybe, maybe...

"What are you doing here?" West looked between me and Beck, his bright-blue eyes blazing with annoyance.

"Unwinding. Supposedly." I smacked my lips together. "Against my will."

"Should've listened when you said no," Beck muttered.

"Told you," I snapped.

"Why do I get the feeling I'm missing something?" West asked.

"You are!" Vicky chirped up, grinned, and moved to the other end of the bar.

Boy. This was fun.

I didn't want to get drunk anymore.

Actually, I kind of wanted to go home and get in the shower. Then, if I cried out of frustration, I could pretend I wasn't. That was a winning thought right there.

"You brought her to unwind...here?" West asked Beck. "Why?"

"Honestly," Beck answered him, casting a glance at me, "I don't know. I don't think it's worked."

"What clued you in?" I asked sarcastically.

"Mia." West touched my arm and pulled me away from Beck.

I managed to shoot him one final halfhearted glare as West dragged me through the door and into the hall. As the door shut, the music dulled enough that we'd be able to talk without yelling at each other.

"What's wrong?"

"Nothing. I'm fine." *Vicky was spot-on with her explanation. I feel like...* Fuck off.

"You don't look fine." Concern flashed in his bright-blue eyes. The ones that had probably just been eye-fucking the bride-to-be. "Tell me what's wrong?"

I took a deep breath, met his gaze, and opened my mouth to answer.

I couldn't.

The lump in my throat combined with the darting flash of memory of him dancing with the woman tonight rendered me silent, and the only words I could form were inside my head and they summed up the situation perfectly.

How had everything changed so quickly?

"I have to go," I said thickly, stepping away from him and back toward the door.

"Mia—"

I tugged the door open and disappeared through it, cutting him off.

"Mia!"

I just about heard him call my name through the music, but instead of stopping like my heart wanted me to, I marched to the bar, grabbed my purse while ignoring Beck, and turned away. My eyes stung, and as I darted past West, I felt like the biggest idiot in the world.

I wasn't allowed to have feelings for this man, yet I did. I'd allowed myself to let them form into something that stung me.

Even the blast of warm air as I stepped outside didn't soothe me. I ignored the couple of cabs lined up outside and turned the corner. I couldn't run in my heels, but I could walk fast, so I did. I walked as fast as I could, away from the club, to my apartment, holding in everything that'd come to a head inside me tonight.

I held it inside until I'd gotten upstairs, and then, the moment my door slammed behind me, I leaned back against it and screwed my eyes shut.

Don't cry. Don't cry.

I was begging myself even as I pushed off the door and the tears stung my eyes. Even as I kicked my heels off, peeled my clothes off, and stood beneath the shower, allowing my makeup to run down my face.

Don't. Cry.

I did. I went against everything I'd told myself not to do and I cried, letting the tears roll out of my eyes, letting the hot stream of emotion battle with the equally hot water that dripped across my skin.

I cried all of my frustration out, and when I was done, I braided my hair, climbed into bed wet and naked, and buried myself under the covers.

I woke up with a renewed sense of determination.

My cry last night had been therapeutic. I managed to get out every negative emotion I felt, and somehow I'd managed to sleep for ten hours straight. Maybe it was because I'd had a damn good cry. Everyone knew that, when all other routes were sending you for a trip up shit creek without a paddle, sitting your ass down and crying was the only option.

I was headed up shit creek without the fucking boat, and it stunk.

Thankfully, last night's cry had given me a cruise ship for the trip.

As I dressed in a white blouse and my favorite red skirt, I reminded myself what I needed to do. Clearly, West and I couldn't work together. There was an obvious...well, not conflict of interest. The problem was the interest was all too mutual. So there.

There was an obvious mutual interested that almost rendered our professional relationship untenable. Don't get me wrong. I had no issue with going to work and getting hit on by him. I was female. I had an ego that needed stroking too, except mine came less in the form of a stroke and more in the form of a two-fingered nub-rub.

The problem was the feelings I'd developed for him. They were making it impossible, and something had to give. Since I unfortunately couldn't just flick a switch and have the feelings fuck off, I had to stop our physical relationship.

I also had to figure out how to grow the balls to tell him that we couldn't sleep together any longer, but that was another issue. I would focus on it later.

Or, you know. Just avoid him.

Yeah... It seemed like the best idea, but it wouldn't work.

Why, out of their businesses, did it have to be Rock Solid I was needed for? Why couldn't it have been The Landing Strip, the female strip club next door? Why couldn't their ladies need some marketing love, huh?

I sat on the end of my bed and blew out a long breath. I was getting frustrated again. I was a frustrated crier, so what I was feeling didn't bode well for me. I needed to calm down or there was a chance I'd burst into big, ugly tears at a random point in the day. Like a volcano.

It'd happened before.

It wasn't my finest moment. I was an uglier crier too. I had pictures Allie had snapped that would give Kim Kardashian GIFs a run for their money.

I fluffed my hair with my fingers and stood up. Starbucks. I needed a Starbucks refresher. That was the only way to calm myself, wasn't it? Yes. It had to be true.

God, now, I was rambling to myself. I'd completely lost my train of thought when I'd started thinking about my ugly crying.

Unfortunately, the reminder was never far away that what I was doing was to tell an insanely hot man with hips Shakira would cry over that we could no longer sleep together.

My vagina wanted to cry. Seriously.

Crying was in the air.

The emotion I'd felt last night had been too real and too strong. It didn't matter how hard my vagina begged me not to take him away, I had to do it. For my sanity, if anything else.

I couldn't believe I'd given in in the first place. Nothing ever, ever, ever should have happened between us, because look where it'd gotten me.

Shit Creek Cruises was open for business, bitches.

At least, if this career didn't work out for me, I had another option. There was also the option of writing a book: *How Not to Date*. That I was a pro at.

Which meant that, technically, what I was about to do should have been easy.

Technically.

It wouldn't be. I never did anything easily.

It was going to be a long, long day.

By the time I'd crawled through the Starbucks drive-thru at a pace slower than a snail's and gotten my refresher, I was contemplating going back to bed.

Not seriously.

Well, probably seriously. Mostly *not* seriously. Mostly, it was another avoidance technique I'd mastered. If you don't wanna do something, go back to bed. Pretend to be sick or something. It'd worked for me so far.

My biggest issue was, I'd realized while waiting for the barista to get her shit together, that I had to see West. I probably should have thought of it earlier, because seeing him meant I had to explain my disappearing act last night, and I didn't actually have an explanation for it. I was definitely more of a winging-it kinda girl, but the closer I got to Rock Solid, the more I thought I probably should have planned an excuse.

With any luck, it'd be another thing we wouldn't discuss.

It was unlikely, but I could hope.

Hope was about all I had left. I hoped we wouldn't talk about it. I hoped I could just break this off. I hoped I could go back to San Diego and forget all about him.

I pulled into the parking lot and killed the engine, turning to stare at the side of the building. Was it wrong that a part of me hated it? A part of me regretted having booked Allie's party there. Maybe a quiet night at the movies at home like she'd originally wanted would have been best.

No, there was no maybe about it. It would have been for the best. I was such a stupid idiot for not listening.

Even if I'd ended up going there in Michelle's place for this job, I didn't think the outcome would have been the same. I wouldn't have known anything about West Rykman. I didn't know a huge amount as it was, and I was glad. I wished I'd never asked questions.

I wished I'd never asked about Charlotte or his family. I wished I'd never heard Beck tell me stupid stories from their childhood. I wished I'd never asked him to go to Allie's wedding with me.

I wished I could go home. It'd only been two days since I'd been with all of my girls, but I felt like I needed their strength in this stupid-ass situation.

Why did the crappy stuff always happen when you were alone?

A van pulled up in front of the club as I got out of my car, my purse hooked over my shoulder. Was that the fliers already? We'd known about the color schemes for Lili's cocktails, so I'd photo shopped pictures of cocktails onto the designs before West ordered them on Sunday afternoon. How were they already printed?

"Mia O'Halloran?" the van driver asked, sizing me up.

"Uh, yes. Can I help you?"

"I have a bunch of boxes for you, care of a West Rykman. Sign here please." He thrust a device with a small, plastic pen at me and tapped the box for my signature.

I took it and scribbled in the box, a little dumbfounded. Why would my name have been put on them, not his?

They couldn't have been the fliers, but there was nothing else I knew of that could have possibly been coming for me.

"Anyone in there who could help me with this?" The guy waved toward the club. "I got ten boxes, darlin'."

"Oh." I looked at the parking lot, finally paying attention. Both Beck's and West's cars were there. "Sure. Let me grab them a minute for you."

"Thanks." He put the device in the front seat and pulled a box of cigarettes out.

Nice to know my inability to help him lug the boxes in was providing in a smoke break. I hoped he choked on it, lazy bastard.

"Hey, Vicky," I said, catching sight of her almost as soon as I walked through the club. "Are West and Beck here? I think the fliers have just been delivered and the van driver needs a Snickers."

She snorted on the water she'd been sipping and put her glass down. "They're upstairs. Want me to call?"

"Oh... No, it's okay. I'll go up. If it's the fliers, I'll need the floor space to sort them." I smiled and walked through the door that linked to the stairs, brushing off the memory of West pulling me through it last night. Those kinds of thoughts weren't going to help me.

"I just think—" Beck's voice traveled through the open door, making me pause.

"Forget it, Beckett," West said sharply. "Give it a rest."

I lightly rapped my knuckles against the door after a moment. "Hello?"

"Mia." West got up from the sofa.

I pushed the door open. "Hey—I think the fliers just got delivered. The van driver said there's ten boxes. He seems pretty intent on some help."

Beck pushed up off the sofa and stretched his arms over his head. "I'll go give him a hand," he said, passing me.

"Great. I want to check that they're all there before he leaves." I turned to follow him, but West snatched my hand and pulled me back.

Tingles shot up my arm from where he had a hold on my hand, and I had to swallow hard as I looked up into his bright-blue eyes.

He kicked the door shut so hard that it slammed, and then he touched the backs of his fingers to my cheek. "Why did you leave like that last night?"

Okay. I guessed we were talking about it.

Damn it.

"Doesn't matter." I stepped away from him, but he pulled me right back, this time clasping an arm around my waist so I really couldn't move.

"Mia," he said in a low voice, his breath skittering across my mouth. "Tell me why you left so quickly."

"I said it doesn't matter. I was tired and overwhelmed by all the people. I needed to leave. Now, please let me go, because there's work to do." I tried to get out of his grip.

I couldn't.

It was like stone.

He wasn't letting me go until he was ready to.

"Did I do something?" he questioned, concern in his gaze.

"No." That was a big, fat lie. "I just told you why I left."

"You're lying. I can see it in your eyes. They don't hide a thing, angel." He touched my cheek again, stroking the backs of his fingertips down until they curved under my jaw and he could cup my chin. He tilted my head up so I couldn't look anywhere but into his eyes. "You're angry with me. Why?"

"I'm not angry," I replied quietly. "I don't want to discuss this right now. I have work to do." I pushed at him even though I knew he wouldn't let me go. It was a futile attempt to put distance between us, but it made me feel better.

He wrapped one strong hand around the back of my neck and lowered his mouth to my ear. A shiver ran down my spine when his lips ghosted over my skin.

"Fine," he said. "Have it your way, angel. For now. But you will tell me why you left—what I did to make you leave. Even if I have to bend you over and spank it out of you. You'll tell me."

He released me, and the moment he stepped back, I inhaled deeply. Not because I could breathe again, but because I felt like I couldn't. The threat... No. It hadn't even been a threat. It'd sounded like a promise, and I had no doubt he was right.

West Rykman got what he wanted. Always.

Then again, I was used to getting what I wanted too.

I cleared my throat and smoothed my skirt out, momentarily dropping my gaze to gather my bravado. When I met his eyes, he was standing tall, adjusting one of the sleeves of the shirt hugging his muscular body. The way it fit reminded me of every inch of perfection that hid beneath it, and that only made my next words harder to say.

"We can't see each other in a personal capacity anymore. From now on, it's professional only. No more grabbing me or kissing me or anything else. It never should have happened in the first place. And no—it isn't up for discussion, no matter what you say." I held his gaze for the longest second to prove to him that I was serious before I stepped through the door and took the stairs down.

My hands were shaking. Even though I held them clasped against my lower stomach, I could feel trembling against my skirt. I didn't know what I'd expected, but it hadn't been for him to stand there and not argue.

I guessed I'd wanted him to argue. Wanted to hear him tell me to shut up because we both knew it wouldn't happen because we were unable to resist the other.

But he hadn't. And I had no idea how I felt about that.

Fucking stupid, contradictory feelings.

When I walked into the main area of the club, Beck had the boxes on the stage and was in the process of opening them with Vicky's help. I counted—there really were ten.

Wow. How many had he ordered?

"These look amazing," Beck said as I stepped up beside him. "Take a look."

I took the one he was handing me and scanned it. Huh. He was right. It did look good. Even the back. It was the basic one that had every night's plans and deals, from the cocktails to the theme nights.

"They printed so well. Are they all here?"

Beck looked at all the boxes. "I sure hope so."

I grinned and patted his arm. "Don't worry. I'm sorting them."

"Thank god for that." He immediately relaxed. "I need to get back next door. I'll open these all up for you. Do you want them upstairs?"

"Um..." That had been my plan, but West was still up there. "No, it's okay. I want to get them out on the tables tonight. Lili will be here soon, and she'll teach Vicky the cocktails. She's a great teacher."

"Lili... The hot cocktail friend, right?"

"Yes. The hot cocktail friend."

The lesbian one too. Boy, I couldn't wait for him to find that out.

He glanced at the watch on his wrist and muttered beneath his breath. "I can be back in time for that."

"Of course you can," Vicky put in, climbing up on top of the stage. Her jeans covered her modesty—a luxury I didn't have.

I'd be flashing my panties everywhere if I tried to climb up there, mostly because my skirt was so tight that I'd have to hike it up around my hips like a hooker to stand a chance.

"Hey." Beck made a gun with his fingers and pointed them at her. "You. Stop it."

She snorted and took the penknife from his hand. "I can open these. We're fine. Go next door so you can be back in time for the cocktail chick."

He held his hands up and didn't argue as he backed up. I watched him go, a smile on my face, and then straightened the boxes up for Vicky.

"Is the cocktail chick actually hot, or are you just saying it?" she asked, ripping open one of them.

"Oh, she's hot." I grabbed the trash bag she'd obviously brought over before and gathered the extra packaging. "She's also a lesbian."

She paused, the knife stuck in tape, and looked up at me. "I'm assuming he doesn't know that."

My smile widened, and I gave her a small, sheepish shrug. "Maybe. Maybe not."

"Oh, you evil woman. I like it."

"Not evil. Just...up for some amusement."

"I can't wait for this. I'm so glad there are security cameras that'll catch this. I'm going to have a copy made to take home and keep forever. Think how safe my job will be."

I laughed and walked around the stage to dump the trash bag on top of it. It was quite amazing how big it was—the stage, not the trash bag—and moved back to the stacks of boxes. I peeked inside the boxes and shifted them around, organizing them based on their contents. There were the every day fliers, plus the specialized ones based on particular deals that, in my head, I named Thursday, Friday, Saturday. The annoying box was the last one I moved—those were mixed, which I guessed was overflow.

They couldn't just send them in smaller boxes, obviously. At least they'd wrapped each design separately so I didn't need to organize them all.

Vicky sliced the last box open and eyed me. "That'd be easier if you were up here with me."

I took three steps back and pointed to my skirt with both hands. "I can barely walk up stairs in this thing. Getting up onto the stage is going to flaunt my underwear."

"Well, you're in the right place for it, and there's actually nobody here to see it." She laughed and tugged the bag toward her. "Just use a chair."

I looked down at the Devil Shoes. "Uh...I'm not sure Christian Louboutin had chair-climbing in mind when he designed my shoes."

"Oh lord, you're a special snowflake today. Take them off, doll. They're just feet. As long as you don't have any bunions or anything, we're good."

"No. I don't." I bent forward at the waist and pulled my shoes off. I set them on the table closest to me before swinging a chair around and attempting to step up onto it.

My skirt didn't give. At all. It didn't rip, either, so that went in my favor too.

Even when I hitched it up and tried to sort of bounce off my other foot, it wouldn't give enough. Vicky could have helped, but when I almost fell backward, she burst into peals of laughter and leaned back on her hands.

I sighed.

"What on Earth are you doing?" West walked from the bar to us, his hair messed up where he'd obviously been running his hand through it. "Are you practicing for an audition for Cirque du Soleil?"

I gave him the look. You know the look—the sarcastic, dry one that said, *Are you fucking kidding me?*

"Yes. That's exactly what I'm doing. How did you guess?"

"The awkward barefoot bouncing clued me in." His eyes twinkled. "Do you want a hand?"

"I'm good." I waved him off and rolled my skirt up another inch. Now, it was just above my knees. "My skirt wasn't made for climbing."

I made another attempt to get onto the chair, but I still couldn't do it—and I didn't find myself all that surprised when West grasped my waist and effortlessly lifted me to sit on the edge. I gripped his arms, my teeth sinking into my lower lip.

Boy, they were nice arms. I wanted to squeeze them.

"Thank you," I said quietly.

"Any time." His eyes lingered on my mouth before he stepped back, forcing me to drop my grip on his upper arms. "How do they look?"

"Hm?" Apparently, my hands had dropped, but my focus hadn't, because I was staring at him. "Oh. The fliers. Right."

Vicky laughed again.

I glared at her. "I've only seen the general one, but... Hold on. Let me grab one. I've pushed them around." I scooted back on my butt before rolling onto my knees and crawling across the stage. At least it was super clean...

And I just stuck my butt pretty much in West's face.

I peered over my shoulder, my teeth once again in my lip, and looked at him. He was standing perfectly still, his eyebrow raised, his eyes shining with a lusty burn, and his lips curved into his dirty, sexy smirk.

"Sorry. I didn't mean to force my butt into your face." That's an apology I'd never thought I'd have to make.

"I'm not complaining," he offered. "If that makes a difference."

Yes, it did, but it shouldn't have. Damn it. Why couldn't we put our attraction in time out? I'd have had our mutual one in the naughty corner quicker than you could set the timer.

This went against everything I'd said not twenty minutes ago.

"Here's the general flier." Vicky cleared her throat and handed it to him, glancing at me. "We didn't unpack the others yet."

"And Beck just left you?" West asked, taking the flier.

"No. He wanted to get stuff done next door before the hot lesbian cocktail chick gets here."

"He doesn't know she's a lesbian. Got it." West scanned the flier before looking up at me. "These are amazing."

My cheeks lightly flushed, and I shrugged a shoulder. "They're not too bad."

"Not too bad? You're not giving yourself enough credit. Mia, these are brilliant."

"Thanks." I smiled a tiny smile and tucked my hair behind my ear. "I hope the others are good."

They were—just as good, if not better. They were better if you listened to West, and Vicky did, which meant I had to too. They were pretty good; I had to admit that much at least. We unpacked stacks of each together, and then West clapped his hands once.

"Vicky," he said, breaking through the easy silence that had descended. "I need to submit the order this afternoon. Can you check the inventory in the cellar? The order form is upstairs on my desk. I think I have most of it, but I did it yesterday, so after last night's craziness, we probably need more."

"Sure. No problem." She handed him the closed penknife and jumped off the stage. Then she disappeared through the door, leaving us alone together.

I swallowed hard and grabbed the pile of fliers that advertised the Sunday-through-Wednesday happy hour. I wanted to at least get these on tables with the general ones tonight. They were super shiny, so I hoped the worst-spilled drinks would slide right off them without damaging them too much.

I scooted myself to the edge of the stage and jumped down. Then I grabbed both piles of fliers. I almost dropped one pile, and I had no idea how I kept it in my arms.

"Here. Let me take one." West took the happy hour fliers. "You want them out now?"

I leaned over and pointed to the days. "Might as well. Get as much as possible before the online advertising goes out. We really need to talk about social media too."

"Yep."

"I think they're best on the table." I put my flier down on the clean, wooden tabletop. "Put two of yours next to it, but a little bit on top. As soon as they sit down, they'll see them. They'll probably put them in the holder with the drinks menu after they're done reading, but most people will pay attention to it. Maybe even take them for future reference, which is why you need two."

He put his two down, but I couldn't see there was two. I leaned over in front of him, licked my finger, and split them. The bright colors combined with the important text in white would be readable even in the low club light.

"Ah. Got it."

For a businessman, he wasn't good at placement. I had to redo another two of his as we slowly made our way through the next few tables. Awkward silence surrounded us as my parting words from not so long ago hung in the air. The tension thickened every time we put fliers down and our hands touched. I couldn't fight the sensations that zinged across my skin whenever our fingers brushed.

I needed to speak to cut the tension and break the silence. So I said the first thing that came to my head. "Last night's craziness, huh?"

"Hm?"

"What you said to Vicky."

"Oh, yeah." West fiddled with his sleeve and put a flier down. "The bachelorette party got a bit excited. One of them threw up in the restroom but missed the toilet. The bride wooed herself one of my guys and made out with him quite enthusiastically. Her cousin slipped and sprained her wrist when it hit a table, and one of the girls put a napkin with her phone number on it down the front of Vicky's shirt."

"Wow. Sounds like that was a load of fun."

"That's not even the worst part. Honestly, it all paled in comparison to the moment the maid of honor asked me how much I'd charge her for, and I quote, 'the privilege of being able to suck your fine-as-fuck dick.'"

I looked at him. "How much did you charge her?"

He stopped dead, but I carried on, even as his hot gaze burned into the back of my head.

"You think I let her?" he asked.

"I was joking."

"No, you weren't."

"Fine. I wasn't. It was genuine curiosity that had me asking."

"Had you asking what? How much I charged, or were you really asking if she did?"

"Both, honestly." Especially considering I'd gotten to do it for free. Several times.

"Mia." He put his fliers on the table and moved in front of me.

I hugged my pile of papers to my chest and refused to look at him, so he pried them from my hands. I didn't let them go easily, but he managed it and set them on the table next to me.

"Do you really think I'd let someone else do that?"

I trailed my gaze up the row of buttons that ran up the center of his fine body until it grazed over his stubbled jaw and finally met his eyes. "I have no idea."

"Is that why you said what you did earlier? That our personal relationship has to end?" His eyebrows drew together.

"No." It wasn't a lie. I assumed the maid of honor's request had come after I'd left. "I said it because it does, and I told you it's not up for discussion." I tugged my arm out of his grip and grabbed my pile of fliers. I still had a little over half the club's tables to put them on and I needed more, so I moved to stage, and—

And West pounced on me, his strong hands grasping my waist and pushing me back to the stage. I dropped the sheets in shock, and they scattered all across the floor of the club, but that didn't seem to matter as West hauled me up and laid me back.

My heart pounded ferociously as he jumped onto the stage too and lay over me. He grabbed my hands and threaded his fingers through mine, pinning them to the floor. Then he rested his knees on either side of my hips. His upper body pressed against mine, and I struggled to breathe easily as the heat from his body seeped through the material separating our skin.

I was on fire. I felt him everywhere, even in the places he wasn't touching me. I was aware of every movement he made, from each exhale to every twitch of his fingers. The only sound that filled the club was of our breathing, which broke through the silence in an extraordinarily loud way.

I was looking down, but the force of his gaze pulled mine up to meet his. The blueness blazed back at me, enthralling me even as I knew I should try to get him off me. But I couldn't. I was frozen, and it felt like time had frozen too.

That was the problem with looking into West's eyes. They were captivatingly beautiful, surrounded by thick, dark lashes, and the emotions that swirled inside them hooked you and reeled you in.

He was fishing for my attention.

And he had it.

Hook. Line. Sinker.

I was caught in him completely.

"She didn't touch me," he breathed out, his voice rough. "Just because you and I met that way doesn't mean I'm going to take up any woman who offers to suck my cock. I'm not a cheater, Mia, even if all we're doing is having sex. I told her no and told her that, if she made more lewd comments to me or any of my boys, she would be asked to leave. Even if we weren't sleeping together, I wouldn't have touched her."

"Were having sex," I managed to force through the lump in my throat. "We *were* having sex."

West dragged my hands closer together and lowered his face. "We'll see about that. I don't mind telling you that I'm humoring you, angel. You want to be professional? Fine, but I don't see you trying to wiggle your sexy little body out from under me right now. I also know you're hiding why you left here last night, but I don't know why. Things that are hidden rarely stay that way."

"You're humoring me?" Annoyance tickled the back of my neck. "You're humoring me? Are you kidding me? In case you haven't noticed, I can't move. You've pinned me to the stage."

His lips curved upward. "So I have."

A mischievous glint brightened his eyes, and the small smile on his face turned playful. A tremor that was both excited and nervous spun through my veins, and I stilled as he slid his knees back and his erection brushed against me.

"What are you doing?" It came out a whisper.

He flexed his hips, and the brushing of his hard cock against my lower stomach made me gasp.

"Don't you know?" he asked. "This is my job. I'm being professional."

"That's not what I meant!"

"Then what did you mean?" His voice was low, seductive, and it made my heart thump hard. "Because you didn't say, did you?"

"You wouldn't listen anyway."

"No. I wouldn't, because I know it's not what you really want." He released my hands and flattened them on either side of my head. He had more strength now, and his mouth half brushed mine as it found my ear. He kept moving, never wavering in his skillful flexes. "You don't really want to stop what we have. You're worried because of what I do—how we met. But know this, angel: I've never taken a woman I've danced for until you. I couldn't resist you then. I can't resist you now. I don't know what the fuck you're doing to me, but I know I can't get enough of it. I don't want to get enough of it. Of you, Mia. I can't get enough of you."

He stopped moving, lifting his head and looking me in the eye. My hands traveled to his sides, and my nails lightly trailed down to his hips. His words were... His words were *doing* something to me. I was scared and thrilled and excited, and I wanted to run away. I didn't want him to talk anymore. I wanted him to get off me and stop, but I also wanted him to just drop his mouth on top of mine and kiss me.

"And I don't know why," he said, his voice still husky and low and sexy. "I wish I did. All I know is that you feel the same. I can feel your heart racing and you clenching your legs together. If you could look in your eyes right now, you'd see what I do—desire, confusion, shock. So yeah, I'm fucking humoring you when you say you're done with our relationship. You can run, but I'll catch you, and if you hide, then I'll find you, and I'll probably fuck you right on the spot."

"Please stop talking," I whispered, my throat closing up.

He put one finger over my lips then traced them with the tip. "Perfect," he murmured. "Completely perfect."

"West..."

"Oh, one more thing." He trailed one of his hands down my side, following the curve of my body, and grabbed my ass. His fingers dug into my flesh as he pulled my hips up toward him, his grip possessive and singing of ownership.

Why do I love that?

"Next time you come in here and I'm dancing, expect me to clear the stage, throw you in the middle of it, and let a good two hundred people see exactly how I feel about you."

He dipped his head and brushed his mouth down my neck, and I shivered as the warmth from the touch spread through me. He smiled against my skin. Then he pulled back, held my gaze for two seconds, and got off me.

I pushed myself up to sit and shuffled toward the edge of the stage. My feet had barely touched the floor when, once again, he pulled me against him and snaked his hand down to my ass. The grip was just as tight, just as possessive, just as owning as it'd been before, and that same possessiveness shone back at me through his eyes.

"And I'm not dancing this week. Unless you come in." He gave my ass a quick squeeze. Then, as soon as he released it, he smacked his palm against my ass cheek.

I squealed and clapped my hand over it as the sharp sting radiated across my skin. I was still rubbing it as he went back to the table to get the pile of fliers. Mine were still strewn across the floor, and he stopped, his hand hovering over his own pile, and sighed heavily.

Then he dropped to his knees and started the slow, arduous process of picking them up.

I joined him, elbowing him as I got down. "Smack my ass like that *ever again* and I'm going to bite your balls off."

He grinned, turning his face toward me. "I'm counting on it, angel."

16

I put the phone down and slumped forward onto the stage. Lili had been here and left, but right as she'd left, my mother had called.

Did I have a date for the wedding? The seating chart said I did. Who was he? What was his name? What did he do? Did I meet him in Vegas? When am I coming home? Am I in a new relationship with my date?

They were but a handful of the questions she'd asked me in the space of not very long—but, at the same time, way too long. I knew that, one day—Saturday— it'd come back to bite me, but I'd mumbled my way through the entire thing as West had watched with knowing amusement.

At least I'd gotten to see Lili shoot Beck down before they'd both left with Vicky. Lili to meet a *friend* and Beck to work—Vicky in tow. I figured he just didn't want to restock The Landing Strip's bar by himself.

Not to mention I'd put my heels back on before Lili had arrived and, now, my feet were hurting.

"Your mom?" West asked, bending over me and lifting a chunk of my hair.

I eyed him. "Yes. I'm exhausted about this weekend already and it hasn't even started yet."

"I can't wait to meet her. Do you think Allie would mind an impromptu strip at the reception?"

"You'd give my mother a heart attack." I straightened then paused. "Although, on second thought..."

He laughed, leaning back against the stage and gripping the edge of it. It made his muscles pop, and my gaze slid downward before... Shit. I was staring at him.

He coughed, and when I looked back up, his eyebrows had shot up and he was smirking.

"Nothing," I said, scooting away from him and moving fliers on the next table.

They didn't need it. I just needed to do something with my hands before I did something stupid like stroke his arms. Like a newborn kitten or something.

"Stop being so skittish. Believe it or not, I don't mind when you stare at me like you want to push me back and climb on top of me." West's tone was so cocky that I wanted to slap it right out of him.

"I did not look at you like that!" I put my hands on my hips. "You're so arrogant, you know that?"

"Yes. But I'm hot, so it works."

"You sound like a sixteen-year-old trying to impress the head cheerleader so she'll suck his dick."

"I'm a twenty-nine-year-old trying to piss off this hot marketing guru I know so she'll suck my dick."

"I'm not going to suck your dick, West. Our relationship is platonic now."

"Of course it is, but I can still try."

I glared at him. "You're getting on my nerves."

"Good. The fact that I can't bend you over that table and fuck you is getting on my nerves."

I didn't have a response for it. I so badly wanted to fire something back at him, but instead, my cheeks betrayed me once again and I blushed red hot.

Damn my cheeks. Why did they always have to give me away? Damn red hair and fair skin. I was at an unfair disadvantage in the art of aloofness.

"I love it when you blush like that."

I covered my cheeks with my hands.

"No." He pushed off the ledge and closed the space between us. His fingers were cold as they wrapped around my wrists and pulled my hands away from my face. "Don't cover it up. Please."

It made my cheeks burn hotter.

"Why do you like it?" I asked. "I hate it. It's my least favorite thing about myself."

"Why do I like it when you blush?"

I nodded. Only his gentle grip on my wrists was stopping me from covering my cheeks again.

"I guess..." he said softly, lifting one hand to my face. He brushed his thumb right along my cheekbone, his eyes on mine. "It's the way your eyes shine. I could look at them shining like that all day and never be bored of the view."

I swallowed. God... He was on a roll today.

"Have dinner with me tonight."

I stilled. "I... I can't."

West frowned, small indents furrowing in his brow. "Of course you can." His fingers stretched out and he cupped my cheek.

Involuntarily, my face turned in toward his palm. "I can't, West. I shouldn't even be here right now." I pulled his hand away from my face and spun away. My purse was on the bar, so I made a beeline for it.

"Cute, Mia."

"Excuse me?"

"Cute. I didn't ask you to have dinner with me. I told you."

I spun back around on my heels and stared him down. "Told me? You freaking told me to have dinner with you?" I stormed to him and jabbed my finger at his chest while he stared down at me with too much amusement. "Listen to me, West Rykman. You don't tell me anything. You can throw me on that stage and grab my ass and whisper your dirty talk in my ear like you own me, but you don't. You can spank my ass like you own that too, but you still fucking don't."

I went to turn, but his lightning-quick reflexes twirled me and pinned me against the stage. I gripped the edge of it and hit him with a dark glare.

He responded by grabbing a fistful of my hair and pulling my face close to his. "That's where you're wrong. I *do* own you, Mia. Not in the conventional sense, but in the sense that you can't stay away from me. I owned your pussy the first time I bent you over that hotel bed and fucked you senseless. I owned your mouth the first time you took my cock to the back of your throat. And, if I have to put you on your knees, spread your tight, little ass cheeks, and fuck you there so you believe I own your ass too, then I damn well will."

He leaned in closer, so close that our noses touched. Our breath mingled in the tiny space of air between us, and my nerves sang as desire-fueled adrenaline pumped right through my body.

"And, angel? The moment you looked into my eyes, I owned you. So it wasn't a fucking request for dinner tonight. You come to my place for it or I'm gonna bring it to yours."

I stared him down as best I could. I didn't let my gaze waver, even as he released my hair and grasped the edge of the stage the way I was, boxing me in. Even as his cock pressed against the apex of my thighs and my clit throbbed.

"I don't know what kind of women you usually have relationships with, but rest assured, I'm not them," I said quietly. Strongly, but quietly. "And, even if I am turned on right now, demanding shit of me won't get you what you want, West. I'm sticking by what I said this morning."

And he didn't need to know why. Even if he thought he owned me. That he couldn't resist me.

He didn't need to know I was falling for his tender, blue eyes, his rough grip, his powerful presence, and his dirty mouth. He didn't need to know I was falling for him.

"I know you're not." His voice was quieter now, the same volume as mine. "Because you're the first woman I've fucked without her putting a single dollar in my pants in years."

"Should I be flattered by that?"

"I don't know. Does it sound flattering? I meant it to, but I'm not sure it came out that way." He looked so thoughtful, so confused, that I had to bite the inside of my cheek to stop myself from breaking out into a massive smile. "It didn't come out that way, did it?"

I grimaced, still fighting my amusement, and shook my head.

"Shit." He stepped back and folded his arms across his chest. "I probably could have worded it better?"

"Or not said it at all," I offered as a better solution.

"Yes... That's probably the preferable option."

"You think?"

"I'm blaming you for this." He unfolded his arms and touched his finger to the end of my nose.

"Me?" My jaw dropped. "How is it even close to being my fault?"

"Because you're so damn cute when you get mad." He cupped my chin and pulled my mouth toward his. "Combine that with the fact that it's hard to think straight around you at all and nothing I want to say is going to come out right."

I leaned back. "So, literally everything you've said to me today has come out wrong?"

"No. Just the dollar thing."

"You're a dork." I smiled.

"So, will you have dinner with me?"

I mock gasped. "You're asking?"

"Don't get used to it, angel. I'll be back demanding unless you answer me soon."

"You're a double dork."

"One... two..."

"Yes," I said, breaking through his counting. "I'll have dinner with you. As long as you keep these"—I grabbed his hands—"to yourself during it."

He slid his hand down the curve of my back and grabbed my ass yet again—the other cheek this time. I was going to have imprints of his fingertips permanently sealed onto my skin at this rate.

"You got it, angel."

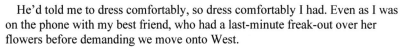

He'd told me to dress comfortably, so dress comfortably I had. Even as I was on the phone with my best friend, who had a last-minute freak-out over her flowers before demanding we move onto West.

"So, he's coming with you?"

I sighed. "Yes."

"Even though you're not actually sleeping together anymore," Allie confirmed.

"Yes."

"Riiiiiiight."

"What does that mean?"

169

She laughed. "It means I think you're crazy. You're probably in Vegas for another seven full days, max, and you're worrying about this now? Just screw him, Mia."

"You know, it's getting ever more worrying that you, my virgin best friend, are giving me an increasing amount of advice about sex."

"And I keep telling you. Just because I haven't done it doesn't mean I can't tell you to do it."

"Yeah, all right. Whatever."

"Mia, obviously, you like this guy."

"And that's why I'm not having sex with him. It makes me like him more." So did his laying me down and dancing on top of me, but that was beside the point.

"I just think you need to stop worrying. I know you're the queen of all dating disasters, but honestly, I think part of your problem is that you take it too seriously."

This from the one about to get married.

"I told you last week. If you're really this attracted to each other, trying to ignore it is only going to make things worse."

"They can't get much worse."

"You could be pregnant. That would be worse."

"Why would you do that to me? You know I'm on birth control. And you know I don't want babies yet. You're the worst best friend ever."

"I know. That's exactly why I think you should go over there, thank him for dinner, and then get your nasty on."

"I thought you were the sensible one in this friendship. If you start being the crazy one, I have no idea how I'm going to end up. You're my voice of reason, and without the reason, you're just..."

"Telling you exactly what you want to do?"

"Exactly. And I can't. I told him I can't. I told myself I can't. I won't do it, Allie. I am not going to take my panties off for that man tonight." And he's not slipping them to the side, either.

"Call me if that happens. If not, I'll sleep well knowing you'll sleep well, and I'll see you on Friday morning."

I pulled into West's driveway. Despite his insistence to get me after my agreement, I'd put my foot down and told him in no uncertain terms that I would be driving myself.

Of course, part of the problem with that was that his nosy neighbor, Mrs. Evans, had seen my car, and she was running a bag of trash out to the can at the exact moment I got out of the car.

"Helloooo, dear!" She wriggled her fingers at me, a giant smile on her face.

"Good evening, Mrs. Evans," I called back, holding my hand up in greeting.

"Dinner with dear West?"

"Yes, ma'am."

She excitedly pursed her lips. "Well, you two have fun, won't you?"

"Thank you." I smiled and waved again as she disappeared inside her house. Did she keep something by her front door for times like these?

West's door opened almost immediately. He stared across the street for a moment before he even acknowledged my presence by pushing the door wide open. "She means well, but I think she has something by her door at all times."

"I literally just thought the exact same thing."

"Great." He took my hand and pulled me up onto the step next to him. "Now, I know she'll be watching, so don't kill me for this."

He clasped the side of my neck and dropped his mouth to mine. I'd expected him to do it, but I was shocked all the same. I leaned into him, practically melting against him as his lips moved across mine so tenderly and honestly that my toes curled inside my shoes.

I felt warm everywhere, and I almost forgot why I was fighting against this.

Almost. Not quite.

West pulled back from me and slowly opened his eyes. The raw honesty I saw reflected back at me clenched at my heart.

That was, perhaps, the realest touch we'd ever shared.

And we both knew it.

"I thought you said you'd keep your hands to yourself," I said softly, breaking the silence.

"I did." His eyes flipped from raw and emotional to playful in seconds. "During dinner. I made no promises about before or after it."

"West Rykman, you are a sneaky little shit."

He grinned, grabbed my hands, and pulled me into his house. He shoved the door shut behind me, and then he cupped my face and kissed me once more.

It felt exactly the same.

From the soft pressure of his lips on mine to the dizzy hum of delight through my body to the way my heart beat double time.

It felt like the more I was so hesitant about, but I couldn't pull away. I couldn't make myself step away from him and break the contact. I couldn't pull my lips from his, because damn it all, he was right.

He did own me.

West Rykman owned my body, and he owned it entirely. It was almost as if he'd cast a spell over me that meant I couldn't fight him, that I had to surrender, because when it came to his touch, there was no reasoning with myself.

I craved it.

I craved the sensation of his skin against mine. Craved the way I felt when he ran his hands up my sides. When he kissed me. When he dragged his mouth over my neck. When his lips brushed my ear when he whispered dirty things to me.

More dangerously, I craved *him.*

He was a natural disaster of immense force, and the devastation he'd leave me with would be irreparable. I was sure of it. He'd shaken my world up in more ways than he'd ever know, because telling him... It was crazy.

Impossible.

"Come out to the deck," he said, finally releasing me but keeping my face between his palms. "I'm grilling steak out there."

"Okay." I followed him when he dropped his hands. I set my purse on one of the pristine kitchen counters and went out to the back deck. It was still early, so the sun was still visible in the sky, but the roof of the deck blocked most of its glare out.

I pulled my shoes off as I curled up on the rattan sofa with bright-blue cushions. I hadn't really paid attention to it before, but now, I loved it. The black-and-white, stripy throw pillows that adorned it lent it a certain modern charm, and I wondered if he'd picked it out himself.

I had to admit that I couldn't see this six-foot-three hunk with muscle on top of his muscle strolling around Ikea with a cart.

I could, however, see him grilling steaks on that big-ass machine at the other end of the deck. A beer bottle was sitting on the side bit that jutted out, and he swigged from it before stepping back and pulling his shirt over his head.

I gulped.

Didn't even swallow. It was a legit gulp that was probably heard from outer space.

His back was a piece of art. The way the muscles dipped and curved in their natural ways. The way even his shoulder muscles just crept up, something I rarely saw when he was wearing a shirt. The dimples at the base of his back, right above his butt.

Lord...he was hot.

"If you keep looking at me like that, we'll skip the steak," he warned.

"How do you know if I'm even looking at you? You have your back to me."

"I know. And I know how you look at me."

"How is that, oh smart one?"

He peered back at me over his shoulder, a shit-eating, smug-as-hell grin on his face. "Like you want to push me over and ride me."

Well...that was pretty hard to argue with. I was relatively close to thinking such a thing now, if I was honest with myself—and, after the two kisses we'd just shared, being honest with myself was something I needed to start doing. Fast.

"Can I ask you a question?" I needed to change the subject and fast.

"Go ahead."

"Did the maid of honor really ask you how much it'd be for the honor of sucking your cock?"

"My 'fine-as-fuck cock,' you mean," he corrected me with a wide grin. "And yes, she did. Quite shamelessly and loudly, actually. I was almost impressed."

"Almost impressed?"

"Well, it was her guts more than anything." He paused, flipped the steaks, the put the spatula down, and grabbed his beer. "She quite literally grabbed my dick and asked me."

My eyebrows shot up. Wow. "I'd almost be impressed too."

"Oh. You're not getting angry with me this time?"

I pursed my lips. "It can be arranged."

"Would it help if I said the steak was ready?"

"It'll delay it, not necessarily help it."

He caught the teasing tone in my voice and flashed me a quick grin before he put the steaks on the plate. He carried them over to the table near the grill, and I joined him there.

"Do you want a glass of wine?" he questioned, setting the plates down. The next thing he grabbed was a large wooden salad bowl.

I shook my head. "I'm driving."

"Are you sure?"

I eyed him curiously. "If I didn't know better, I'd say you wanted me to so I can't drive home."

West sat down, looking the picture of absolute innocence, his eyebrows raised. It didn't wash with me—I knew that the man was the embodiment of temptation, of the ultimate sin.

"Me?" he asked. "What makes you say that?"

I spooned salad onto my plate. "Because it falls in line with absolutely everything I know about you."

He dropped the innocent look and smirked. "You know me better than I thought you did." He cut into his steak.

I wrinkled my nose at the look of the almost-raw meat and the blood that was very visible.

"What?"

"I think your steak is still mooing."

He paused, his steak knife still stuck in the meat, then laughed loudly. "And it's delicious when it moos."

"Is mine like that?" I pointed my fork at mine. "I mean, I'm all for a little pink, but I don't even know why you cooked yours."

"No, yours isn't still mooing, as you put it. I hedged a bet on you being a medium-well kind of woman."

"What made you think that?"

He was right, but I was interested. Guessing someone's steak preference was quite the talent.

And it actually made perfect sense that he, alpha extreme, liked his steak still half mooing.

"Most of the women I know like it cooked until it's virtually charcoal. You're not like most of the women I know. You're in a completely different league."

My brow furrowed as he took a big bite of his half mooing dinner. "Different league? Is that a good thing?"

He swallowed his food, and his lips twisted up into a smile. "Yeah. You're like Major League Baseball, and they're...throwing-the-ball-in-the-backyard league baseball."

I blinked at him. "So, basically, they're collecting quarters in their piggy bank and I'm a millionaire?"

"Pretty much. Let's just say they never got to see me enjoy eating a cow."

"That's still mooing."

"Definitely not one that's still mooing."

"What an honor. I can barely contain my amazement." Or my disgust at its redness.

"Sarcastic shit." He smiled then sipped from his beer.

We fell into an easy silence as we ate. Unlike the others from earlier, it wasn't awkward or tense, and it didn't promise anything except comfort. It was a little scary, how at ease I felt here with him, just eating.

I lied. It was a lot scary. Despite the fact that I'd been hungry when I'd arrived, I couldn't finish the steak or the salad.

There were too many thoughts whirling around in my mind—thoughts that morphed into questions I needed answers to. It was easy for Allie to tell me that sleeping with him and then leaving was the easiest thing to do, but in fact, it was the hardest.

I cared about West, and leaving someone you cared about was never easy.

"Can I ask you another question?" I asked as he brought out a filter jug of water and two glasses half filled with ice.

West set them between us, the glasses clinking as they went down, and poured the water into them. "You're inquisitive tonight."

"The last question wasn't really serious. I just wanted to know if it'd really happened or you just said it to get back at me for what I'd said."

"Get back at you? I'm almost thirty, Mia. I don't have time for games like that." He sat back down. "If I did and I wanted to get back at you, I'd have told you I didn't charge her and let her suck me for free."

"Fair enough," I muttered.

"Ask your question. Something is obviously on your mind."

I knew I shouldn't, but it tumbled out of my mouth before I could stop it. "Why did you get married?"

West stilled. Yet again, my abruptness had caught him off guard. I really needed to work on not blurting shit out.

"Wow. That's...random." He chuckled quietly. "It's as simple as I told you. I was young, I was stupid, and I thought she was the one. I got caught up in the success of the business and I wasn't careful. She was an aspiring singer working a part-time job, and I should have gotten a prenup to protect myself, but you know I didn't. I wish I could tell you some long, romantic story about how she broke my heart, but she didn't."

I pushed my plate to the side and sipped my water. Then I propped my chin up in my palm. "Is it really the reason why you don't...have serious relationships?"

"Mostly. I also don't have much time to dedicate to one."

"You've given me enough of your time. Enough for a relationship."

"Yes," he said slowly, his gaze locking with mine. "But I want to spend time with you. There's a difference between making time for somebody and time creating itself for them. Time creates itself for you. You just...fit."

My stomach flipped. "Doesn't that scare you?"

"Terrifies me."

"Then why do you let it? Why do you let me fit into your life when you know this won't be serious if it scares you that badly?"

"Because, sometimes, the things that scare us most are exactly what we need, and that's why they're scary."

I looked down at the table. Was he right? Was I so scared because this...this *connection* we had was exactly what I needed?

"Mia," he said, drawing my gaze back up to him. "I'm terrified of you. You're the scariest person I've ever met because there shouldn't be time for you in my life. I shouldn't have time to take an evening off to have dinner with you—for the second time in a week. I shouldn't be able to drop work for three days this weekend to take you to Allie's wedding, but I can, and I am. I would work through the night if it meant I could lie in bed all morning with you. That's not who I am, but with you, it's who I become. I figure that's why, even when you come and tell me we can't see each other anymore, I can't for the fucking life of me give up on you."

"I think you should." I smiled sadly. "When I told you before that I can't do personal relationships, I wasn't lying. I am so bad at them. I even have the nickname of Queen of Dating Disasters at home."

That cracked a smile from him.

"I don't have a lot of time, either. What you don't see is that I can sit down at my laptop to design stuff at eight p.m., the sun setting, and look up five hours later in the middle of the night. I literally lose time, so I know I sure as hell won't be able to find it anywhere."

"Yet here you are. With me. Finding it."

"I didn't find it."

"Because it found you."

I opened my mouth, but he was right. I had stuff I could have been doing for work—not immediately pressing, things I did have time to do, but I was always early. I always had everything done way before it needed to be because I hated knowing I had a to-do list longer than my arm. The only to-do list that was allowed to be that long was a celebrity crush one.

Yet...there I was. I had time, and I was spending it with West. Out of choice—kind of.

I took a deep breath and looked away from him. This had escalated beyond anything I'd imagined when I'd blurted that question out. I hadn't thought it through at all, had I? Mind you, I could have, and we probably would have ended up having this conversation anyway.

That was how it worked with us. It didn't seem to matter where we started. We always end up in the same place.

Back to us.

There was still one question, one burning question, I'd asked him several days ago and hadn't received an answer for. One I needed an answer for.

"What do you want from me, West?"

"I want you to be honest with yourself and stop fighting this. Stop fighting us."

Another deep breath filled my lungs, but it didn't feel like it was enough. The frustration I felt at this entire situation balled tightly in my stomach and traveled up through my body until it was a hard lump in my throat and a threatening sting in the backs of my eyes.

I stood up from the table and went inside. I needed a minute to breathe—where he wasn't there. I needed air he couldn't take from me, because that happened all too often. Too many times, he'd stolen my breath.

"You know your problem, angel?" He'd followed me. "You're so concerned about doing what you think is right that you're ignoring what feels right. You can't tell me this—we, us—feels wrong."

"No, it doesn't. You're right." I turned and met his gaze, my hands flattening against the top of my stomach. "But that's the entire problem, isn't it? It does feel right, and yeah, time is making itself for us right now when we're in the same city, but when we're in different ones? Then what, West? Would our time for each other be nothing more than phone sex? Dirty picture messages? I have this much time that you fit in because this isn't my life. My life is in San Diego, where most of what qualifies as my spare time is spent fending off my mother and hanging out with my friends." I pressed my hands harder against my stomach and licked my lips to wet them. "Do you not understand that the more time we spend together that isn't work, the more you matter to me and the more it's going to hurt when I leave Vegas and go home? We're almost done. I've got a red-eye flight on Friday morning, and then I might not even have to come back."

He watched me, but he didn't say anything. His eyes blazed with a mix of emotion I couldn't tell apart, but he kept it in check as I spilled out all the things I'd been thinking for the past few days.

"You're afraid of a relationship that will fuck up. Every relationship I have with a man ultimately fucks up. Do you not understand how insane that is when you put those two things together? It's a recipe for disaster. It's like asking a hurricane and a tsunami to hit the exact same spot at the exact same time. Chaos, West. We'd be chaos."

"We already are, angel. We're the kind of chaos people send armies to fight, but I think that kind of chaos is worth it."

"You're crazy." I ran my fingers through my hair. "I fall hard and I fall fast, and then I fuck up. It's like the slogan of my entire life. And you?" I paused, exhaling a shuddery, painful breath. "You could fast-track me into falling in love with you in a heartbeat. And that's why we can't do this anymore. That's why it has to stop. I can't fall in love with you and then leave you here and go back to my life because I have absolutely no doubt that the hole you would leave would always be there."

He quickly closed the distance between us, framing my face with his hands. He swiped beneath my eyes with his thumbs and brought his face close to mine. Our noses brushed, and his slow exhale coated my lips with the taste of beer and steak and spice.

"And you think I can let you walk out of my life without leaving a hole in it? Don't think it. I don't think I can let you go. I can't stop wanting you, Mia. I can't stop needing you. Yes, it's all scary, but I think if we want it badly enough we can do it."

"Do you?" I whisper. "Do you want it badly enough, even knowing that the chance it'll fuck up is greater with me than with anyone else?"

"I don't think it's greater with you at all." He pulled back and looked into my eyes. "I think the idiots you've dated didn't deserve you or your time. I believe in coincidence, but I also believe they happen for a reason. And I believe the reason we met again is because of one thing."

"Which is?"

"You were meant to be mine."

I stared into his eyes for a long moment.

Was he right? Did coincidences happen for a reason—supporting the theory that there's no such thing as a coincidence? I wasn't a kooky, crazy lady who lived by psychic rules or anything like that, but I did believe that things happened for a reason.

Every time I'd broken up with someone, I'd told myself that it was because their suit of armor was so shit that it wasn't even made of tin foil, just wet paper that'd been painted silver.

"You were meant to be mine," West repeated, this time with conviction strong in his voice. He slid his hands down my face to my neck, his thumbs brushing my jaw, and pressed his lips against mine. "Believe it, Mia. You're mine. It's not something that will change. It's not something I will let change. You. Are. Mine."

The words thrilled me. They echoed through my mind, tugged at my heart, twisted my stomach, formed goose bumps all over my skin. Everywhere the words could touch me, they did.

"What if I don't want to be?" I whispered, looking into his eyes.

"Decide. Either way, I'm going to convince you I'm right." His eyes flashed darkly, in a way I was all too familiar with.

I knew the look. It was the look that told me I was about to get fucked.

Hard.

I didn't move. I didn't decide.

I didn't need to.

I already knew I wanted to be his.

I just wanted to know how badly he needed to convince me.

"Convince me," I whispered.

He took my mouth in a kiss that was almost aggressive. I staggered back at the primal force he put behind it, and my back slammed into the wall. I narrowly missed the side table by the armchair, but if he noticed, West didn't stop.

He dropped his hands from my neck, slid them down my body, kissing me hard, and grabbed my thighs. Before I could wrap my arms around his neck, he lifted me up, his fingertips digging into my skin, our mouths still touching, and hooked my legs over his hips. He pressed his entire body against me. The heat that seeped from his bare torso through the thin material of my dress set my heart racing.

His tongue flicked over mine at the same time he pressed his cock against me. It rubbed against my clit, and a small gasp escaped me as the desire took hold. He was flawless in his execution of every seductively rough move, from the deep kiss to the probing way his fingers moved closer to my ass. He held me effortlessly, like I weighed nothing, yet the need aching between my legs was so strong that it felt heavy.

He held my ass tight with one hand and pulled my dress up with the other. The kiss momentarily broke as I reached between us to pull it up and over my head, but the second it hit the floor, West had his lips on mine again. His free hand undid the clasp of my bra, and somehow, I didn't know how, he slid the straps over my arms and threw it to the floor too.

My nipples hardened as they rubbed against his hot, bare chest, and I moaned when his cock pressed against my clit again. He laughed low and bit my lower lip. His teeth dragged across it as he released it and I shivered, unable to control the feeling it sent bursting through me.

West hiked my legs up from his hips to his waist, kissing his way down my neck and over my heaving chest. I moaned the moment he closed his lips around my nipple and greedily teased it with his tongue. My fingers wound themselves in his hair, and I felt his smile as he tugged hard then released it.

The other received the same needy treatment, and I gasped when he moved farther down my body.

Before I knew it, he was on one knee, and my feet had hit the ground. He grabbed the sides of my panties, yanked them down my legs, and carelessly threw them to the side once I'd stepped out of them. They slid across the floor, but I had no idea where they stopped because he hooked my legs over his shoulders, grabbed my ass, and pulled my pussy close to his face.

His breath tickled across my clit, and I breathed heavily when he ran his nose along the side of my thigh.

"Look how wet your pussy is, Mia." He kissed the mound of skin right above my wetness. "Look how fucking wet it is for *me*. Because it knows it belongs to me. Even your sweet, tight little pussy knows it's *mine*." His tongue licked a teasing trail from my ass to my clit then flicked back and forth over it.

My hands found their way into his hair again as he licked my pussy. I writhed against his face, held up by his iron grip on my ass and my shoulder blades against the wall. I couldn't help but move and flex and fuck his face right back as he fucked me with his tongue.

He was intense in his tongue's assault of my clit, and within minutes, I shook with the heady force of my orgasm as it consumed me.

I'd barely recovered when he was standing, guiding my legs back to his waist, and pushing his cock into me.

He wiped his mouth with his hand then swallowed my cry with a kiss as he buried himself deep inside me. His palm connected with my ass cheek as he pounded into me. It turned me on more, and my nails scratched up his back, marring his perfect skin as his relentless fucking came faster.

West wrapped one arm around my lower back and grabbed my face, forcing me to look at him. Our gazes connected, and everything else disappeared. There was just him, desperately moving inside me, touching me, holding me up, fucking me until I felt like I couldn't breathe anymore.

He said one word.

"Mine."

I nodded as I felt a new orgasm rapidly building.

"Say it, Mia," he forced out between labored breaths. "Fucking *say* you're mine."

"I..." I couldn't form the words.

Everything was building, and just when I thought I could, his name left my lips in a desperate cry to the tune of my pleasure. My entire body clenched as my blood pumped red hot around my body. I couldn't control how tightly I gripped him or how I whimpered when he groaned my name as he came inside me.

I'd lost control completely, and it was all his fault.

Still, when we'd stopped and he was still holding me, still inside me, I buried my face in his neck and I whispered, "Yours. I'm yours, West."

His grip tightened. He didn't say anything, but he did pull me away from the wall and carry me to the stairs. His cock rocked inside me as he carried me up, but he pulled out of me after he'd placed me gently on his bed.

He leaned over me and kissed me, slowly gliding one of his hands up my thigh. "Stay," he whispered between kisses. "Stay with me. All night."

I touched his face. "I can't. I don't have anything I need."

"Then we'll go get it." His blue eyes seemed brighter as he gazed down at me. "We'll clean up, go get your stuff, then come back."

"Why do you want me to stay so badly?"

"Because I'm not done with you yet." He sucked my bottom lip. "You're mine, and I'm going to fuck you so hard and deep and dirty that you won't ever doubt it."

"You drive a hard bargain."

"Twelve hours ago, you were done with me. Now, you're lying on my bed, having just been fucked against my living room wall, with my come inside you. There's no bargaining, angel." He smirked down at me, his hand back on my ass. "This is a done deal. So, if you want the things you apparently need—and clothing doesn't fall into that bracket—then we need to move now before I change my mind and keep you here all night."

I linked my hands behind his neck. He was right. Twelve hours ago, I didn't want to do this anymore.

Good thing I'd finally made my mind up, wasn't it?

"Let's go." I kissed him.

He got up, disappearing into the adjoining bathroom. He threw a towel through the door at me.

"Although I do need clothes. Work has to happen, you know."

"Yes, it does. I supposed I can allow you clothes for that." He leaned against the doorframe of the bathroom, naked save for the towel he was using to clean his still-hard cock off. "Just for that though. You really won't need them for what else I have planned for you."

I raised my eyebrows, but I didn't question it. Instead, I stood and stuffed the towel between my legs in a very undignified way. West fought laughter as I waddled to the door. Why'd he have to bring me up here?

"Then I guess I better go find my panties."

"I guess you better," he said, laughter echoing in his words. "You'll be losing them again soon enough."

I hadn't needed my panties. Or clothes. Or anything at all, really. He had been very right. I didn't know two people could have sex as many times as we had last night.

He was very determined to convince me once and for all.

I was still apprehensive. If he was too, he was hiding it well. Maybe he had more confidence in the art of relationships than I did. In fact, that was a given. Everybody had more confidence in the art of relationships than I did.

Especially one that would ultimately prove to be a little long distance.

My doubts were exactly why I was sitting at West's kitchen table while he slept, in my underwear, with one his shirts as a robe. His shirts were super soft and comfy. Massive, yes, but it only seemed to add to the comfort factor.

I'd Googled just about everything I could. It was a short flight, but who wanted to deal with the never-ending crap of airports on a regular basis? And a five-hour drive—that was insane if it was a regular thing. Hell, I didn't like driving farther than L.A. for a weekend break.

Would he do that? He was busy. He might have had time for me, but for traveling? That was a whole lot of extra time that was needed. Hours extra.

That was a lot. It would add up. And lord forbid if the relationship got super serious... Who would move where? Who'd live where? Who'd do what?

I buried my face in my hands. This—this was when all the fuck-ups happened. The anxiety about the seriousness of relationships. Almost every time I'd gotten anxious in a relationship was when it'd gone wrong. Maybe I was asking for it. Maybe it was coincidence. Maybe I knew that it was going wrong and that was why it went wrong.

Or maybe all of those bad experiences had turned me into the one thing I'd never thought I was: a commitment-phobe.

Oh my god.

Was I a commitment-phobe? I felt like one. Even after we'd spilled out our feelings to each other and spent the entire night talking and having sex, I was still trying to figure out all the ways this could go wrong, which gave me all the reasons for not doing this.

I had a ton of reasons why this was a bad idea.

I had only one reason why it should continue: I wanted it to.

I had no idea if it would be enough. I guessed it would have to be enough.

I opened a new tab on my Internet browser and clicked on the search bar. *Commitment-phobe,* I typed, hitting the Enter key after. Every result was an article by this expert or that journalist, and after clicking through three pages and finding nothing other than magazine or website articles a la "10 Signs You're A Commitment-Phobe," I went back to page one.

The first article had to be better than the others.

It wasn't. Too much professional jargon. Thankfully, the second one down gave me the eight top signs of being a commitment-phobe. Apparently, I fit a great deal of them, but I still had doubts.

Jesus. Now, I was doubting my doubt.

I needed to get off the Internet.

"What are you doing?" West appeared behind me as if by magic and looked over my shoulder, his hands resting on the back of the chair. "'The Top Eight Signs You're A Commitment-Phobe,'" he read off the screen. "That would explain a lot."

I turned and smacked my hand against his forearm before he moved away. "I'm wondering if I am. It would make a lot of sense why I just spent forever Googling easy ways to travel between San Diego and Las Vegas before deciding it was all far too time consuming and not worth the hassle."

"And you did all of this while wearing one of my shirts."

I shrugged. "It's comfy."

"It's sexy—that's what it is."

"Funny. I feel the same way about you when you wear them."

West grinned and, with his finger hooked beneath my chin, tilted my face up to his. "Good morning, angel." Then he kissed me softly, letting his lips linger over mine for a minute.

I sighed when he let me go. It really wasn't fair that he was so handsome and could half turn me on with just a simple good-morning kiss.

"Morning."

"And back to your freak-out..." he said, pulling a mug down out of a cupboard, his back to me. He was wearing nothing but tight, black boxer briefs, and I had to admit that I was enjoying the morning view. "The flight is ninety minutes, if that. An hour at the airport before. Ten minutes to get out. Less than three hours each way. It's not as bad as you think it is."

I wrinkled my face up even though he couldn't see me unless he'd suddenly developed eyes in the back of his head. "But that's a lot for a weekend. And what about weekends we can't see each other because of work? You own clubs. You're not always going to be able to get away. Sometimes, most of my work has to be done on a weekend."

"You're panicking."

"Yes. Yes, I am."

West put his mug down and turned. The kitchen was big, but not so big that it took him more than four or five steps to get across it to where I was at the table. He flattened one hand on it and leaned forward, shutting my laptop with the other. My lips pursed as he pulled the computer away from me and kept his hand on top of it.

"It's something we might have to figure out as we go. We both have flexible jobs and set our own schedules for the most part—it doesn't have to be a weekend."

"But what if—"

He silenced me by putting a finger to my lips. His gaze met mine in earnest, and in it, I saw a strong determination I wished I'd had the conviction to keep myself. "This can and will work, Mia. Making us work is my number-one priority, no matter how hard it is or how long it takes or how many times I have to calm your fears."

"Okay." I nodded.

Satisfied, he pulled back.

"But just one more thing," I said to his abs. What? They were distracting.

"There always is." His half smile was both annoying and amusing.

"What happens if we plan time together and"—I paused, swallowed, and then forced myself to continue—"and someone requests you. In Rock Solid. For a dance."

His smile slowly disappeared from his face. His eyes, bright and raw, searched mine. "It's no longer an option."

I felt as though time froze. "No longer—you're stopping?"

He walked around the table and tugged me up. He lifted me with ease and set me on the kitchen table. Then he eased his way between my knees. His shirt, the one I was wearing, fell to the sides, exposing my black bra and panties, which looked so dark against my lighter skin.

He trailed one fingertip down the curve of my jaw, ghosting it over my neck until it reached my chest. He continued its journey over the swell of my breasts, each touch tender and caring, right down my stomach to where it stopped at my hip. My skin buzzed as he spread his hand, grasping my hip, and then held the other.

"West?" I said, my voice quiet. "You can't stop. You love what you do. Not just for me."

"True. I do love it, but I *am* almost thirty. I can't keep doing it forever, and even now is a bit questionable, isn't it?" His smile was genuine. "I mean it though, angel. No more private shows. I know the bachelorette party was why you left on Monday night."

I nodded, finally admitting it. "I didn't know what to do. I hated, and I mean *hated*, seeing her touch you like that, but I knew I shouldn't. It wasn't my place to hate it. So...I left."

He touched his lips to my forehead then pushed my hair from my face. He let his fingers run all the way to the ends, and I decided I liked this West. A lot. This tender, loving West was just as great as the dirty, sexy West.

"Then it stops." He lightly squeezed my hip and stepped away, his eyes lingering on my body for a second too long.

No, that was ridiculous. When a man like him was checking you out, it could never be for too long.

"As much as I hate to say this, you need to go and get dressed."

"I do? But it's so early."

"Yes. I know." His eyes sparkled. "We have a plane to catch."

"We have a what? Why? What did you do?" I grabbed the waistband of his boxers and tugged him right back against me. "West!"

He grinned down at me, mischief bright in his eyes. "We're going to San Diego. Today. Our flight is in four hours."

My throat closed up as an emotional lump formed. "We're not supposed to be going until Friday. It's Wednesday."

"I know." He leaned in and kissed the tip of my nose. "But time decided to give us some spare. How about that?"

There was one giant obstacle I hadn't anticipated when I got home. I hadn't cleaned up before I'd left on Sunday.

That meant, unfortunately, I had a pair of dirty underwear in a crumpled ball in the middle of my bedroom floor, a bra dumped on the coffee table, and a box of tampons on my kitchen island.

Not that I needed the tampons right *then*. They'd just happened to be on sale, and hey, I was a woman, and those suckers were expensive. Fifteen percent off things that would go up my lady bits and ultimately be flushed? Yes, please.

Basically, entering my apartment with West in tow had made me blush ten times before I'd even put my suitcase down.

The man was smarter than I'd given him credit for. Coming to San Diego before we were completely done with the marketing overhaul meant I had to go back to Vegas—and so did the fact that half the things I'd originally taken were still in the apartment I was staying in.

Of course, San Diego was where it all was likely to implode. Between my mother, my crazy friends, and having to spend the entire day on Saturday with my ex, I knew one thing for sure: If we got through these few days and the man still wanted me, we'd be just fine.

The challenge was getting through the next few days.

The current and more immediate challenge? My mother had heard from Allie's mom that I was coming back today instead of Friday, and within an hour of walking through the door and doing a food inventory in my kitchen, she'd shown up.

West was hiding in my bathroom. At my insistence.

"Why didn't you tell me you were coming home?" Mom demanded, her hands on her hips. She looked like she was trying to scold me for having stolen a cookie out of the jar.

"Because it was a last-minute choice."

"How last minute?"

"Two hours before I took off," I lied. What? It wasn't a huge lie.

Mom sniffed. "Fine. It's good you're back anyway. Allie needs you to help her get ready."

I rolled my eyes and walked to my fridge. There was nothing in it, but pretending to look for something was better than the righteous eyes of my mother.

"Her nails are getting done Friday morning," I said, "and she had her hair cut and colored yesterday. She needs me for nothing until after her nails are done, at which point I'll already be at the venue making sure everything is falling into place. I've listened to her plan her wedding since she was five and watched Cinderella. I think I've got this, Mom."

"I know, I know." She pressed her hands against her chest. "I'm simply so excited for her and want her day to go off without a hitch."

I paused. "Or with a hitch."

"What?" She stared at me, confusion in her green-gray eyes.

"With a hitch. You know. 'Cause they're getting hitched." I snort-giggled at my own joke.

Mom didn't laugh.

"Never mind." I grimaced. "I really need to take a shower and go to the store, so..."

It hung in the air for a moment before Mom got the message. "Fine. But call me tomorrow." She spun around then stopped. "Whose suitcase is that?" She pointed to the plain, black one next to my deep-purple suitcase.

"Mine."

She turned around. "You don't have a black suitcase. Yours broke right before Christmas, which is when your father and I got you the purple set."

"I bought another." I blinked quickly. "You know. Backup."

"There are three large suitcases. Is that not enough backup?"

The lock on the bathroom clicked, and I froze as the door opened and West appeared.

Mom's head swung around to him, then back to me, then back to him. Her mouth opened for half a second before she obviously decided better and closed it again.

Good lord.

My mother was speechless.

West Rykman was my new hero.

"Mrs. O'Halloran!" West injected a little too much enjoyment into his voice, but Mom was too busy blinking at him to notice. "It's lovely to meet you. I've heard so much about you. I'm West Rykman."

She still didn't move, even when he lightly grasped her shoulders and kissed her cheeks.

"And, if you don't mind me saying, now, I understand why Mia is so beautiful. She obviously inherited your good looks."

Oh, man. He's laying it on thiiiick.

"West. Hello." Mom blinked again, visibly flustered, and then...

Ho. Lee. Shit.

She blushed.

She fucking blushed.

Was I being punk'd? Where was the camera?

"Thank you," Mom finally managed to string two words together. "She didn't say you were here. Why was that, Mia?" She side-eyed me.

I shrugged. I didn't have an answer, so I wasn't even going to bother. She knew I had been deliberately hiding him.

"She wasn't hiding you in the bathroom, was she?" Mom asked him, her gaze landing back on him.

I didn't blame her. He looked really freaking hot in a white shirt and blue jeans with little rips.

"Oh, no, ma'am." West gave her one of his dazzling smiles. "Coincidental timing."

They both looked at me, and he winked. She didn't notice.

"Yes, great." I rubbed my hands together in front of me. "As you can see, Mom, houseguest and all that. I really need to go shopping."

"Of course." She looked at me for two seconds longer before going back to West. "West, will you be joining Mia at the wedding this Saturday?"

"Absolutely. I can't wait." His phone rang then, and he pulled it out of his pocket and glanced at the screen. "Beck," he said to me then looked back to Mom. "It's my business partner. I have to get this. Excuse me." He stepped away with a, "Hello?" into the phone and shut my bedroom door behind him.

I sank my teeth into my lower lip and waited as Mom slowly dragged her gaze from the closed door to me.

She stared at me. Hard. For a good ten seconds.

Have you ever been stared at by your mom for ten seconds? Especially right after you'd just been caught hiding a hot man in your bathroom? It was terrifying. I was ready to run out of my own apartment just to escape it.

She let out a short breath, glanced at the door while shaking her head, then met my eyes yet again. "Marry that man, Mia, and then have his babies."

My jaw dropped, and I just stared after her as she turned without another word and left my apartment.

I was still standing there two minutes later—my mouth shut—when West surfaced from my bedroom.

"You look confused, angel," he noted, amused.

I blinked hard. "You just won over my mother. In the space of, like, three minutes." I turned my face toward him. "And you made her blush," I said slowly. Very. Slowly. "Are you sure you're human? Because she has never, ever, ever liked any guy she's met. And you made her blush." I felt dumb for having repeated that, but it was important.

"I'm a likable person." He grinned and put his phone on the island. Then he wrapped his arms around my waist.

I was still blinking up at him—a habit I had, apparently, inherited from Mom. Along with her good looks, if you asked the man in front of me. Who was, by all accounts, an expert on good looks.

"No, no. You don't understand. She doesn't even like *me* a lot of the time, but you... I knew there was something wrong with you," I finished on a mutter. "Rich, successful, sexy as shit... You're an alien. It's the only explanation I have."

He laughed, pressing the side of his face into my hair. "Fuck. You got me."

I slid my arms around his waist and grinned up at him. "Knew it. But I still can't believe she didn't hate you."

He smiled, winked, and pulled me in for a long, deep kiss. When he released me, I felt dizzy, but he only had one thing on his mind—and, for once, it wasn't sex.

"I'm hungry," he said. "Let's get food."

This hadn't been in my plan, but I should have known that it would happen.

The twenty-minute drive between San Diego and Imperial Beach passed in a blur. West had insisted on renting a car although my own car was perfectly fine. I chalked it up to his alpha male complex and needing to drive everywhere himself.

Either way I looked at it, I was going to meet his grandparents. And I was freaking out.

Like I-want-to-jump-out-of-the-moving-car kind of freak out.

It seemed like the only option. His meeting my mom had been an occupational hazard of coming to the wedding with me, and yesterday had been a giant mistake. He should have stayed in the bathroom, damn it.

Though knowing that my mom wanted me to marry him and have his babies made it a little easier. It was the closest she'd ever get to telling me that she liked him. That or she accepted that we'd have beautiful babies.

I glanced at him. We would have beautiful babies.

Whoa now. Why was I thinking about babies with West?

Damn it. Mom had gotten into my head.

Now, I wanted his babies. Why did I want his babies? We weren't at babies.

Then again, we weren't at meet the grandparents, either, but there I was, entering Imperial Beach, getting ready to meet his grandparents. Since his parents had died, this was meet-the-parents territory.

I wasn't ready for meet-the-parents territory. It hadn't mattered that he would meet my mom because I hadn't thought she'd like him. She didn't like anybody.

I wanted to throw up.

"You look like you want to throw up," West commented, quickly cutting his eyes to me.

"I want to throw up," I confirmed. He'd read my mind again. "I'm not sure I'm ready for this."

"Will it make you feel better if I tell you my grandfather is likely to try to hit on you?"

I turned in my seat, grabbing my ankle as I moved it onto the cushion, and shook my head. "I don't meet parents, West. Or grandparents. Or anyone."

"Because you're a commitment-phobe?" He raised an eyebrow. "Is that what Dr. Google told you?"

"For one, yes," I confirmed. "And, for two, it's because my relationships never last that long."

"But they meet your mom."

"Not by choice, but because she shows up unannounced on a regular basis. Like you experienced yesterday."

He bobbed his head in agreement. "That was a shock. Luckily, she didn't seem too bothered that you hid me in the bathroom."

"I didn't hide you. I was trying to protect you."

"From your mother? Mia, she couldn't even speak to me at first."

He didn't need to remind me.

"Yeah, well," I said, "you're not like other guys I hide in my bathroom, okay?"

His blue gaze slid to me. "You hide other men in your bathroom?"

"No." I shook my head. "I've never done it in my life. That's not the point. The point is you're not like other guys I've dated."

"I guessed that. Most guys you've dated—and no offense, angel, but I'm starting to think 'dated' is a loose term for your previous attempts—probably let you go when you get all freaky about a relationship."

I would have been pissed off if I hadn't thought saying that I'd dated them all was playing fast and loose with the word *dated*. More like...sampled. Like wedding cake.

Yep. That was it. Most of the guys I'd ever dated had been samples. I was waiting for the three-tier-knock-your-socks-off cake.

And I think I've found him.

"That's unfair," I argued, coming out of my head. "Those guys are the reason I get all freaky about a relationship. If they didn't do stupid shit like tell me they're gay or cheat on me or make me pay for dinner, I wouldn't need to be freaky about relationships."

"I don't do cheating, I have no attraction to men whatsoever despite my business, and I promise to never make you pay for dinner." He'd easily reeled them off. "Does *that* make you feel better?"

"Oh, that's just the tip of the iceberg," I muttered as he pulled into the driveway of a gorgeous little house.

The front yard was the complete opposite of West's—where his was barren desert with cacti serving as décor, this was a mishmash of bright color and gorgeous greenery.

"Whoa."

"Nan loves her yard," he said, fondness in his tone. "Granddad, however, has not only a black thumb, but black arms."

"Like you and your cacti, then."

"Exactly like me and my cacti, which I happen to be very fond of."

"Why? Because they essentially water themselves?"

"Ahh, she learns so fast." He grinned and kissed my cheek. "Come on. Let's go in."

I slowly got out of the car. "Do they know I'm coming?"

"Of course. You think I'd just show up with you?"

"I don't know. Maybe you would."

"Mia, be quiet." He touched my upper arms and kissed my forehead. He took my hand and led me to the door, where he didn't even knock before it swung open.

Standing there, wearing a bright-blue dress, white hair in perfectly permed curls, and the biggest, brightest smile known to man on her face was West's grandmother. And she was adorably small—not that it was a reflection of her personality if what he'd told me was anything to go by.

"West!" she exclaimed, holding her arms out.

He bent right down to hug her, and she squeezed him tight.

"I missed you, buttercup!"

Buttercup? Was that a general nickname or one just for him?

Judging by the way he glanced at me, it was just for him.

Oh. My. God. He let her call him buttercup. That was the cutest thing I'd ever heard in my life.

"I missed you too," he replied, straightening. "Nan, this is Mia. Mia, this is my grandmother, Virginia."

Warm, brown eyes with flecks of amber scanned my face, and she smiled. "Well, aren't you lovely, dear?" She hugged me.

I returned her embrace and eked out an awkward, "Thank you."

She tapped one short, light-blue nail against her chin and looked at West. "You can't bring her in. You know what kind of inappropriate comments are likely to be directed her way."

"Don't worry." West's lips tugged up to one side. "She's well acquainted with Beckett. I think she'll handle Granddad and his warped sense of humor."

She sighed and looked at me. "My apologies, dear. He's rather lewd."

Well...so was her grandson, but I wasn't going to tell her that, was I?

"Don't worry. I promise to play along." I didn't have much of another choice.

"Where is he?" West asked, following her into the house. He pulled me behind him.

"In his chair. Where he always is." She rolled her eyes, but it had been said fondly.

"West!" a man bellowed. "Bring her in! Let me see her!"

My eyes widened.

"Oh, for goodness' sake, Jeff," Virginia scolded him, shuffling past West into what I assumed was the living room. "It's not a livestock auction!"

"Told you," West muttered. "Hey, Granddad. How are you?" He tugged me into the room after him, giving me the view of his grandfather.

He was tall, almost identical-looking to West—it was obvious to see. That and I recognized him from the photos on the wall at West's house.

"Oh!" his granddad exclaimed when his gaze landed on me. "She's a pretty one, ain't she? Now, I know you didn't get her by yourself. How much did he have to buy you for to impress me, darlin'?" he asked, directing the last question to me.

I glanced at West. His eyebrows were raised expectantly, and he had a smile stretching across his lips.

I grinned and looked back to his grandfather. "It's just a loan, sir. He can't afford me, really."

"Ha!" he barked out, grasping his cane and pointing it at me. "You 'ear that, Ginny, darlin'? She's pretty and sassy! The boy doesn't stand a chance at keeping her!"

"All right, Granddad. Give it a rest," West said, but he couldn't stop grinning as we sat on the sofa. "Did they change your meds again?"

"Sure did, boy." The older man's eyes lit up. "And I tell you what," he continued, putting a hand on the arm of his chair and leaning forward. "They're fucking *magical*."

I bit the inside of my cheek so I wouldn't laugh, but Virginia rolled her eyes.

"Stop being so eccentric, Jeff, and mind your language. You'll scare her off," she told him.

He barked out another laugh. "West'll do that by himself. She's way too pretty for him. Look at her. She should be in those commercials I tell you I don't record."

"Can I get anyone a drink?" Virginia asked to break through his ramblings, her lips pursed. She was clearly amused but just good at hiding it.

I politely declined, but West took a coffee, and as soon as she'd disappeared, he turned to his grandfather and asked, "What commercials are you recording this time?"

"Them Victoria Secret ones." He cackled, leaning back in the chair and loudly tapping his cane against the floor once. "Got some right beauties on 'em."

So. Five minutes in and West's grandfather thought I should be a Victoria Secret model. That might have been one of the most flattering things that'd ever been said to me.

"How's Beckett?" he asked. "Still sleeping with the ladies?" He punctuated it with the waggle of his eyebrows.

Again, I had to force myself not to laugh.

"If, by ladies, you mean strippers," West replied dryly, "then no. I told him he had to stop."

EMMA HART

"Pish! This is why you're the boring one." His grandfather looked to me. "How did you meet?"

I clicked my tongue and looked at West. "At my best friend's bachelorette party."

"O-ho!" His grandfather laughed.

I was sure I'd never met a happier person in my life.

"At the bachelorette party, eh?" More eyebrow waggles.

Oh my god. I couldn't hold it in any longer, and my giggles burst out of me.

"There it is," he exclaimed proudly. "She's succumbing to my charm! West, move over, boy. I'm keeping her."

"Oh, here we go," Virginia added as she came in. She glanced at me as I finally got my laughter back under control. "You'd think the man was sixty years younger, wouldn't you?" She handed West his coffee and turned.

"Speak for yourself, woman!" Jeff tapped her backside with his cane. "I'm as young as the women I pretend to feel—and let me tell you, those lingerie adverts are keeping me twenty-one!"

"Those new pills are making you too excitable. I'll call Dr. Regis in the morning."

"Don't you like me excitable, Ginny?" Eyebrow waggles again.

Honestly, I'd never met an elderly man like him.

You could give this man a Facebook page—The Randy Granddad—and he'd probably go viral.

"I think we should fly him to Vegas then sit him outside Rock Solid," I whispered to West as Virginia told Jeff not to be so crude. "He'd get everybody's attention."

He laughed quietly, resting his hand on my knee. "I told you he was crazy. He keeps life interesting, that's for sure."

I met his gaze. *And so do you, West Rykman. So do you.*

Stop.

"What are you doing?"

"I'm making grilled cheese."

West raised an eyebrow. "Do you always make grilled cheese on a George Foreman grill?"

I closed the top of the grill down and turned to him. "Yes."

"Why?"

"Because it grills both sides of the bread evenly so I don't have to flip it over. Plus it does both sides at the same time which means it's done quicker."

He blinked at me for a long moment, and I swore I saw a light bulb ping over his head. "That's both lazy and genius."

"I'm going to ignore the part where you called me lazy." I sniffed and peeked inside. Almost done. "It's genius. Do you know how many times I've burned one side of the sandwich?" I lifted the grill again and using the spatula, carefully guided the sandwich out onto the chopping board.

West boxed me against the kitchen counter and gripped the edge of the counter. He watched over my shoulder as I sliced the sandwich in half and cheese oozed out of the middle. "I have to admit, that looks better than doing it the normal way."

"Mhmm." I smiled, put the slices on a plate, and turned. I only just avoided his hard body forcing the plate up and against my chest. "Here. I know you said you didn't want one, but now I think you do."

He grinned down at me and took the plate from me. "You think right, angel.

EMMA HART

Thank you." He leaned down to kiss me, then sat at the kitchen island.

I rolled my eyes as I turned back to the grill. He was a typical man. It was exactly why I'd sliced twice as much cheddar as I'd needed.

And so what? Yes, I was maybe a little strange in how I made my grilled cheese. Allie had said the same thing until she tried it, and now she won't eat it any other way.

There was method to my madness, and both the method and the madness were brilliant.

I put the second sandwich under the grill. "Well?"

"It might just be the best one I've ever eaten."

I smiled over my shoulder. "I told you. It gets it perfect."

"And it really does get done quick, doesn't it?" He put the empty plate next to me.

I peered down at it. "They disappear quick, too."

"No comment." He kissed the side of my head and sat back down. "What time is the rehearsal dinner?"

"Six-thirty. Eating at seven. So, naturally, I have to be there at six." I removed my sandwich, cut it, and joined West at the island. "Allie is going to be losing her shit right about now, so the first thing I'll do is hand her a shot of vodka to deal with her constantly feuding relatives, and then I will have one myself to cope with the horror of sitting by my mother all night."

"If Allie's freaking out, shouldn't you be with her right now?"

I snapped my gaze up to him, chewing slowly, and shook my head.

He frowned. "Call her at least?"

"You don't call Allie when she's in a freak out. You wait for her to call you, or she'll say two works: Fuck off."

"Really? But she is getting married."

"Okay, no offense, but you're starting to sound like my mother and I don't know if I like you anymore."

He laughed, leaning forward. "I'm sorry. I've only been to two weddings, and they were the cousins who took after my grandfather, so you can imagine just how eventful they were."

I didn't want to think about that. Quite frankly, the thought of thinking about it was giving me a headache. Instead, I shook my head and finished my sandwich. "Honestly, Allie is just about the calmest person I know until the day before a big, life-changing thing happens. The fact most of her family has flown in today, coupled with the fact her dad's sister hates her mom, her grandmas have never gotten along, and her first cousin once screwed Joe's brother at an orgy... Hell, I should probably call the restaurant and ask them to pack more vodka."

"Wow. That's... crazy."

"Right? It almost makes the relationship I have with my mom look normal." I licked my fingers and pushed the plate to the side.

West tilted his head, looking at me contemplatively. "What's up with that? You and your mom. Every time you talk you look like she's going to give you a heart attack."

I slowly nodded. "Something like that." I paused, then leaned forward and rested my chin in my hands. "Honestly, we just don't get along well. We never really have. She has a very... traditional... view of women and relationships and careers. It's not one I share, so we butt heads about my job all the time."

"Isn't she proud of you?"

"I think so, in her own way, but she'd be prouder if I allowed my cervix to expand ten centimeters bigger than it should be to push out a watermelon attached to a body with a mad set of lungs."

"And there goes any desires I may ever have had of having babies with you any time in the next five years."

"You thought about having babies with me?" I froze. "Five years?"

"No. Tell your inner commitment-phobe to pipe down, angel." His eyes twinkled. "I was just saying."

I relaxed with a whooshing exhale. "Okay, good."

"You're going to have to stop getting crazy every time I mention something that'll last longer than your period."

I pursed my lips. "I wasn't crazy. I'm not getting crazy. It was just very random."

He raised his eyebrows, his eyes sparking with amusement. I knew that look—he was thinking I was cute, and I didn't want him to think I was cute, so all it did was make me pout. Which, in hindsight, probably didn't help my case.

"Mia." He got up and walked around the island. His hands were warm as they grabbed mine, his fingers intertwining with mine to pull me up. He pinned me against the island, and I pushed up on my tiptoes to perch on the edge of it, but he let go of my hands and pushed my back, slipping himself between my legs.

Our eyes met, and I blinked up at him. "What?"

"Do you want me?"

"Yes," I answered quietly. "I do, but I'm afraid."

"I know you are, but you need to trust me." He swept his thumb across my forehead, pushing hair from my eyes. "There's no way this will work if you don't. It's okay to be afraid, but it's not okay to not believe we can do this—and don't lie to me. I can see it in your eyes, Mia. You don't believe we can make this work."

I opened my mouth to argue, but nothing came out.

Unlike before, I didn't have a reason.

I had nothing.

"I'm afraid too, but no matter how much I want you, I can't put myself in a relationship that is more likely to fuck up than be successful." He cupped my chin gently and titled my head back. "I think you need some time alone, so it's probably best if I don't go with you to dinner tonight. I'll book into a hotel tonight and see you at the church tomorrow. Okay?"

Was he right? Did I need to be alone?

But what if I was alone and my fear took over and made a choice I wouldn't ordinarily have?

I nodded anyway. My throat was closing up, because although a part of me knew he was right, that I did need to be alone to work out what I really wanted and if I could give it my all, it still felt a lot like he was saying goodbye to our relationship.

The same thing I'd tried to do many times.

The same thing I'd failed to do.

He touched his lips to mine in a kiss that was so light it was barely a brush, but at the same time, so strong I felt it all over my body.

He kissed me like he was saying goodbye.

I didn't move as he pulled away from me and walked into my bedroom. The sounds of him gathering his things went through my heart like arrows, but I still couldn't move.

I was afraid—of everything. I was afraid of losing him, of trying to make it work only for it blow up in my face, of the entire situation. I didn't know how thinking it through, alone no less, would make it better.

It wouldn't make it better.

"West." I jumped off the counter, then paused.

He was standing in the middle of the kitchen, his suitcase behind him. My heart hurt with how beautiful he was, from his handsome face to his strong body, but as always, it was his eyes that drew me in and grabbed hold of me. The blue eyes that swept across my face, that traced the lines of my lips as he waited for me to speak, that finally came to rest on my own bright green ones, shimmering with questions.

"I'm sorry," I said softly, dropping my eyes to the floor.

"What for?"

For being afraid. For not believing. For not holding my ground before when I said it was enough. For wanting you as badly as I do.

"Everything."

He released the handle of his case and crossed the room to me. His hands framed my jaw, and he touched his forehead to mine. "Don't apologize for being you, angel. Just, when you think, remember one thing for me. Remember how badly I want you, yeah?" He kissed me once again, this time with more pressure, and I leaned into him, committing the curve of his lips to memory. "See you tomorrow."

I nodded and watched him go. My stomach dropped with every step away from me he took, and my heart clenched when the door shut.

I dropped onto a stool and leaned over the island, my face in my hands. I slid my fingers through my hair until my head had completely fallen forward, and I gripped my hair a little tighter than normal for one reason.

The sting across my scalp was sharper than the one that kept shooting through my heart.

Regardless of the pain and the fear and worry, West was right. I needed to decide what I wanted, and if what I wanted was him.

I was pretty sure it was, but committing was the thing I needed to think about.

My thoughts were cut short by the ringing of my phone. I grabbed it and slid it toward the counter for me. *Allie.* "Hey."

"I need you!" she cried down the phone. "Joe's brother has disappeared with my cousin, my mom and aunt are already arguing over where to place the cake during the reception, and there's no alcohol left."

"I'll pack my things for tonight and stop by the store on the way over." I got up, pushing the thoughts of West to the back of my mind.

"Aren't you with West?"

"I... no. Not right now."

"I'll—" she paused as screaming echoed in the background. It sounded awfully like her mom. "I'll meet you at the wine bar a block over from my mom's. Otherwise I won't survive until the wedding tomorrow."

Our two-person wine date had quickly morphed into four. Apparently the fact I wasn't with West right at this second was highly worrisome to my best friend and she'd called Jaz and Lucie.

The worry line was probably bullshit, and it was more she wanted distracting, but I needed focusing, so it worked.

"You blew off the hot stripper?" Jaz got straight to the point.

"I didn't blow off the hot stripper," I shot back at her. "I'm..." I didn't know.

"Thinking about blowing off the hot stripper?" Lucie offered helpfully.

"I think that's exactly what she's doing." Allie took a big mouthful of wine and gulped it down. Yep, she was stressed.

"Whoa—slow down, chicken." Jaz touched her fingertip to the rim of Allie's glass and pushed it down until the base touched the table. "You don't need to be hung-over for tomorrow."

"Nope, but I do need to be sane. Can we get back to Mia and West now?"

"Do we have to?" I asked, groaning and leaning forward. I rested my head on her shoulder, and she reached up and patted my cheek. "He doesn't want to pursue a relationship that isn't going to be serious. He had a bad one in the past, and he's made it clear he's not willing to have another."

"Hold on." Lucie massaged her left temple as she stared flatly at me. "You're unwilling to have a relationship with *West?* That super sexy stripper you invited back to your hotel room after your biggest conversation being his dick flexing in front of your face? The same sex god you've been face-fucking and cock-sucking and rough-sexing for the past two weeks?"

"Gee, say it a little louder," I hissed.

"When she puts it like that, it does sound insane." Allie patted my cheek again.

I sat up with a sigh and leaned back in my chair, gripping my glass by the stem and twisting it on the coaster. "It is, okay? It's insane. I am insane."

"So call him," Jaz said.

As if it was that simple. I wouldn't have let him go if it was that simple.

Maybe I shouldn't have let him go.

"I'm trying to get my head around this." Lucie leaned forward, propping her chin up on her hands. Her elbow almost slipped on a wet patch on the table, sending her hand toward her wine glass, but Jaz's lightning-quick reflexes saved it from certain death. "Thanks," she said to her before turning her attention back to me. "Seriously, Mia, all joking aside. If he wants a serious relationship with you, what's the problem? I know you don't exactly have... well, anything that remotely resembles even mediocre success in the dating pool, but he isn't like the guys you usually hook up with."

"She's right," Jaz agreed. "He's older than them. He's successful—owns a business, his house, his car. Doesn't want a casual hook up which is always a plus."

"And lives in Las Vegas," I pointed out. "While I live here."

All three of my friends blinked at me. "That's the excuse you're using?" Jaz demanded before anyone else could say a word. "Seriously? All of those amazing qualities that are like right up there on the list of the perfect guy and you're worried because he lives an hour's plane ride away?"

"Well..." I squirmed in my seat.

"Course she is," Allie said absentmindedly. "It's how she's justifying her fear of commitment and general lack of trust in the male species. He doesn't live within reasonable driving distance, so they may not see each other regularly, even if you consider the flexibility of their jobs. On from that, he owns two strip clubs, both of which in one way or another are filled with gorgeous, attractive women who would give an ovary to spend an hour with him, so why would he wait until he could see her again when he could get an itch scratched right there and then? Not to mention the fact he *is* older than her, so is he thinking about marriage and babies sooner than she is? Because that's a helluva big turn off if he's emotionally further in the relationship than she is. And when it gets serious? Who moves? He can't because of his business and she's got roots deeper than a hundred year old tree which, ironically, if she stopped being such a pussy would probably die."

"That's completely unfair," I muttered.

Except, it was entirely true. And it *stung*. I could feel the sharpness of the truth as it crawled across my skin, forcing the hair on my arms to stand on end.

"Not to mention there has to be something wrong with him because he's so perfect." She was on a roll. "I mean, come on. Hot, successful, wealthy, good in bed? He has to be a serial cheater or something equally outrageous because it's impossible to find a guy who is all of the above *and* faithful and committed."

I squirmed.

"So, to sum up, yes. That's the excuse she's using because she's not willing to delve into herself and see all the shit she's making up inside her head to justify her irrational fear of relationships."

I opened my mouth and then closed it again. See, that was the problem with a lifelong best friend. You couldn't hide shit from them.

She'd basically just ripped my soul out of my body, flipped through it like a book, and gave a very public reading.

And hearing it out loud, from someone else, even without judgment in their tone? How *stupid* did it sound? How completely and utterly irrational was my brain?

"It's a viable excuse," I said weakly. "It's a long-ish distance relationship."

"It's a bullshit excuse," Lucie responded, matter-of-factly.

The evidence apparently supported that. I didn't really have another argument to make. Allie had summed up everything I'd been thinking in the past two weeks in less than five minutes, completely ripping my thought processes apart.

Jaz and Lucie had helped there too. Bitches.

"Now I'm not saying it is," Allie said, twirling her wine glass between her finger and thumb. "In a roundabout way, it makes sense."

"Don't encourage her!" Jaz nudged her.

I glared.

Allie rolled her eyes and flicked her blonde hair over her shoulder. "West is a big risk. Long distance relationships require almost more work than ones where you're together. I'm pretty sure that when Joe went away for work for a month last year it was the hardest time in our relationship, and we currently have Family World War One being hosted right here in San Diego. So, yeah. He's a risk, and the dedication they'd both need is insanely crazy."

"Thank you." *Finally*. She was seeing it from my side.

"But, Mia..." She sighed and looked at me. "I don't think it matters. I think that if you really want him, that stuff won't matter. It's only time, and time flies. If two people are meant to be together, neither time nor distance will keep them apart. If two people are meant to be together, then they will be, no matter what distractions or issues or disagreements rock their world. I love you, and I know you're beating yourself up something mad right now, but, babe, he's right when he says you need to think."

Jaz glanced at her then leaned forward, more serious than I'd maybe ever seen her. "Don't think whether or not you can do it. Don't think about how badly you want him or how hard it'll be to make it work. That won't give you the answers you need."

"She's right," Lucie added, her tone gentle and soothing. "You need to think about how you'll feel if you don't try. You need to think about how West makes you feel, and if you can live without feeling that way ever again. If you can, then you can't do it. But if you think even a day without it will be too hard... Then you might have to take the risk."

I sucked my bottom lip into my mouth and looked down at my wine glass as they paused just a second before they changed the subject to Allie and her family, making her groan in exasperation. The pink alcohol swirled as I twisted it, desperately trying to occupy my hands. There was too much sense in what they'd just said, and I both loved and hated them for making sense of the situation when I couldn't.

That was the sign of the best friends a girl could have. They could make sense of every mess in your life in less time than it'd take you to get into the mess, and they'd sure as hell give you the answers you needed, even if you didn't think you had any questions.

They'd given me the answers I didn't know I needed, but the new problem was that I now had more questions than I knew what to do with. It wasn't even that I had a lot, it was that the questions I had to answer were bigger and more important than I'd thought.

How did West make me feel?

That was an easy one—like everything. He had the craziest power over my emotions and my body, able to set me alive with only the barest glance. His touch burned me in the best way, exciting me and soothing me simultaneously. Each time he held me it felt like I could fly, and every kiss had me drowning, losing myself within the beautiful chaos that we were.

He made me feel like I was the most beautiful—and only—girl in the world. Like I was the center of my own universe and the entirety of his.

And he did it all without trying. He only had to *be*. It was thrilling and terrifying and completely insane, but it *was*, and there wasn't a damn thing I could do about it. I couldn't change it or stop it. I could only live it and breathe it and allow myself to be consumed by everything that he was.

He consumed me even when I didn't allow it.

If we weren't meant to be, why did we feel so good? Why did my fingers fit perfectly between his? Why did my face tuck into his neck just right?

If we weren't meant to be, why did the thought of not touching my palm to his or laying my head on his chest or watching him sleep or coming apart beneath me make me feel like I wanted to throw up?

Why did that hurt so badly? Like I was tearing a piece of me out of myself?

I couldn't help but doubt my feelings, still, I swallowed hard and beat them back. The girls were right—the irrational feelings were ruling me. But West wasn't a boy. He was a man, older and better than any of the other guys I'd dated. He'd taken all my issues in his stride until this afternoon.

Then he'd put his foot down, told me to decide, and left me to do just that.

"Okay?" Allie asked as I stepped off my stool.

"Yeah." I gave her a small smile. "I'm just going to the bathroom."

I wove my way through the tables to the back of the bar where the restrooms were, then pushed into the women's. It was mercifully empty. Apparently everyone else had something to do on a Friday at three p.m.

I locked myself into a stall, put the toilet lid down, and sat on it. It was silent minus the air condition lightly blowing, and I leaned forward, my elbows on my knees, and propped my chin on my hands. The plain white door was the best blank canvas for my thoughts as I played them out.

How would I feel if I couldn't hear West's voice every day?

How would I feel if I couldn't feel his skin against mine?

How would I feel if I couldn't curl myself into his arms?

How would I feel if I couldn't hear his dirty whispers in my ear?

How would I feel if I couldn't tease him only to give in?

How would I feel if I couldn't lie my naked body against his and have him kiss the top of my head?

How would I feel if West Rykman wasn't one of the most important parts of my life?

Incomplete.

My eyes burned with tears.

Incomplete. I'd feel incomplete, because he was one of the most important parts of my life. I had no idea when it'd happened, but it had, right under my nose, probably when I had my eyes closed.

Wasn't that always when it happened?

Didn't you always fall in love when you were living the emotion instead of deciphering it?

Oh no. I'm in love with West Rykman.

How was it possible? Did it matter? Was falling in love the amount of time you spent with someone, not the length of time you'd known them? Two weeks—but almost every possible hour.

Hour upon hour of touches and looks and kisses and... okay, orgasms.

But was I in love with him, or the way he made me feel?

I closed my eyes. His face came to mind instantly, and the one I could see was the one that had laughter in his hypnotic blue eyes and that irresistible dirty, sexy smirk curving his soft lips.

Could I live without it?

No.

It was the tiniest, most indiscernible whisper from my heart. No. I couldn't live without it. Or him.

God.

I couldn't live without him, and he'd given me the chance to.

It wasn't a chance I could take.

"Mia?" Allie's voice was soft. "Are you okay?"

"Yes." I got up and unlocked the cubicle, pausing in the doorway as I looked at her concerned face. "Yeah, I'm okay."

"Honestly?"

"Promise you." I smiled.

"Do you know what you're doing?"

I nodded and walked to her, grabbing her hands. A lifetime of friendship, and she was still my biggest rock. "I'm going to go sort out my best friend's family and remind them whose weekend this is, and then I'm going to go to her rehearsal dinner. Then, tomorrow, I'm going to watch my beautiful best friend walk down the aisle and marry the man of her dreams. And, then...then I'm going after the man of my own. So come on. Let's get this show on this road."

Allie smiled, stopped me from moving, and hugged me tight.

I had the best friend in the world, because that hug said everything she needed to.

e: Promise me you'll be there today. I want you to be.

I stared into the mirror as my hair was fixed. Loose curls hung over one of my shoulders, held in place with bobby pins. The soft white robe I was wearing had my name on the breast, a gift from Allie's mom to me, Jaz, and Lucie for being her bridesmaids. Allie herself had given us each the most gorgeous bracelets, set with our birthstones.

They'd be the only things that'd defer from the white and baby pink color scheme she'd settled on.

Lucie was already sitting on the sofa in the living room, painting her toenails, while Jaz was next to me getting her hair done too. Allie's hair was done thirty minutes ago, and she'd been MIA ever since. I was dying for my hair to be finished so I could go and find her. The house was a buzz of activity, so it was amazing nobody had pulled her out of hiding.

She was scared. It had been written all over her face. This day had literally been eighteen months in the plans, and despite the almost-fight at the rehearsal dinner last night that I'd lost my mind over, it was going to go perfectly.

Not that she believed it.

Even informing her that I'd personally haul assholes out of the building hadn't done it.

I honestly thought she was going to throw up, so the moment my stylist put the sparkling headband in my hair, I got up, tugged my robe around me, and went in search of her.

This was the freak out she had to cope with me for.

I checked every room, downstairs and up, until I noticed the attic door was slightly cracked. Her parents had renovated it fifteen years ago for a 'hangout' area for us. Since Allie had moved out, it'd become half hangout, half storage, and I knew I'd find her up there.

She'd always hidden there.

I jumped four times before I reached the string to pull the door down. The ladder followed, and I climbed up. I seriously hoped nobody came out and walked under it, because they'd get a nice view of my perfectly white panties.

I poked my head through the square door space and looked around.

She was sitting in the corner, head down, surrounded by boxes and flicking through an old photo album. "I thought you'd find me here."

"Don't worry," I said, climbing the last of the ladder and stepping into the attic. "Nobody has noticed you're missing." I pulled the ladder up and shut the door properly. "What's wrong?"

She shrugged. Her blonde hair was pulled into an elegant half-up, half-down style, and the Swarovski tiara that sat prettily on top of her sparkled as sunlight streamed through the roof window. "It's crazy down there. Everyone is running around like the world is ending, and all I want to do is drink my coffee in peace." She raised a mug with a half-hearted smile.

"Are you scared?" I sat down next to her and hugged my knees to my chest.

"Nervous. Not scared. But that's normal, right?"

"Don't ask me. I'm going off what I've seen in movies."

Allie smiled. Properly. "I feel like whatever happens today will happen. As long as I can walk out of the church as Mrs. Joe Walker, I'll be okay. Everything else is just a side note."

We both stilled as someone yelled Allie's name in a panic from downstairs.

She rolled her eyes. "Honestly," she whispered. "You'd think my mom was getting married, not me."

There was that eerie air of panic from her, yes. "She just wants it to go well."

"Would you be saying it if it was your mom and your wedding?"

"No. I'd be jumping out that window." I pointed to the square-shaped glass.

"Head first."

"There you go." She sipped her coffee and put the mug down on the wooden floor next to her, along with the photo album she'd been looking through. "I think it's all so insane. This fancy wedding is all for our families, and all I want to do is just marry the guy, Mia. I just want to wake up next to him and call him my husband and share his name and know that he's mine forever. I could marry him anywhere and it wouldn't matter. Is that insane?"

I opened my mouth, then paused. Was it?

No.

Not at all.

"Oh, god, it's insane, isn't it?"

I shook my head and squeezed her hand. "No. It makes perfect sense."

She tilted her head to the side. "Wow. You agreed on something all lovey-dovey without barfing."

I tapped my fingers against hers. She was the worst. "I just agree with you, Al. It's all just... stuff... isn't it? All the dresses and tiaras and flowers."

"And seating charts and menus and name cards and confetti and all the other shit I won't remember."

"Exactly. If you want to marry someone, it doesn't matter if it's like Prince William and Kate's or in a barn surrounded by pig shit."

Allie paused. "Well. The barn would be okay as long as there was a limit on the pig shit."

She had a point. "Still... I think if someone said to me it's a barn full of pig shit or you could never get married, I'd take the barn."

"Hold on. You've used the l-word and the m-word in the space of 24 hours and you haven't passed out? Are you sick? Running a fever?" She reached forward and touched my forehead with the back of her hand. "No. Well, damn, Mia O'Halloran. I'm not gonna lie, of the things I'm looking forward to today, talking to West Rykman is right up there on the number two spot after getting married."

"Don't be stupid." I batted her hand away just as her mom yelled for her yet again. You wouldn't believe we were twenty-five years old. Sitting up here hiding made it feel like we were thirteen again. "We should go down before she calls the police for a search party."

Allie sighed, but nodded, and crawled across the floor to unlatch the door.

"Watch out below!" she shouted a whole five seconds before she let it go and the ladder slid down with a crash. "I'm done with my coffee now."

"Allie! Do not tell me you were hiding up there to drink your coffee!"

I crawled over next to her and smiled down. "Hi."

Her mom looked up at us. It was the worst attempt at a frown I'd ever seen—there was too much love in her eyes. "I should have known. The make-up girls are here. Let's go."

We both got down from the attic, and when we went back downstairs to where the make-up girls were waiting, I saw my phone flashing with a notification, and I swallowed hard as I picked it up and opened the text.

West: *I'll be there. Waiting...*

West's eyes had been on me the whole time.

From the moment I had to walk down the aisle with my ex, to when I stood at the front and dared glance back at him, and to the moment I had to fight my tears as I watched my best friend marry the man she loved more than anything in the world.

Even as I walked back down the aisle, somehow with a tiny three-year-old bridesmaid attached to me in place of Darren, West had watched me.

His gaze burned red hot every second it was on me. I felt it dancing over me, touching every part of my body in turn. He explored my body entirely at his leisure, and from where I was standing, it felt like he'd missed everything that had happened around him, like all he'd seen was me.

That was him. That was how he made me feel, and it was the simplest thing in the world.

I felt wanted—no, needed.

Even now, as we were sitting and waiting for Darren to finish his speech, there was one set of eyes on me, and they belonged to one person. West Rykman, the red hot stripper with the body of a saint and the mouth of a dirty sinner.

Darren finished his speech, and all eyes turned to me. Yeah—this was the one part of the wedding I wasn't looking forward to.

Still, I stood, smoothing out the wrinkles of my fitted, pale pink dress, and took a deep breath. The little square of paper I'd tucked under my plate stared at me, so I picked it up, then looked out. "I wrote this speech about two months ago. I can't even remember what I wrote, but it doesn't really matter, because that was a long time ago, and it was probably the equivalent of a two-year-old writing Shakespeare. So." I threw it over my shoulder to the floor to low hum of laughter. "I could come out with a long rambling speech about everything stupid we've ever done, but there are children in the room, and it's not appropriate. Sorry, Mom. And Mom Two." More laughter.

Hey. I was good at this.

"So, instead I'm going to say this. I am blessed with the best friend a girl could ever ask for—so is she, for what it's worth, I'm awesome." Even more laughter. "And I've done a pretty good job of putting up with her for this long. But, Joe, it's my obligation to tell you that if I want tacos at eleven-thirty and I call her, she's coming to get tacos, and she has an obligation to answer my needy texts at two-thirty. You're both leaving me high and dry here with this marriage thing, okay? I'm going to need adjustment and possibly a bedroom at your house for a while. And if you hurt her, I've watched enough Netflix documentaries that I know how to kill someone without leaving evidence. That's also why I need the bedroom. It'd be easier if I didn't have to break in, you know?"

He laughed into his hand, watching me.

"In all seriousness...watching someone you love find someone who loves them the way you know they deserve is one of the best things I've ever experienced. So thank you for loving my Allie like that. And she is still *my* Allie." I winked at him. "I guess I'm sharing her with you."

He raised one eyebrow.

"Joe! Not like that. There are children in the room." I rolled my eyes dramatically and flung my arm in his direction. "You can't even take a man to his own wedding." Everybody laughed again. "As much as Joe loves Allie, then I need to keep looking because clearly I drew the short straw." Laughing. Again. "But that's a good thing. I'm blessed to have two wonderful people to call not only my best friends, but my family."

My eyes scanned the room, but they didn't have to look long before they landed on the smiling face of West Rykman.

I couldn't look away as I spoke.

Even if my throat felt like it was going to close up.

"And somewhere along the way, they made me believe in love again. And that's pretty special. Not even Disney did that because I'm still waiting for the birds to do my laundry." I paused, and West's smile faltered, emotion flashing in his eyes, even through my joke. "So I'd like everyone to raise a glass," I grabbed mine and finally looked back to Allie. "To the best friend in the world and her new husband. To Mr. and Mrs. Walker."

Everyone echoed it, and Allie's eyes shone with tears. She squeezed my hand hard as I sat down, then pulled me into a giant bear hug. "I love you."

"I love you too," I whispered back.

"You know he hasn't stopped looking at you."

"Yeah. I know."

She pulled back, tears still in her eyes, still smiling. "I'll get your bed ready if you go get him."

"Deal." I wiped under my own eyes. "But I'm eating first. I'm hungry."

"Of course."

Chaos ensued after dinner. Between the plates being cleared, tables being moved, children running to let off steam, and everyone coming to congratulate Allie and Joe before the evening got in full swing, I lost sight of West.

I was also tired, emotional, and in desperate need of fresh air.

Mercifully, I stepped out onto the patio that was decked out in fairy lights and flowers and took a deep breath. Even this sticky air was better than inside, because the light breeze that fluttered the petals of the roses held a welcome freshness. I grasped the stone wall that surrounded the patio and leaned forward, watching as the kids from before chased each other around the grass.

I'd barely relaxed when I was boxed in by a strong body and familiar hands appeared on the wall, either side of mine. His warm breath tickled across my cheek, and I couldn't help but smile.

Twenty-four hours. That was how long it had been since I saw West. It felt like it'd been a lifetime, and for the first time, the fact I was so relieved to be near him didn't scare me.

He did, but my feelings didn't. And he didn't scare me in a bad way—it was in a heart-pounding, this-feels-so-real kind of way.

"I've seen you look so many different ways," he said in a low voice, his mouth right by my ear. "And you look beautiful even when you're frowning at your laptop, your hair a mess, wearing nothing but underwear and a white shirt. But right now? You're breathtaking, Mia, and I don't want to do anything but look at you."

"Well, what can I say? Professional stylists are useful to have around." I blushed. Damn it.

He laughed quietly. "Yeah. It's the stylists. Not the happiness in your eyes or the smile that won't leave your face."

"That probably helps, right?" I craned my neck back to look at him.

"It's everything, angel." He pushed a loose strand of hair back into place. "Absolutely everything."

I swallowed hard. He was wearing the suit damn well, but like he was saying to me, there was something else about him that had my heart pounding. "We need to talk. Or I need to talk and you need to listen. One of those."

He raised his eyebrows. "Right now?"

"Right now." I nodded, then turned around and leaned against the wall. "You were right. Yesterday. To give me space."

He didn't say anything, just patiently watched me with hesitance in his eyes.

"Do you want to go somewhere quieter?" West asked when I didn't continue. He brushed back another strand of my hair that had fallen in front of my face.

I nodded, and he took my hand. I lifted my dress as we walked down the few steps from the patio to the grass. I'd changed out of my heels before dinner to rest my feet—Allie had stashed flats under the table—and thankfully, I hadn't changed back, or walking across the grass would have been near impossible.

The further away from the building we got the quieter and more relaxed the air became. Even if West did have to kick a soccer ball back to the kids two or three times because it'd rolled a little too far. After a couple of minutes though, we reached a part of the grounds where there was silence except for the tweeting of birds and water from the small fountain in the middle. The sweet scent of roses filled the air, and I perched on the edge of the seat of a wooden bench. He sat next to me, and we both watched as the water shot up from the center of the fountain then splashed back down into the pool.

I swallowed hard as what I wanted to say clogged in a lump in my throat. My chest felt tight, and the thought of speaking sent chills down my arms.

Why was it so hard to form words? Was I overthinking what I had to say?

Of course I was overthinking it. I overthought everything. That was why we were in this situation where this conversation was even necessary. I'd overthought every little detail and risked everything because my mind had the uncanny ability to create problems that didn't even exist—that probably never would.

"Is it crazy if I tell you I missed you last night?" West's quiet words broke through the silence we were sitting in.

"Is it crazy if I tell you *I* missed *you* last night?" I asked right back, still watching the fountain. "Because if it is, then the answer is yes. It's crazy."

"It's crazy," he confirmed. "But then again, I've been crazy since the moment I met you."

I looked down at my feet. The stones crunched beneath my shoes as I stretched my legs out a little. "I met with the girls yesterday, after you left. Once they'd got past their horror at the fact I let you leave, we actually had a good conversation about everything."

He waited again. God, he was so patient. For talking, at least. Not so much for the other stuff.

"They told me to stop thinking about what my life would be like with you in it and start thinking about what it'd be like without you."

I felt his gaze as he turned to look at me. "Did you?"

Slowly, I nodded. Emotion closed up my throat again. I knew I had to be honest with him and pretty much pull my heart out of my body and give him the option to break it, so I stood to put some physical distance between us. It was the only way I'd be able to close the emotional canyon I'd created.

"I hated the thought of it," I admitted, watching the fountain water splash into the pool. "I hated knowing it meant I wouldn't hear your voice every day—even your laugh. I know I'm a little hard work. I create endless scenarios of disaster in my mind from the realistic to the impossible and all the stupid in between, but more so with you than anyone else I've ever met. Now I've realized, it's because I care about you more, and that means there's more to lose." I turned, my teeth sinking into my bottom lip, and met his eyes. "There's so much of you worth keeping that losing any of it at all would hurt. Bad. I'm not afraid of you. I'm afraid of losing you. The only way to avoid losing you, in my mind, is not to have you at all."

His lips pulled up to one side. "Hate to break it to you, angel, but you already have all of me."

"And I can't make that change, so it's scary. The way I feel about you is scary too. Everything you are, we are, is petrifying to me, West. If something went wrong and I lost you, I'm almost certain I'd lose a part of me too."

He got up and closed the distance between us. My eyes fluttered shut when he cupped my face and dipped his down to mine. He ran the tip of his nose down the bridge of mine, and when he exhaled, it was a shudder of hot air across my already parted lips.

"Mia," he said in a low, rough voice, forcing me to look at him. His eyes swam with raw emotion, the kind that sent tingles across my skin and made my heart clench tightly. "I'm falling in love with you. It's fucking scary, but not being able to love you is even scarier. Let me love you."

"I don't have a choice." My voice cracked. "If I didn't, then I'd have to stop falling in love with you too, and I know I can't do that."

He pulled my mouth to his. The kiss was hard, hot, possessive. I wrapped my arms around his waist and gripped the back of his jacket, even as my eyes burned with tears at the way I'd just exposed myself to him.

At the way he had to me.

At the fact two people who'd screwed up so badly in the past could be brave enough to say fuck it and fall in love anyway.

"I believe in us, West," I whispered against his lips. "I believe we can do this."

"I know we can do this." He pulled back and looked deep into my eyes. "We just need to go back in there and survive your mom—if she can talk to me this time."

Oh god.

My mom.

"Oh no. She's going to yell at me for running away." I groaned and dropped my head back, making his hands fall away from my face. "It was bad enough last night. 'Where's West? Why isn't he here? Did you scare him off already?'" I mimicked her endless questions and finished on a heavy sigh.

Amusement replaced emotion in his eyes. "What did you tell her?"

I looked him dead in the eye and said, "I told her she terrified you and scared off the only decent guy I'd met in the past three years."

He laughed and wrapped one arm around my waist, pulling me into his side, guiding me away from the fountain. "And she said..."

"I had to give you her phone number so she could apologize. And then hire you for their next book club meeting because their current read is about a male stripper."

"I thought you said she didn't know I was a stripper."

"She didn't. Then she Googled you and told me last night during dinner."

"She... Googled me?"

"Yes." I clicked my tongue. "It's not something she usually does, but she's pretty insistent on having pretty grandbabies and she apparently singled you out the moment she laid eyes on you, so she made it her personal mission to find out as much about you as possible."

"I'm not sure if I'm impressed or should skip out this party."

I nudged him with my elbow. "Please don't do that. I told her you had to deal with work stuff last night, and if you run away now, she's going to know I've scared you away."

He laughed loudly and spun me around to the front of his body, then locked his arms around my waist. "What if I skip out and take you with me?" he asked suggestively, a lusty shadow passing through his gaze, full of promise. He lowered his voice. "We could go back to your apartment. I could take off that dress, pin you down..."

I squirmed, his words turning me on instantly. "I don't think I can escape."

"You're right." He kissed beneath my ear. "You'll just have to wait until later."

"For what?"

"For whatever I want to do to you." His eyes sparkled. "But I promise you'll like it."

I was giggly.

I'm not saying it was the champagne or the fact I had a handsome guy taking me home, but it was definitely the champagne and the fact I had a handsome guy taking me home.

"Sssh," I said, pressing a finger to my lips and looking back at him. "You have the footsteps of a herd of elephants. You'll wake the neighbors."

"I'm not sure it matters." He wrapped his arms around my waist and kissed the side of my neck. "They'll hear you screaming my name while you fuck my face within the next few minutes."

I gasped, finally getting the key inside the door. "Sssh! They'll hear!"

He pushed me through the door, slammed it, then pinned me against it. "That's the point." His lips descended on mine, his strong body pushing against me and flattening me against the door. "They're supposed to hear." He slipped one hand behind my back and undid my zip in one swift movement. "They're supposed to hear that you're mine." He tugged my dress down, and it pooled at my feet.

I squeaked as he grabbed my ass and lifted me against him, guiding my legs around his waist. A tiny laugh escaped my lips as he carried me through my apartment to my room, and an even bigger one left when he threw me back onto my bed.

I scrambled to right myself as he whipped off his tie and threw it to the side. His jacket was in the car, and his shirt was stretching across his muscles. I chewed on my bottom lip as he stared hungrily at my body and undid his shirt, then shrugged it off, revealing his toned stomach.

Watching him undress was a thing of beauty.

And that wasn't the champagne talking. It was my vagina.

His pants fell to the floor and he stepped out of his shoes and the pants, then grabbed my ankles and pulled me down the bed. He wasted no time exploring my body with his mouth before he settled his face between my legs and kissed me through my underwear.

My hips bucked against his mouth as he moved the fabric to the side and ran his tongue over my clit. His grip on me was tight, and before I could so much as breathe properly, he pulled an orgasm from me, holding me as I rode it out, and flipped me onto my front.

It was quick. It was rough. It was perfect.

West opened my legs from behind and lay over me, pushing his cock inside me easily. I gasped as my pussy stretched around him and he buried himself right inside me. He thrust into me deeply, and he fisted the back of my hair, tugging my head back so my back arched and my moans couldn't be muffled by the sheets.

Hard. Deep. Harsh. So much emotion was packed into every movement although it shouldn't have been, and I sobered as pleasure came at me in waves.

He pulled back just long enough to put me from my stomach onto my hands and knees, then grabbed my hair again and leaned over my back.

"You say my name when you come, Mia," he demanded into my ear, slamming his cock deep inside me. "You fucking *scream* it."

I didn't need telling twice. The roughness in which he came at me was enough to drag his name from my lips as I gave in to the orgasm. I moaned it, shouted it, screamed it, over and over, as he continued his fast rhythm of thrusting into me.

Then he stopped, his whole cock buried inside me, groaned, and came as I clenched around him. He let go of my hair, and I dropped my head forward. My arms gave out and I fell forward onto the bed, my heart beating wildly against my ribs.

West laughed and collapsed on the bed next to me. "Noted."

"What is?" I flopped off my knees onto my side and peered at him through my now-messy hair. I reached up to pull out the numerous bobby pins he'd dislodged and threw them on the floor, one by one.

"Most women would prefer slow, gentle love-making after the 'falling in love' conversation, but you like dirty, rough sex."

I smiled, throwing the last pin to the floor. "Well, if you love me as passionately as you fuck me..."

His laugh rang out around the room, and he rolled me onto my back then leaned over me. His eyes shone as they caught mine, and I reached a trembling hand up to stroke his stubble-dusted jaw. "Dirty, rough sex it is," he murmured, kissing me gently. "I'm going to lock your door."

I stared after him as he stood and walked out, his cock still hard and bobbing with each step.

Locking the door was good.

I was snuggled under the covers when he came back in, every glorious of inch of him, and he climbed into bed next to me. He yanked me against his body and wrapped his arms around me, holding me close, and kissed my forehead.

"You know," he muttered, "If you'd told me you didn't want me, I would have fucked you until you changed your mind."

"Really? The thought you'd do such a thing never crossed my mind."

"Hey. You're the one who watched me strip then went upstairs in the club with the sole plan of sucking my cock."

I tilted my head back and looked at him. "Will you really stop?"

"Stripping?"

I nodded.

"Angel." He brushed his thumb over my cheek. "I promised you. I mean it. No more. I'm all yours."

I smiled, but the thought he wouldn't do something that he enjoyed made me feel a little sad. Plus I did really like watching him do it. "What if..." I paused.

"What if, what?"

"What if you still did it? Just not... personal. Just on the stage. Where they can't really touch you."

He stilled. "You want me to keep stripping?"

That did sound a little insane.

West reached over me and switched on my bedside lamp. Soft yellow light bathed the room, and he looked down at me. "You want me to carry on?"

"I want you to do what makes you happy. You can't stop just for me. Besides." I tried to wriggle away from him. "I like watching you. It's hot."

Amusement flicked across his features. "Who said I have to stop? I can do it for you."

"You'd striptease for me?"

"Yes, with the added bonus I get you fuck you right after. That's far more appealing than having fifty pairs of hands attempt to get inside my pants."

I could see his point. "Fine, but I'm going to need convincing that you doing it just for me is going to be that hot."

His dirty, sexy smirk played with his lips. "Sounds like a dare, angel."

"It is." I turned off the light, kissed his soft mouth, and snuggled into his side. "Night."

"Night, Mia."

<hr/>

We were back in Vegas, and the moment we'd walked through the door of my apartment, West had grabbed all my things and taken them to his house. Apparently, that was the only option for sleeping arrangements.

I was also trying not to focus too hard on the fact I *knew* this was my last week in Vegas. Dragging this job out wasn't an option, and unless he hired MM Marketing almost immediately to re-market The Landing Strip, I'd be spending a lot more time in San Diego.

Except... I had a crazy idea. A crazy, risky, un-Mia-like idea.

I was a city girl. It was in my blood, and despite being raised in San Diego, I wasn't a beach girl. Red hair and the sun aren't a great mix. I preferred the bright lights to the ocean, and I tried to tell myself that was why this thought had taken up root in my mind and refused to let go.

It also solved every problem that had made me hesitate about a relationship with West.

I could move.

Sure, I'd be leaving my family and friends behind, but I had the kind of job that was applicable at anytime, anywhere, and San Diego was only an hour flight away.

Plus I couldn't shake the feeling it was time to a take a risk, and West Rykman was the risk worth taking.

After all, I was surrounded by risk takers whose chances had paid off. My parents, even Allie and Joe had only known each other a month before he proposed, and a year and a half later, they were married.

And it was Vegas. Sin City. Gambling central. If I couldn't do it here...

"Yo, Mia." Beck snapped his fingers three times in front of my face and pulled me out of my thoughts. "He only left ten minutes ago. You can't be losing your mind already."

I hit his hand away. "I'm pretty sure I don't have a mind left to lose."

"You chose West over me. Of course you don't."

I side-eyed him, but I was smiling. "That's it. That's what I'm figuring out— how I made the wrong choice. What was I thinking?"

He grinned and leaned over the table. "You're thinking you should have asked me to strip before you decided."

"There it is. You nailed it. Why didn't I think of that?"

His deep laugh echoed through the empty office space above the club. "On a serious note, what's up?"

I huffed out a breath, put down the fliers I'd been attempting to sort, and turned to face him. "You'd tell me if I did something stupid, right?"

"Yes..." He leaned back, his black shirt creasing as he did.

"What if I move?"

He blinked at me, his long, girly eyelashes fluttering. "By move you mean..."

"Here. To Vegas." I held my breath until my lungs burned. He stared at me, and I felt sick. "It's stupid, isn't it? It's only been two weeks and that's insane and why did you let me say it out loud?"

"What did he let you say out loud?" West walked back into the room, and I froze. "Are you speaking before you think again?"

Yep. Yep, I was.

"She's thinking about moving here." Beck nodded toward me.

"Beck!" I hit his knee. "Why would you say that?"

"Because you said it first."

My cheeks burned, and my eyes crept toward West. He was standing in the middle of the office, staring at me hotly, a muscle in his cheek twitching.

Yep. It was a stupid idea.

"Why?" he asked. Not meanly... Just... asked.

"Because it's really crazy, but it feels like it makes sense?"

"Are you asking me?" He fought a smile. "Because I'm not gonna tell you no."

"Is it crazy?" I asked Beck.

He leaned forward and grabbed his mug of coffee. "Yeah. It's fucking insane, Mia."

That was reassuring.

"Then I'm gonna do it." The words tumbled out of my mouth. "I'll move. Here."

West smiled—no, grinned. Wide, bright, infectious. He took a few strides toward me and pulled me up against him, locking his arms around me. "Good choice. What about work?"

"I'll start my own company. And then you can hire me for The Landing Strip."

Beck laughed. "I like how you think. You're hired with immediate effect."

I smiled at him over my shoulder, laughing and falling against West. God—I was crazy. I had to have been. But... I felt free. Like this was the decision I needed to make all along, like Vegas was where I was meant to be.

"Then I just need to find an apartment."

"No you don't." West's tone was final. "You live with me."

I leaned back. "What? No. I can't live with you."

"She's right," Beck agreed. "That's insane."

West looked around me at him. "Fucking really? She's moving to a different state to be with me and I'm the insane one for telling her she's living with me?"

"You're right." Beck got up then slapped him on the shoulder. "You're both fucking insane. I'm going to call you a doctor." He tugged on my hair before turning and disappearing into the adjoining kitchenette.

I dragged my eyes back to West. "It is a little insane."

"I prefer the word *chaos*," he said softly, taking my chin in his hand. "It's all we've ever been, angel. Beautiful chaos."

EPILOGUE
West

SIX MONTHS LATER

Mia frowned as she looked around The Landing Strip. The last six months had been a whirlwind of her finishing up her clients at MM Marketing, moving to Vegas, and forming her own company. She'd spent just about every second working her tight little ass off to make it happen, and after taking on two small contracts under her company, O'Halloran PR, we'd finally gotten around to her coming to the female club and looking at it.

"Have you guys learned nothing this year?" She turned to me, her hands on her hips. Her fiery hair flew around her shoulders as she shook her head in despair. "Offers, West! Why are there no offers? Men like cheap booze too!"

Shit. I was feeling appropriately scolded. "This is Beck's lair. Not mine."

"And? You own fifty percent of the building, which means you own fifty percent of the marketing."

"So does he." I felt like a child blaming him, but I had a point. He did own it, and Landing was his responsibility. It'd been that way since we bought the building and he decided to stop dancing. It made more sense.

Mia narrowed her emerald eyes as she stared me down. "Your petulant argument isn't working in your favor, honey."

"If I didn't know better, I'd say you just called me a child."

"Well," she said, spinning away and stalking to where her purse was on the bar. "It's a good thing you know better."

I grinned, and my gaze dropped to her ass as she walked away from me. *Fucking hell.* It'd been months, yet I still got as hard as I did the first time I led her into the back room in Rock Solid to dance for her. Shit, just the thought of her lithe little body made my cock hard.

Combined with the knowledge of the deep purple lingerie she was wearing...

I adjusted my pants over my erection and joined her at the bar. She ignored me when I sat next to her. One look at her face told me she'd moved into what I called her 'work mode.' Trying to talk to her when she moved into this zone was like drawing blood from a stone—or common sense from Beck.

She scribbled furiously on a notepad. I could usually read her handwriting, but this time, it was like reading a doctor's note. Letters scrawled everywhere, her sentences veering off the ruled lines on the paper.

Yeah. She was definitely in her own little world.

It was quite amazing to watch her, actually. I didn't know how she thought up the kind of ideas she did, but there hadn't been a single one that hadn't worked for Rock Solid. Even the random ones she yelled at me out of the shower had boomed business, and one of those was free fucking popcorn with every round of four drinks on the theme night.

I was considering doing it once a week. Apparently drunk women enjoyed popcorn while watching pretty much naked guys dance.

Granted, it made a royal fucking mess, but it brought people in. Even if it sounded stupid.

"Stop staring at me. You're distracting me." Mia continued writing even as she said it.

"Yeah, I can see it. Also down your shirt."

She tugged her blouse up and over the glimpse of cleavage I could see.

I reached out and pulled it right down, then undid the top button.

She sighed and slammed her pen on top of the pad. "How do you expect me to work if you're undressing me?"

I rubbed my hand through my hair as my lips formed a dry smirk. "Really? You should know by now that if I wanted you naked, angel, you'd be fucking naked already."

Her cheeks flushed dark pink. "West."

"Mia."

"Stop it. It's almost time for the bar staff to come in. You can't keep talking like that."

"Oh, come on. You're not still embarrassed about Vicky almost catching us last week, are you?"

"Yes!" Yet again, her cheeks burned brightly. "You might not care about your staff seeing you naked—"

"They used to on a regular basis, in my defense."

"—but I do! And if you carry on, I'm going to start wearing pants to work."

"What if I hide all your pants?"

"Then I'll kick you in your sleep."

I stared at her. It sounded like it was worth it, if I was honest. Easy access to her sweet cunt on a regular basis for a nightly kick at two a.m.? Yeah, it was fucking worth it. "I'm gonna hide your pants."

She sighed heavily and packed her things inside her purse. She tucked her hair behind her ear and stood, grasping her purse tightly. "Come on. I think I have enough to get started."

I followed her lead. I took her hand in my as I caught her up and ignored her eye-roll. So I liked touching her—always had. Always would. Touching her every second I could wasn't something I was going to compromise on, even if she did roll her eyes at me when she deemed it unnecessary or ridiculous.

"I'm going to pretend you didn't roll your eyes at me," I said as we stepped onto the sidewalk.

She flung her hand out toward Rock Solid. "It's like twenty steps, West."

"And your point is what, exactly?"

"It's twenty freaking steps."

"So you don't have a point." That's what I'd heard.

"I'm not even continuing this conversation. I'm going to go upstairs and get to work on re-branding The Landing Strip." She pushed open the door, releasing my hand.

Once again, my gaze fell to her ass. It wiggled as she walked. It was those fucking heels and figure-hugging skirts she wore. *Fuck me.* My cock was hardening again—I needed more than simply staring at her.

I needed her pussy to hug my cock before I could think straight and let her work.

My addiction to her was a little unhealthy, but I loved the fuck out of her, and I couldn't stop.

I caught her up and swept my arm around her waist. She squealed loudly when I pulled her back against me then spun her around to face me.

"West, don't you dare!"

She knew me well.

I threw her over my shoulder, ignoring her warning, and smacked my hand across her ass. She squealed again, this high-pitched noise drawing Vicky's attention from behind the bar.

"You should probably get lunch," I told her, carrying my wriggling, fussy woman through the club. "She gets loud."

"West!" Mia beat her fists against my back, and her purse whacked me in the legs several times. "Ignore him, Vicky! He's being an ass!"

I'd show her ass if she carried on—except it'd be hers in the air in front of me.

I pushed the door open and carried her up the stairs. She slumped halfway up, giving up the fight, and sighed with resignation. She could pretend all she liked. I could feel her heart beating against her chest when I put her down at the top of the stairs and pressed her against the door to kiss her.

The way she gripped my collar with one hand and kissed me back just as hard as I kissed her gave her away too.

"Your own fault," I said in a low voice, opening the door to the office and pushing her through. She dropped her purse to the floor. "You wear those fucking skirts with those shoes and I'm not responsible for how hard I fuck you when I get you out of them."

"Dirty," she muttered.

I slammed the door behind us and pushed her back onto the sofa. She fell back with a smile stretched across her face, and I leaned over her, my hand sliding up her thigh beneath her skirt. Her skin was soft against my palm, and I kissed her deeply as she dove her fingers through my hair.

Still couldn't fucking believe she was mine.

My cock pressed against her lower stomach as her skirt rode up around her hips and she wrapped her legs around my waist. Yeah—she complained about how much I loved touching her until her pussy got wet. Then I couldn't touch her enough.

My girl had a greedy pussy, and I loved it.

She reached between us and unbutton my shirt before she shoved it down over my shoulders. Her nails skimmed across my skin, leaving goose pimples in the wake of her touch. I shuddered when her hands dropped to my waistband, and then—

"Oh, Jesus," Beck groaned. "Can't you get a fucking room?"

I released Mia's mouth and dropped my head forward as she scrambled back on the sofa and pulled her skirt down. "We have one."

"A private room," he shot back, walking straight through into the kitchenette.

Mia sighed and straightened herself out. Her green gaze swung to mine, and she pursed her lips, but she was smiling behind her mock annoyance. "And that's why we need to stop having sex at work."

I made a mental note to pencil in sex time at least three afternoons a week when she was working in one of our clubs.

I got up and shrugged my shirt back on. "He sounded pissed off. Just me?"

She shook her head, running her hands through her hair and shaking it out. "No. He sounded really mad." She pulled off her shoes, then stood and walked toward the kitchen.

Beck beat her to it, appearing back in the main office. He had a tight grip on a glass of water if the whiteness of his knuckles had anything to go by. But it wasn't his grip that had me staring at his hand.

"What?" Beck snapped, looking at me. "Never seen a guy hung-over before?"

I scratched my jaw, my lips forming a smirk despite my best efforts. "Yeah. Seen you hung-over more times than I can count. Never seen you with a fucking wedding ring on your finger though, have I?"

Mia gasped and grabbed his arm before he could hide it. Water sloshed out of the glass onto the floor, and Beck put the glass on the desk as she clawed at his hand.

"Beck!" she cried. "What the hell?"

He tried and, surprisingly, failed to get his hand out of her grip. "I meant to take it off." He covered the plain, white-gold band with his other hand.

Mia smacked it away. "Take it off? What the hell did you do last night?"

"Yeah..." I was confused. I was the fucking idiot who got married on the fly, not Beck. For all his jokes, relationships were one thing he took deadly serious. "Shit, man. You had dinner with us at six then went to work. The fuck did you do?"

He finally managed to pull his hand away from Mia and tucked it into his pocket. "Involved a woman and tequila. Will you leave it at that?"

"No!" Mia shrieked. "Leave it at that? No. Tell me what you did right now."

"Leave it, gorgeous," he said to her.

He was still the luckiest son of a bitch I didn't punch him every time he called her that. He was basically my brother, and I knew it was just his term of affection for her. Like she called him sweetie. Mostly when he was being a dick.

"No. Sweetie, I don't understand how 'involved a woman and tequila' involves you wearing a wedding ring."

Like that.

Beck sighed heavily and dropped onto the end of the sofa. He buried his face in his hands and shook his head. "Finished work early. Met a woman. Got drunk out of my mind. Got married."

"Get an annulment then," I told him. What was the fucking problem? Apart from the obvious.

"Can't." He slid his gaze to me. "I fucked her after."

That was the problem.

"Beck." Mia said his name softly and sat next to him. "What are you gonna do?"

He blew out a long, tortured breath and looked at the wall. "Wait until she comes into work next and talk to her about a quickie divorce, I guess."

"Wait." I leaned forward. "What the fuck do you mean you're gonna wait until she comes into work? Are you telling me you got a member of staff drunk, married her, then fucked her?"

"Yeah. One of the girls. She was off her game so I took her for a chat, threw back a couple of shots with her—"

"Sounds like more than a couple."

"Yeah, well, it was. Don't worry, yeah?" He looked at me. "I'll handle it. She sees it for the mistake I do. Easy fixin'." He got up and walked back into the kitchen.

This time, Mia didn't follow. She slid along the sofa and tucked herself into my side. Her teeth sank into her bottom lip, and she peered up at me, concern in her eyes. "Oh no," she whispered. "This is bad, isn't it?"

I gently squeezed her and kissed her head. Her worry for him was palpable. "Yeah. Yeah, angel. This is bad."

THE END

Sign up for Emma Hart's New Release Notifications:
http://bit.ly/EmmaHartNewReleaseNotification

Join Emma Hart's reader group:
http://bit.ly/EmmaHartsHartbreakers

Read on for more on STRIPPED DOWN.

STRIPPED DOWN

What do you get when you mix a bottle of tequila, a single mom moonlighting as a stripper, and her sinfully sexy boss with an impulsive side?

Married. You get married.

Rich. Demanding. Hot. Crazy.

That was Beckett Cruz in a nutshell.

Not to mention wild, determined, dangerous, and forbidden.

He was my boss—and, after a drunken moment of insanity, my new husband.

An annulment was impossible... so was keeping him.

I was taking my daughter and leaving,

determined to give her a quieter life.

But Beckett Cruz had never taken no for an answer.

And he wasn't about to take mine.

What happens in Vegas... might just keep you there.

COMING AUGUST 30TH.

Pre-order is now available at all e-book retailers.

BOOKS BY EMMA HART:

Stripped series:
Stripped Bare
Stripped Down (August 30th)

The Burke Brothers:
Dirty Secret
Dirty Past
Dirty Lies
Dirty Tricks
Dirty Little Rendezvous

The Holly Woods Files:
Twisted Bond
Tangled Bond
Tethered Bond
Tied Bond
Twirled Bond (coming July 21st)
Burning Bond (coming Fall 2016)
Twined Bond (coming late 2016/early 2017)

By His Game series:
Blindsided
Sidelined
Intercepted

ABOUT THE AUTHOR:

By day, New York Times and USA Today bestselling sexy romance author Emma Hart dons a cape and calls herself Super Mum to two beautiful little monsters. By night, she drops the cape, pours a glass of whatever she fancies - usually wine - and writes books.

Emma is working on Top Secret projects she will share with her readers at every available opportunity. Naturally, all Top Secret projects involve a dashingly hot guy who likes to forget to wear a shirt, a sprinkling (or several) of hold-onto-your-panties hot scenes, and addictive, all-consuming love that will keep you up all night. She likes to be busy - unless busy involves doing the dishes, but that seems to be when all the ideas come to life. This has recently expanded to including vacuuming, a tedious job made much more exciting by the voices in her head. Naturally, it also takes twice as long to complete.

You can connect with Emma online at:

Website: www.emmahart.org

Facebook:
www.facebook.com/EmmaHartBooks
Instagram: @EmmaHartAuthor
Twitter: @EmmaHartAuthor
Pinterest: www.pinterest.com/authoremmahart

Email: emma@emmahartauthor.com /
assistant@emmahartauthor.com
Publicity: Danielle Sanchez at
dsanchez@inkslingerpr.com
Representation including subsidary rights:
Dan Mandel at dmandel@sjga.com